GRAVE

SECRETS

LINDA

SWINK

Copyright: 2014 Red Engine Press

All Rights Reserved. No part of this book may be reproduced or transmitted in any form or by any means, electronic or mechanical, including photocopying, recording, or by an information storage and retrieval system (except by a reviewer who may quote brief passages in a review to be printed in a magazine, newspaper or on the Internet) without permission in writing from the publisher.

Library of Congress Control Number: 2014932282

ISBN: 978-1-937958-58-9 Trade paperback

ISBN: 978-1-937958-59-6 eBook

Red Engine Press

Bridgeville, PA

Cover design and layout by Joyce Faulkner

Printed in the United States.

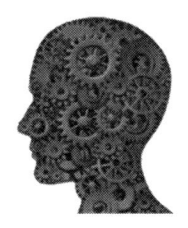

To My Mother

A crescent moon slices across the night sky

leaving in its wake slivers of dark, gray clouds.

Cryptic messages scratch the air — air hungry for warmth.

Tiny circles of light from street lamps cast ghostly halos onto the empty street below,

but fail to light the coal-black night — a night hiding behind its secrets.

A dog howls. An owl calls an eerie, ominous warning as

sinister shadows snake along the ground — crawling under bushes — hiding, waiting.

The town sleeps.

No one hears its soft, rhythmic breathing,

not even the child — the child creeping along the street toward the graveyard.

~ CHAPTER 1 ~

Normally Police Chief Hank Blankenship wouldn't have paid attention to the boys' claim that Mr. Harper lay dead on the floor of his house, passing off their jabbering as youthful exaggeration. Harper most likely had passed out after one of his three-day drinking binges. Even though checking on town drunks wasn't part of his job, when the Taylor twins said they thought Harper was dead but couldn't get too close because of the awful smell, Blankenship thought he should check it out just in case.

If the boys had been thirty minutes later, Avery Kunkle, the night shift patrol officer, would have been on duty and Blankenship would be sitting in the warmth of his landlady's boarding house enjoying a pile of creamy mashed potatoes cradling warm, brown gravy. Instead, he was sitting in a hard, cold saddle guiding Mingo, his bay Morgan, through the entrance to the Willoughby Cemetery.

Once inside the gate, he dismounted and led Mingo along the footpath into the far side of the graveyard. Blankenship removed his hat and bowed his head as he approached the section, not yet eight-years old, where nine white tombstones marked the graves of gallant men who died at the battle of Shiloh. Each headstone heralded a name and the date, April 1862 — 41st OVI. Dry, rust-colored leaves lay around the stones — lifeless as those they covered.

The late September evening air caused a chill to crawl around Blankenship's neck. He pulled his coat collar closer to his ears and tried to push the images of war from his memory, but failed. He never had been able to forget the crack of gunfire, the boom of cannons, and the screams of raw, untrained soldiers as they charged across open battlefields. Even after all these years, the cries of the wounded still reverberated in his head and stung his heart.

He whispered a prayer for their souls and continued on.

Harper's house stood on the west edge of the cemetery property near the railroad tracks at the north end of town. Owned by the city, the house was part of the caretaker's pay for maintaining the cemetery, preparing gravesites, and lowering the dearly departed into their final resting places.

As Blankenship tied Mingo to a nearby tree, a hound dog let out a baleful howl, lumbered over, sniffed at his legs, and then followed him to the house. Mangy cats of various sizes and colors, acting as if they hadn't been fed in days, swarmed around his feet. He stepped over one cat, but another ran under his next step. He shuffled along until he reached the front porch.

Light from the waning moon created deep shadows across the house. With no smoke pluming from the chimney, and no light coming from the two front windows, the house sat like a dark specter.

Aged boards sagged and creaked under his weight as he climbed the steps. He knocked and called out to Harper. When no one answered, he tried the latch. It opened freely. He pushed open the door and stepped inside.

Instantly, the foul odor of human decay assaulted him. Not since the war, when men lay dead on the battlefield with wounds seeping gangrene, had he smelled anything so vile.

The boys were right about the smell.

Unable to stand the stench, Blankenship staggered back outside, gasping for breath. He swallowed hard in an attempt to keep his stomach from revolting, grateful now that he hadn't eaten supper. He sucked in a lungful of fresh air and stood leaning on the porch railing until his head cleared.

After gathering his courage, Blankenship stepped back inside. Groping in the dark, he found a lantern, lit the wick, and turned up the flame.

A flicker of light fell across a body lying face down in a pool of dried vomit next to an overturned chair. Blankenship held his breath and approached and then gently turned the body over. Harper's eyes, glazed with death, stared up at him. His body was cold and stiff and flies had already laid their eggs. There was no need to feel for a pulse.

The boys were right about Harper being dead, too.

Harper appeared to have been in his sixties. Sparse strands of oily, gray hair clung to his balding head and days-old stubble covered his chin. He had on the same tattered clothes he'd worn whenever Blankenship saw him wandering around town. His shoes — one on, one off — were caked with dry, gray mud.

At first it appeared as though Harper had just keeled over and died. Maybe his heart had given out, but the empty whisky bottle lying nearby gave proof that he had probably drunk himself to death.

Blankenship covered the body with a blanket he found in an adjoining room, and taking one last look around, bolted for the door before he finally puked.

~ Chapter 2 ~

Blankenship breathed in the clean, invigorating autumn air as he strolled through town on his way to the jail the next morning.

The weather would have been perfect if the unusually heavy rain the day before hadn't turned the streets into a quagmire. Wagons bogged down in it, sometimes blocking the roads for hours. Horses plodding through the sludge pelted the planked walkways with mud and splashed ladies' skirts. The town council had promised to pave Erie Street with bricks, but here it was two years later, and not a single brick had been laid. Budget restraints, he was told.

Willoughby was a friendly place where men greeted each other by name and tipped their hats to the ladies. Women, dressed in their finest, paraded down the street twirling their parasols, nodding to friends. The citizens were well-meaning, God-fearing folks who understood hardship but also took every opportunity to flaunt their self-importance like a badge of honor. They would rush to anyone in need of help and never objected to a good piece of gossip.

Upon first arriving in the small town a little more than two years ago, Blankenship had inquired about the town's history and discovered it was first settled in 1787 along the banks of the Chagrin River that flowed into Lake Erie. Over time, a sawmill and gristmill sprang up along the river, bringing workers. Soon coopers, cobblers, and chimney sweeps as well as tailors, seamstresses, and wheelwrights arrived, and the town began to prosper. Along with tradesmen came doctors, attorneys, and bankers who made Willoughby their home. When the Cleveland, Painesville and Ashtabula railroad was built in the mid 1850s, linking Buffalo and Cleveland, Willoughby became a thriving community. Residents no longer needed to go long distances for basic needs or wait weeks for goods because of wagon delays.

Blankenship ambled along Erie Street observing merchants as they began opening their stores for the day's business. Bernie Holtzman rolled out his fashionable green and white awning with the words *Holtzman's Jewelry* printed across the front. In the store's window hung a poster announcing the Annual Charity Walk that was to take place this coming week to raise money for the county orphanage.

Many children had become fatherless after the war, and mothers, left without an income and unable to care for their children, had only one of two options--letting their children starve or relinquishing them to the care of the Sisters of Charity Orphanage. Each year the Catholic nuns paraded the children through town taking donations from passersby. "Morning, Chief," Bernie waved and called to Blankenship from across the street.

Bert LaRue, the bank president, tied his horse to the brass-knob hitching post in front of the bank and exchanged pleasantries with Bernie. LaRue, noted for sporting a thick mustache that turned up on the ends, wore a bowler and carried an ivory-handled cane, and always arrived in town in his carriage.

Down Second Street, Ned Potter, the barber, swept debris from his stoop. Next door, a young boy came out of the telegraph office and took off running down the street with an envelope in his hand.

Willoughby was coming alive.

At the corner of Maple Avenue, Blankenship glanced down the street in the direction of the house where Katie Wilson, the schoolteacher, lived with her widowed aunt. His heart beat a little faster knowing that in another hour he would walk her to school as he had done almost every day since classes began three months ago.

The jail on River Street, used to hold detainees until they were formally charged with a crime and transferred to the county jail in Painesville, was a one-story building with a back entrance that opened onto a small courtyard, beyond which was a stable that held the three horses and police wagon. Blankenship checked on Mingo and refilled the horse's water bucket. The stable boy would come by after school to feed the horses and clean their stalls.

Carl Stanger, the youngest and newest member of the police force, was in the office when Blankenship arrived. Finding Stanger at his desk any time of day was a surprise. He had first been hired on a trial basis after flunking out of medical school. Blankenship figured he could put up with him during the couple months probation period.

Stanger sat with his feet propped on his desk, chewing on a licorice stick, engrossed in the front page of the *Cleveland Plain Dealer*. His uniform was in disarray and his boots were in the need of a good rag. Reports that Blankenship had told him to file the day before still sat piled on top the filing cabinet. Blankenship sighed. He needn't bother reprimanding Stanger for not doing what he was told. It hadn't done any good in the past.

Except for the hissing and popping coming from the stove in the back of the room and the tick tock of the Regulator clock, the jail was reasonably quiet. Subdued would be a better description. The black and white rogue's gallery of criminals covered a bulletin board on the far wall. A county map, yellowed with age, hung opposite it. Blankenship saw no reason to take it down. A four-foot map of the United States hanging behind his desk and the American flag standing in the corner provided the only color in the jail.

The chief hung his coat on the coat pole by the front door and tossed his hat on top. It landed squarely on a peg. Blankenship refused to wear the prescribed police helmet as directed by regulations. He thought it looked ridiculous, and besides it made his head hurt. His old Cavalry officer's hat suited him just fine, tattered as it was.

"Morning, boss. How's everything with you this morning?" Stanger asked, looking up over the paper.

As he did every morning, Blankenship went to the stove and poured himself a mug of black coffee. At least making coffee was something Stanger could do reasonable well.

"What do you think about Mississippi getting a colored Secretary of State?" Stanger turned the page and repositioned his feet.

Blankenship stopped at the counter that divided the entrance to the office from the rest of the jail and read the log sheet from the night before. There, he found the usual entries of which doors to which businesses had been found unlocked and whose chickens had gotten loose. Two entries noted where hogs had gotten loose and had run the streets again. Seems the hog reeve had been busy during the night.

After initialing the police log, he closed the book. Out of habit, he checked the gun cabinet to make sure it was locked. He never understood why the town council felt the police department needed to maintain six war surplus Henry rifles. Nothing ever happened in Willoughby that required such defense.

Jake Cranshaw, a regular at the jail, slept on a cot in one of the two windowless holding cells. Jake was known for drinking and getting into fights, after which he'd get himself hauled into jail for public intoxication. He'd stay locked up for the night or until he sobered up. Cranshaw used to end his drinking sprees by taking jabs at anyone who got in his way, but his street brawls ended the night he took a swing at a horse tied in front of the hardware store. The horse, none too happy about being socked, retaliated by rearing and kicking him in the head. Cranshaw hadn't acted right since. Now his stints in jail were the result of just being stinking drunk and unable to find his way home.

"I see here it says that four more southern states have been readmitted to the Union. How many does that make now?" Stanger inquired.

Ignoring Stanger, Blankenship found the latest issue of the *Independent Gazette* under a stack of papers on his roll top desk and tried to catch up on the latest local events.

According to the newspaper, all was well in Willoughby. The Nelsons had returned from summer vacation with relatives back East, as had the Turners. Both families enjoyed their visits with no delay of the railroad or from bad weather. Edna Mathews had held another card party. From the list of names every woman who was anybody had attended. A detailed account of what she served and the prizes won covered a full column of newsprint.

"*Farmers' Almanac* says it's going to be a blustery winter. Do you think it's going to be a rough winter?" Stanger asked.

A notification about the church social this coming Sunday at the Congregational Church stood out on the second page. He planned to attend and hopefully have some time alone with Katie.

"What do you think about President Grant's latest choice of personal friends to fill government positions in the White House?"

Paying no attention to Stanger, Blankenship read on.

One disturbing piece of news, which Blankenship knew he would find, was the retelling of the story about Doctor Richard Haroldson, director of the Willoughby Medical College. After being sick for several months, Haroldson suffered a heart attack, lingered for two days, and then died peacefully in his sleep last week. The college canceled classes for several days in respect for the beloved doctor. The next headline announced the appointment of Doctor Charles Mathews as the college's new director. The article described the doctor's education in New York, listed his many accomplishments, and told about his family and his plans for the college.

There was no news of Pete Harper's death — not yet.

News of the little Mathews child's disappearance had faded from the front page. What more could be said that hadn't been printed and reprinted those first few weeks? How could a little girl disappear so quickly, so completely, without a trace? A seven-year-old child doesn't just walk away from under the watchful eyes of her parents; not in a small town like Willoughby. Even with his experience as a detective with the Pinkerton Detective Agency, he hadn't been able to find her.

Those first days that grew into weeks were the worst experience of his time as a policeman. He had organized search parties and divided them into small groups to scour every inch of town. The hunt for her expanded to neighboring farms and villages and then into the next county. He even questioned a band of Gypsies that had been reported camped outside of town around the time the child disappeared. A thorough search of their wagons turned up nothing. There was simply no sign of her anywhere. She had just vanished.

He still looked for her whenever possible despite knowing finding her alive after four months was unlikely. The loss was personal to him. It was his responsibility to find her, but he had failed. He had missed something.

The memory caused the biting burn in his stomach to return. The same burn that caused a coppery taste in his mouth throughout the many long weeks of searching. It was also the same burn that accompanied him when he told Doctor Charles and Mrs. Mathews he had to discontinue the search for their child because he had exhausted every lead. Their sorrowful expressions seared into his memory and gnawed at his gut. He tried to shake off the image of their sorrowful faces, but every time he thought about the tragedy, the fiery pain in his stomach returned. His failure to find little Anna Mathews would haunt him for a long time — maybe the rest of his life.

Cleopatra, a grey and white stray cat that had made the jail her home, emerged from behind the stove, stretched and padded over to him and rubbed against his leg.

"What's the matter, Cleo? You hungry again?" he asked and picked her up. The cat purred and pushed her head against his chest, scratching a ragged ear on his badge.

As he juggled the cat and the newspaper, an article on page three caught his eye. A horse auction advertised for next month was to be held in Kirtland. The article said that gaited and non-gaited horses, ponies and mules would be placed on the auction block.

"Do you like horses, Cleo? Maybe someday we'll have enough land for a farm where we can raise a horse or two. You could have the entire barn to yourself and all the mice you could catch. What do you say?" Cleo gave no sign that she cared one way or the other. He gave her a pat on the head, and then gently set the cat on the floor.

Blankenship sighed thinking about the horse ranch he hoped to have one day. But land took money, and despite the few dollars he had managed to save each month, he still didn't have enough to start a flea farm, much less a ranch with a half dozen quarter horses and maybe a few Arabian stallions thrown in for style. Dreaming about buying land was all he could afford to do right now.

"Hmm. Price of linseed's gone up again," Stanger said, turning the page of the newspaper. "Are you going to the church social on Sunday?"

Blankenship felt no need to share his comings and going with Deputy Stanger.

"Oh, by the way, there's a letter on your desk somewhere. Came this morning." He pulled a fresh stick of licorice from a paper sack.

Blankenship found an envelope stuck under the edge of the blotter. "The Office Of The Mayor" was printed in bold letters across the top. He ripped it open and read its contents.

"Who in the hell does he think he is?" Blankenship swore under his breath and threw the letter down on the desk. The mayor's meddling in police affairs had gone too far this time and Blankenship wasn't going to take any more guff from the pompous ass.

Blankenship brushed at the stray cat hairs on his shirt, grabbed his hat and coat, and headed for the door. It was about time he told the mayor just what he thought of his interference with the everyday operations of the police department.

"Get off your ass and take care of the office while I'm gone, and sweep up around here. This place is turning into a pig sty," he said to Stanger, motioning to the broom leaning against the wall in the corner.

"Where ya going?" Stanger glanced over his newspaper.

"And don't leave the office unattended again," he ordered.

Leaving Stanger's question unanswered, he slammed out the door.

Blankenship had made it to the street corner when the familiar voice of Adam Norville, the editor and publisher of the *Independent Gazette*, the town's only newspaper, interrupted the speech he was mentally preparing to give the mayor.

"Hey, Hank! Wait up. Anything you can tell me about Harper?" Norville called, from half a block away. With one leg slightly shorter than the other, he huffed and puffed as he hobbled to catch up with Blankenship. The police chief waited for his friend, and then adjusted his longer stride to the awkward gait of his 5'6" tall friend. Norville had a mass of wiry blond hair topping his egg-shaped head that made him looked like an upside down bird's nest.

Blankenship had met Norville the first week after arriving in Willoughby. Claiming he was writing an article about newcomers to the community, Norville wanted to know all about Blankenship: where he was born, where he had lived, what he did during the war, and what he planned to do in Willoughby. At first his endless stream of questions was annoying, but it wasn't long before Norville's frankness and cheerful manner won him over.

"And good morning to you, too," Blankenship needled.

Norville offered a weak "hello" and continued without a pause. "Come on, Hank, you know I'll find out sooner or later." His nose was like a bloodhound's on a mission.

"You're like an old dog with a bone, you know that?"

"You wouldn't be keeping something from me, would you? We've been friends too long for that."

"How did you hear about Harper so soon?" Blankenship asked. The newspaper editor always seemed to know when something newsworthy happened even before it made the police blotter. His ability to sniff out a story was beyond Blankenship's comprehension.

"I have my sources." They walked on for half a block before Norville asked again, "So, what's the story." Norville was tenacious when it came to getting a story.

"Just found him dead. Probably drank himself to death." Seeing Norville's furrowed brow, he added, "Sorry, not much of a bone this time."

"You should hear what men down at Ferguson's Feed store are saying. Harper's the main topic of conversation. They have him dying of everything from drinking and carousing with the women over at Tilly's Tavern to being shot and stabbed by a jealous husband. One man said he saw Harper's throat cut and maggots the size of earthworms taking up residence in his nose and coming out of his eye sockets when the undertaker carried him away."

"And that's your reliable source for news?" Blankenship asked. He knew trying to stop such talk was impossible.

"I never listen to their jabber."

"Why do I get the feeling you're disappointed there isn't more to Harper's death. You need more juice for your newspaper?"

When Blankenship didn't respond, Norville asked, "Where are you off to in such a hurry? You look as if you could chew nails."

"I just got a letter from his majesty hinting that my job was in jeopardy if I didn't run the department in a more efficient manner. If not, he would see to it that a more competent police chief replaced me. More competent my ass! He also wanted to know why I haven't promoted his fair-haired nephew. He wants Stanger in charge so he can worm his way into the police department and run the whole town. As if being mayor isn't enough."

"How's Stanger working out?"

"That fuzz-for-a-beard kid is never around when I need him, and when he is he doesn't do a damn thing except sit on his ass and chew licorice."

"Well, you did petition city council for more officers."

"Don't remind me."

When Blankenship became the chief of police, Willoughby had only four men to protect the town – three worked the day shift and one patrolled on weekends. He had no one to work at night. But the town was growing and there was a need for a larger police force. Blankenship had requested additional men to cover weekends and the two patrolmen for night duty. What Blankenship got was Avery Kunkle and Carl Stanger as assistant deputies. Kunkle doubled as the town's lamplighter and snow warden. He was a reliable sort, always punctual and did what was asked of him. Stanger, on the other hand, wasn't worth his weight in sawdust. Neither man had ever worked in law enforcement, which made the chief's job all the more taxing. But, according to the mayor, Willoughby could now boast that it had a round-the-clock police force.

"I do have to admit it was fortunate having him around when the Mathews' child disappeared. Even though I had to prod him, he did help organize and conduct searches. He wouldn't be so bad if he'd just stay in the office where I need him most. And it really makes me angry that the mayor insisted I hire him just because he is his nephew."

"Life is full of concessions," Norville said.

"I guess so. The compromise was better than creating more conflict."

"Are you sure you want to get into it with the mayor right now? Why don't you wait until you've calmed down and your face returns to normal."

"What's wrong with my face?"

"Other than being beet red and the furrows in your brow deep enough to plant corn and that 'biting-bullets' grimace, nothing."

"Suppose you're right. Let him stew for awhile." Blankenship didn't realize his face had taken on such noticeable anger. "Getting into a shouting match with the mayor isn't going to solve anything and would most likely add fuel to the mayor's attempts to get me fired."

"Good. I'd hate to see my best friend, and news source, run out of town."

~ CHAPTER 3 ~

It was too early to meet Katie and walk her to school, so Blankenship returned to his office. He needed to calm down and attack the reports waiting on his desk. He liked being the chief of police, but the amount of paperwork tested his patience.

Norville, not about to let the opportunity of a good news story slip away, stayed on the chief's heels. The editor had become a fixture around the jail, stopping in sometimes several times a day to see if there was anything newsworthy to print. Blankenship soon learned that Norville never stretched the truth or skirted issues. When he published a story, readers could bank on it being accurate.

"See what I mean? He's gone again." Blankenship said, entering the jail and noticing Stanger's empty chair. The broom still stood in the corner, and Cranshaw was still curled up on his rent-free cot, snoring.

Norville poured himself a cup of coffee from the pot sitting on the back of the stove and made himself comfortable in the chair next to Blankenship's desk. As it so often did, their conversation turned to the reconstruction efforts being made to help southerners restore their economy. The newspaper editor had very strong opinions on the subject and wasn't shy about expressing them. Blankenship, having seen the devastation first hand, also had strongly held beliefs on the subject. Their bantering could go on for hours. They were in the middle of a debate about carpetbaggers when Norville suddenly stopped talking. With a mischievous gleam in his eyes, he said, "Thought you might be interested in knowing that Mrs. Haroldson is thinking about selling the family property."

The mention of the former director's property caused Blankenship's train of thought to turn to Katie.

"Katie. Oh, damn. I almost lost track of the time. I've got to walk her to school." He didn't wait for Norville to respond, but started to get up when Andy Jarvis, the undertaker, came rushing in out of breath.

"Chief, glad I caught you. I've got something I thought you'd want to know." Jarvis pushed through the swinging gate and hurried over to Blankenship.

"It's not about Mrs. Haroldson's property is it?"

Jarvis gave Blankenship a questioning look. "What do you mean?"

"Oh, nothing. What's on your mind?"

"Found something unusual when I went to work on Harper."

"Like what?" Blankenship asked.

"Harper died from poison. Cyanide."

"Poison?"

"Are you sure?" Norville broke in.

Jarvis turned to the newspaperman and said, "Of course, I'm sure. I ought to know if somebody's been poisoned or not. Been in this business long enough. Bright, cherry red blood and pinkish skin can only mean one thing. Cyanide." Turning to Blankenship, Jarvis continued, "I'm surprised you didn't notice it yourself when you found him, but then I guess you wouldn't have in all that stink. Took me quite some time to clean him up. Soiled his pants and puked all over himself, he did."

"How could he have drunk cyanide without noticing the bitter almond taste?" Blankenship asked.

"If he was drunk he wouldn't have noticed," Jarvis offered.

"Harper was known to drink a lot," Norville said.

"But I don't think he drank it accidently," Jarvis said to Norville.

"You think it was intentional? Suicide?" Norville asked. "Why would anyone kill themselves by drinking poison? A gun would be quicker, and far less agonizing." Norville shook his head. "Nope. Never in all my years in the newspaper business have I heard of anybody killing himself that way. No, just too nasty. Too painful."

"Don't think it was suicide, either. From the looks of the bruises on his throat, I'd say he was strangled before he died." Then lowering his voice to a whisper he said, "Chief, Harper was murdered."

"What?" Blankenship sprung forward in his chair.

"Holy mackeral!" Norville exclaimed.

"Didn't you see the bruises on his neck?" Jarvis asked the chief.

"No. It was too dark to see much."

"When I saw the blood in the vomit and the condition of the body, I figured that he died from all the alcohol he had consumed over the years. But his coloring suggested poison, and when I saw the bruises, I knew something else was going on. I'm no detective like you, Chief, but I'd say Harper's death was not a suicide or an accident. He had been murdered. That's when I knew I had to come straight to you."

"You did the right thing."

"Poisoned, then strangled. Seems as though somebody wanted to make certain he was dead," Norville said.

"Well, he did a good job of that. And I've got something to show you, too." Jarvis looked from Blankenship to Norville, then back to Blankenship.

Seeing the curious look on the editor's face, and knowing how he would drill him about whatever it was Jarvis had to show him, Blankenship said, "It's okay, I'm sure our friend here will use discretion."

Jarvis hesitated and then pulled a crumpled piece of paper from his pocket and handed it to Blankenship.

Norville adjusted his glasses tighter onto his nose, and then stood looking around Blankenship's shoulder for a closer look.

The paper, torn across the top, seemed to be of good quality, and the watermark proved interesting. The writing, boldly printed, conveyed the most intriguing message: *What you gave me wasn't enough. If you want my services you'll have to pay me more or I'll tell.*

"Where did you get this?" Blankenship asked.

"It was in Harper's shirt pocket. I didn't see it at first. I was more concerned with cleaning him up, you understand. I didn't go through his clothes until later."

Blankenship turned the piece of paper over, examining it.

"I'd like to take another look at the body."

"Sorry, but I no longer have it. Before I could finish with Harper's body, two students from the medical college came to pick it up."

"Didn't you question that?" Blankenship asked.

"Sure I did. I usually turn a body over to the next of kin, but they said that he didn't have any relatives and I was to release his remains to them. Showed me a form signed by one of the doctors. Couldn't read his handwriting. Anyway, I brought the letter I found on Harper directly to you. Figured something unlawful was going on."

Norville took a pad of paper from his pocket and began writing.

"How long has Harper been dead?" Norville inquired.

Jarvis stroked his chin. "Best I can figure at least four days. Saturday would be my best guess from the looks of him."

"Four days. That explains the condition of the body and the smell," Blankenship said.

"How do you know how long someone's been dead?" Norville asked.

"I've seen enough dead bodies and dead cattle to know when they died, or at least come close to knowing. They get stiff within about eight hours, but the body is usually still warm. After two days the body gets cold and rigor goes away. Harper was well beyond stiff. The eggs laid by flies had already become maggots."

Norville made a gagging sound.

Blankenship hadn't noticed the flies either, but then it was dark. Changing the subject, Blankenship asked, "How long does it take for somebody to die after drinking cyanide?"

"Can be pretty quick if a person consumes enough of it. Even a whiff of the stuff in liquid form can kill within minutes. Haven't you ever seen anyone die from cyanide before, chief?"

"Fortunately, can't say that I have."

"Then again, if a man has just eaten or had enough acid in his stomach it might take a little longer."

"Hmm," Norville said, writing furiously on his note pad.

"If you want my opinion, from what is written on that piece of paper, it looks as though Harper was blackmailing someone and got himself murdered because of it," Jarvis said.

From across the room, Cranshaw stirred, grunted, and poked his nose between the bars of his cell. "Murdered?"

~ CHAPTER 4 ~

In light of Jarvis' news that Harper had been poisoned and then strangled, coupled with the piece of paper with the note indicating he was blackmailing someone, Blankenship had no choice but to return to the cemetery and brave the stench of Harper's house. This time he would look for evidence of foul play.

Norville reached the door before Blankenship had his hat on.

"I guess you're planning to tag along."

"Murder is news and I have an obligation to the citizens…"

"I know," Blankenship cut him off. "Well, come along then mister reporter."

"That's mister editor to you," he jested.

"Someday you'll have to explain the difference."

"Mind if we take my carriage? The cemetery is a far walk for me," Norville said.

They rode toward the cemetery in silence for a few blocks before Norville asked, "What do you make of that blackmail letter?"

"Looks as though Harper was into more than just digging graves."

"That's just what I was thinking."

A black wrought iron gate stood at the entrance of the cemetery and two huge stone pillars on both sides of the gate towered above their heads like guards preventing the dead from leaving. A row of three-foot high hedge surrounded the graveyard. Norville guided the carriage beneath the twisted ironwork that formed the words *Willoughby Cemetery*. The town founders had set aside ten acres of land within the town proper for the resting place of its citizens. Many other smaller cemeteries spotted the county, some private, some attached to churches, but the Willoughby cemetery was the only one allocated to all its citizens.

They continued along the cemetery's wagon path until they reached the caretaker's house. Seeing it in daylight gave Blankenship a clearer picture of the place the caretaker called home. A hovel was a better description. Situated in the northwest corner of the cemetery near the wooded undeveloped section, the unpainted, weather-worn clapboard house sagged like a jilted lover with its tarpapered roof the only barrier from the elements. Even though the town provided the house rent free to the caretaker, its dilapidated condition testified they obviously didn't require the tenant to do much in the way of upkeep. Overgrown bushes were abundant and surrounded the house in front and along the side yard.

Blankenship helped Norville from the carriage and together they approached the house. The same flop-eared hound sniffed at Blankenship's leg, and the same scrappy cats from the night before swarmed around his feet.

"The house is in pretty bad shape," Norville remarked.

"Wait until you see the inside."

Remembering the stench, Blankenship cautiously pushed opened the door and braced himself. Even without Harper's body, the odor of human decay hung in the air. He hadn't warned his friend about the smell; it would serve him right for being so nosy.

"My God! This place stinks!" Norville gagged and covered his nose when he stepped inside.

"Careful there," Blankenship said, motioning to the pile of dried vomit Norville almost stepped in.

A dingy curtain covering a dirt-encrusted window hung on a bent rod and filtered out what little daylight came through the window. Rags had been stuffed into the windowpane apparently to keep out any draft.

Blankenship glanced around at what he guessed was Harper's kitchen, recalling where the body had lain, hoping to find something — anything — that would shed light on why Harper had died the way he had. Dried food clung to dishes piled high on the counter. The stove stood in the middle of the room, its fire-life dead for many days now. A small bowl of stew sat overturned on the table.

"Where do we start?" Norville asked, looking around.

"Investigating a murder doesn't have rules. Clues to a crime don't just pop up and say, 'Here I am.' So, I guess we look for anything out of place. That is, if we can tell in all this mess."

Blankenship stepped over a broken coffee cup. Had it been knocked off the table in a scuffle? With the room in such disarray, it was difficult to tell if Harper fought with anyone before he died. If Jarvis' assessment was correct, that Harper had been strangled, there should have been a struggle.

Norville followed Blankenship through the house shaking his head.

The bedroom, like the kitchen, was dirty and cluttered. A well-oiled shotgun leaned against the wall in the corner and a harmonica and a twist of chewing tobacco sat on a battered table next to the bed. Filthy clothes lay in piles or hung over what little furniture there was in the room. Boxes were piled nearly to the ceiling, and each corner of the room was littered with trash.

Norville uttered a sound of disgust when he tripped over an old tin can full of urine and tobacco spit sitting next to the bed. "How could a man live like this?" Norville grimaced.

Blankenship opened the top drawer of a small bureau and rummaged through, careful not to disturb anything that might have taken up residence there. Tucked under a layer of tattered lace, he found a Daguerreotype of a woman with hauntingly beautiful eyes and an enigmatic smile. There was no indication as to who she was. He wondered if she might have been Harper's wife. The house gave no evidence that a woman lived there. Certainly no woman he knew would allow a home to get in such disgusting condition.

Next to the picture, and hidden under a crochet-trimmed linen handkerchief, lay a Bible. He opened the cover. The yellowed pages gave names and dates of marriages, births and deaths. Names that Blankenship suspected to be Harper's parents, a Lucille and Jacob Harper, were printed above the name Peter Harper, and next to his name was Catherine Harper, nee Westfall. Seems Harper had been married. Blankenship wondered what happened to his wife. On another line were the names Nora Garrett, nee Harper and Joshua Garrett. Apparently, Harper had a sister. Nothing followed that entry.

"Know any of these people?" Blankenship asked, showing the Bible to Norville.

"Catherine is his wife. I never met her, but I heard stories. No two were ever the same. One thing for sure though, she left town in a hurry some years back, as I recall. Heard she was some looker. Don't know anything about Harper's sister or her husband, but I'll check it out when I get back to the office."

Blankenship returned the picture and the Bible to where he had found them and closed the drawer.

Another drawer in the dresser held nothing but a jumble of flannel long johns, shirts with missing buttons, socks, and a blanket, none of which appeared to have been laundered recently. In the third drawer, he found a cigar box. Inside was several gold watches, tie tacks, and tiny pieces of gold molded into strange shapes. Also in it were both women and men's rings of various sizes, one with a diamond of considerable size. Odd. Why would Harper have such expensive items? Could they be keepsakes from another time or family heirlooms perhaps? He held one of the rings to the light and read an inscription on the inside of the band: *To My Loving Husband, Jacob.* Blankenship assumed the ring once belonged to Harper's father. He returned the items to the box and put it back in the drawer.

Crumpled sheets on an unmade, metal-frame bed exposed a stained, straw-filled mattress, probably crawling with lice and bedbugs. Not wanting to touch anything that might have infested it, Blankenship took Harper's shotgun and cautiously lifted one corner of the mattress with the barrel. Stuck deep into the middle of the bed, he discovered a leather pouch. He carefully pulled it out. The pouch, with hand-carved tooling along the edge, contained money, a large amount judging from the size of the wad. Blankenship stopped counting at three hundred while Norville stood watching, his mouth gaping.

"Where did he get that kind of money?" Norville asked.

"I'd say this answers the question about blackmail. Blackmail business must have been pretty good," Blankenship said and stuffed the pouch of money into his coat pocket.

Leaving Norville inspecting the bedroom, Blankenship went outside and wandered around to the back of the house and followed a narrow, well-worn path that led to a shed and an outhouse. The door to the shed stood partly open. A workbench took up space along one wall where Blankenship found a knife like that used to gut fish, a pair of pliers, a handsaw, hammer, and a box of nails. A pile of oil-soaked rags lay on the floor in the corner. Several shovels and a pickaxe leaned against the wall, and above them, hung on evenly spaced pegs, were spools of heavy rope and large links of chain–most likely the tools Harper used in his work. Seeing nothing that looked out of place, he closed the door behind him and returned to the house.

Back inside, he took one last look around the kitchen. Satisfied he wasn't going to find anything that shed light on who had killed Harper, he turned to go. As he did, his foot kicked something. Light coming through the open door reflected off an object lying not far from where Harper's body had lain. Blankenship stooped to pick up a gold watch fob. Had the fob been dropped during a struggle?

He turned it over. On one side was a design that appeared to be a family crest surrounded by four diamonds. An inscription reading per angusta ad augusta was on the opposite side. The fob seemed expensive. From the looks of everything Harper owned none of it was worth a Confederate greenback. The gold watch fob and pouch of money were definitely out of place.

"Can you imagine anyone living like this?" Norville asked, emerging from the bedroom, shaking his head and blowing his nose.

"Just us bachelors," Blankenship said.

"My place gets taken over with dust balls and stacks of papers, but my God Hank, how could anyone live in such squalor?"

"Maybe there's an advantage to all this filth," he said, handing the fob to Norville. "It grows gold."

"Where did you get this?"

"On the floor where Harper's body was. Ever see it before?"

"Hmm. Looks expensive," he said, inspecting the fob. "A lot of men in town have watch fobs. This one doesn't look familiar though. Interesting inscription. Latin, I believe. I have a pretty good eye for details, you know, being a newspaperman and all," Norville said and handed it back to Blankenship then patted his breast pocket, took out his note pad and pencil again, and began writing.

"Adam, I have to ask you to keep this quiet, at least until I've had a chance to investigate and get this pinned down. You can have your story then." He slipped the fob into his pocket.

"You're asking a lot, Hank. This is news and I have an obligation to..."

"I know. I know," Blankenship said. "But I can't see spreading what I... we know. At least don't mention the fob or the money for a few days. I want a head start before rumors begin to fly." He knew Adam loved a good story, but he would also respect his request.

"I want every detail when this is over," Norville said, tapping his pencil on Blankenship's badge.

"You'll get your story. Don't worry. You always do."

"I don't know why I bother publishing a newspaper. News travels faster through the gossip vine than I can print it."

"Yes, Adam, I know. Come on, let's get out of here before something crawls up our pant legs."

~ CHAPTER 5 ~

Once outside, Blankenship took a closer look at Harper's house hidden behind a row of large evergreens. Harper could have easily conducted all manner of business, even blackmail, without interference from nosy neighbors.

"What do you make of all this? Do you think he got all that money from blackmail?" Norville asked as they climbed into his carriage.

"Blackmail's a nasty business. You can push a man only so far before he snaps. My guess is Harper pushed a little too far and whoever he was blackmailing pushed back."

"But why poison him and then strangle him?" Norville asked as he snapped the reins. The carriage lurched forward. "A little excessive, don't you think?"

"Good question, Adam. I have no answer for that. Right now I'm more concerned in who killed him. I'll get to the why later."

"Find the why, and the who will follow," Norville said.

"And now you're an expert on murder?"

"No. It just makes sense."

"The money could have come from any number of sources. Maybe he saved it or inherited it," Blankenship said.

After leaving the cemetery, Norville cracked the reins and the horse took off in a trot.

"I wonder what Harper had on whoever he was blackmailing? The letter said he'd tell. Tell about what?" Norville asked.

"Another good question. Got your reporter's hat on again I see."

"That's my job, and I'm good at it, too. Just remember that."

"I can't forget. You won't let me," Blankenship said and then asked, "How well did you know Harper?"

"He's been a fixture around here for as long as I can remember. He hid out during the war. Never volunteered. Made people pretty sore. Willoughby lost a lot of sons at Shiloh. This is a proud town. Should have seen them the day they marched off, whistling and high stepping. Folks weren't so happy when their sons and husbands came back missing limbs, some unable to think straight. Some never came back. No, a lot of people had no use for Harper after that."

Norville pulled the reins and guided the horse to the side of the street to allow the horse-drawn omnibus to pass. The driver rang the bell and waved hello.

"He was an enigma though," Norville continued. "Never saw much of him around town. Took to drinking sometime after the war. He just dug graves and gambled. Some would say he was a bit of a blackleg."

"Gambled? Blackleg? Blankenship looked at Norville. Gambling seemed to always bring out the worst in men. It was one of the many problems he had to deal with as an officer in the cavalry. He had watched men sitting around a campfire gambling while waiting on orders to move out. Most men didn't have any cash, so they played for matchsticks, but those who played for money seemed to always end up in a fight.

"That's the rumor."

They rode along in silence until Norville said, "If Harper was going to blackmail someone, how would the killer have known he was being blackmailed if Harper hadn't given him the letter? The money was under the mattress, but the letter was still in Harper's shirt pocket."

"Another good question," Blankenship said.

"Of course, he could have been blackmailing someone before this. This might have been going on for some time. Long enough to collect that amount of money we found."

"That's possible."

"The fob is curious, too. It certainly didn't belong to Harper. I doubt he would own anything that expensive and, like I said, a lot of men have a fob. Could belong to just about anyone," Norville said.

Blankenship's hand went to his pocket, reassuring himself that the fob was still there.

"Translate the Latin and I bet you'll find the owner."

"Have you ever thought about becoming a detective? I could always use a wit like yours," Blankenship goaded.

"Bet you never figured you'd be involved in a murder when you took this job."

"That's true enough."

"Ever investigate a murder when you worked for Pinkerton?"

"No. I mostly investigated bank fraud and counterfeiting. Solving murders wasn't one of our duties. That was left to the local police. If we had, perhaps I'd know more about how to go about finding a killer." Then as an afterthought, he added, "Had an exciting time chasing after John Booth though after he shot President Lincoln. That's the closest I ever came to being involved in a murder. Of course, they called it an assassination, but it was still murder."

"Any regrets?" Norville asked.

"Regrets? About what?"

"You know, about staying here in Willoughby. You said that you were going to stay in town for only a year or two, then head on to greener pastures."

"Nope. I've never regretted coming to Willoughby, or staying."

Norville raised an eyebrow and bantered. "Would that school teacher have something to do with you staying around?"

Blankenship muttered under his breath as he checked his watch. He had missed walking Katie to school.

"Care to explain that expletive?"

"No." Blankenship knew what Norville was hinting at. After the war, with his family gone, he didn't have much reason to go back to Chicago where he grew up. He took a job with the Pinkerton Detective Agency as a security guard with a railroad company, but after many months spent riding the rails from city to city the job became tiresome. He wanted a more permanent place to hang his hat.

Hearing about Willoughby from a fellow soldier, he came for a visit, and like Norville said, he chose to stay — at least for a little while. So, he got a job as a bank guard and started saving his money. Then one night the police chief fell off his horse and broke his hip, leaving the town without a peace officer. The scarcity of strong, healthy, able-bodied men, and the fact that Blankenship had been an agent with Pinkerton in some people's opinion, gave him the necessary qualifications for the job. But Mayor Frank Bascom wanted his personal friend, Ward Tucker, for the job and ran a powerful campaign against Blankenship. Bascom wanted a puppet that would dance when he pulled the strings, but a member of the town council recommended Blankenship for the job and the council voted unanimously to appoint him the new police chief, leaving the mayor harboring resentment ever since.

Although Bascom gave the appearance of being friendly in public, he dogged Blankenship's every step waiting for him to make a mistake. The first one came when he failed to find the little boy who drowned in the river. He told the mayor many times he had done everything possible to find the child. Nothing worked. Bascom lit on him like flies on a carcass after they found the boy tangled in a thicket along the riverbank a few miles down stream. He flung accusations and tried to pit the town council against him, hoping to get Blankenship ousted from office. The mayor lost that fight, but Blankenship always felt that Bascom was just waiting for round two.

The missing Mathews child was the second round. But Blankenship made no mistakes that time. He went by the book, and even though he never found the little girl, no one could fault his tireless efforts and procedures in conducting the search. But Blankenship always felt Bascom was waiting for round three.

Much to Blankenship's surprise, he liked being police chief. Except for the loss of those two children, Willoughby didn't leave much for a small police department to do except break up an occasional fight, help round up a stray horse or pig now and then, or referee a traffic jam on Erie Street. The pay was better than his job as bank guard, and he figured in a year or two he'd have saved enough money to buy a couple acres and settle down. And yes, Katie did play a role in his staying longer than expected, but he never admitted it to anyone.

"Okay, what do we do first in finding Harper's murderer?" Norville asked.

"We?" Blankenship chided.

"You always said I have a way of digging for a story. I can help you dig up the murderer. We'd be partners."

"Well, partner, we start by asking questions. Isn't that what you told me a good reporter does to get a story? Ask the right questions and sooner or later you'll get the right answers."

"In that case, do you have any idea who would have wanted to kill Harper?"

"No. But I'm damn sure going to find out," Blankenship said. "And our first stop is the jewelry store to see who this fob belongs to."

~ CHAPTER 6 ~

Reaching Erie Street, Norville drove through the center of town where the bank, clock shop, general store, and apothecary occupied most of the blocks between Third Street and Maple Avenue. Professional businesses, lawyers, dentists, accountants, and insurance companies took up space on the upper floors. Blankenship squinted as the sun reflected off the second-story windows. He liked the way the traditional Roman arch above each window gave the town a refined authority.

The side streets were home to smaller businesses — a dressmaker, harness shop and the dry goods store. A small sign in the window of one of the storefronts on Third Street announced the powers of Madam Olga, a palm reader.

On the town square, street vendors were in full voice ringing bells and tooting horns as they hawked their wares. "Scissors, scissors, razors, razors made sharp. Knives, knives to grind." A young boy called, "Charcoal. Charcoal sold here."

The tempting smell of freshly baked pastries coming from Mrs. Kunkle's bakery on Second Street wafted through the air, enticing them in as they passed by. Mrs. Kunkle, who had a sweet disposition that matched her confections, kept tray upon tray filled with delicious rolls, buns and muffins ready for early morning customers, and her hand-dipped candies were thought to be the best in Lake County. Norville, never one to pass up a sweet, suggested they stop in. Blankenship tried to watch his waistline but couldn't resist the delicious treats.

Norville tied his horse to the rail and followed Blankenship into the store. The chief requested a hot muffin. Norville selected a jelly-filled roll from among a dozen different confections Mrs. Kunkle prided herself in baking fresh every morning. Norville had stuffed half of the roll into his mouth before placing a nickel in the basket.

The jewelry store, sandwiched between the hardware and the bank, was just a short walk and the men ate their sweets on the way. Holtzman's Jewelry Store wouldn't qualify as fashionable by New York standards, but Bernie carried the latest designs in jewelry and his prices were reasonable.

A tiny bell attached to the doorframe tinkled when the two entered. A faded green carpet showed where years of traffic had worn it thin. Two large glass display cases along the wall to the right were filled with cameos, hairpins, and ladies brooches. Smudges of tiny fingerprints showed where a child must have amused himself while his mother shopped. Another small case to the left of the narrow center aisle held men's watches and fobs, rings, and tie studs.

Bernie acknowledged the men with a nod and extended his hand across the counter. "You look like a man in need of a fine piece of jewelry for a fine lady."

"Not today, Bernie."

"Then, how about you, Mr. Newspaper man?"

Norville waved him off and busied himself looking at a watch that had caught his eye.

"What I'm in need of is information," Blankenship said and pulled the watch fob from his pocket. "Ever see this before?"

The jeweler turned the fob over several times in his chubby fingers, took a loupe from his vest pocket and placed it in front of his eye.

While Bernie examined the fob, Blankenship eyed a jeweled hair comb and imagined what it would look like in Katie's golden brown hair. He wondered if buying such a personal item for her would be inappropriate.

"Nope, I've never seen this piece before. Not from my store. Nice work, though. Real diamonds. Good cut. Expensive. Unusual design. Looks to be a family crest," he said, indicating the design on the back. Latin inscription, I believe. My Latin is pretty rusty but I think it says something about Honor. Sorry, I can't be of more help."

Disappointed, Blankenship thanked Bernie and they left the store.

"Guess that was a dead end," Norville said, as they left the store.

"Looks that way."

"Maybe a translation of the inscription will give us more information," Norville said.

"Good suggestion, Adam."

Just as Blankenship was about to pull himself up and into the carriage, he heard the familiar high-pitched voice of Mrs. Douglas calling, "Oh, yooo hooo, Chief Blankenship."

Blankenship turned to see a portly, overbearing woman waddling toward him, waving her gloved hand. He tipped his hat, and pasted a smile on his face. Mrs. Douglas had trapped him again. Nothing short of a natural disaster would stop her constant pursuit of him.

"Gee, look at the time," Norville said, taking a quick check of his timepiece. "Ten o'clock. I need to get back to the presses. I'll let you know if I find anything on those names." He settled himself aboard his carriage, clicked his tongue, slapped the reins, and rode off.

"Thanks a lot," Blankenship called after him.

Blankenship needed to think fast or Mrs. Douglas' operatic cooing and matchmaking would go on all morning, and he didn't have time to listen to her latest commentary on his life as a bachelor.

"Why, Mrs. Douglas, how nice to see you this morning. What a lovely hat you're wearing today. I bet it's a Paris original."

"Why, thank you," she said and patted her purple ostrich-feather bonnet. Her ruffles and flounces rustled as she sashayed along beside him.

Mrs. Douglas wasted no time getting to the point. "My cousin's daughter Gertrude will be visiting us during Thanksgiving vacation. I just know you would enjoy meeting her."

"I'd love to chat with you Mrs. Douglas, but I'm in an awful hurry."

"She's a lovely girl; bright, pretty, and well-educated." She was actually gushing. She talked fast, but walked slow. Not wanting to seem rude, Blankenship clasped his hands behind his back and slowed his steps to match hers. He listened as she recounted the list of all the women in the Douglas family. Seems her family tree was overburdened with eligible young females.

"I don't suppose that a nice single man like yourself has plans for Thanksgiving supper?"

"Thanksgiving is a long way off, Mrs. Douglas. I can't say what I'll be doing then."

"A young, handsome man like yourself should have settled down with a wife and family by now."

Yes, he did have thoughts along those lines himself, but not with any of the Douglas females. He set his jaw and lumbered on, secretly wishing for lightning to strike or the road to open up and swallow her. He made no further comment she could hook onto. When they reached her front gate, she fluttered her eyes and waved the tips of her fingers, "Now, you will give some thought to Thanksgiving supper won't you?"

He gave her a halfhearted grin, and then continued down the street, the same street where last year he had accidentally met the new schoolteacher when she first arrived in Willoughby.

He had just rounded the corner of Maple Avenue when he saw her struggling to pull a large suitcase from her carriage. As she tugged, her foot slipped. Luckily, he reached her before she fell into the mud. Small by his estimation, she weighed no more than a feather in his arms.

A hint of deep auburn laced through a tiny golden brown curl that had escaped her bonnet and fallen over her eyes, and when they met his, he heard the whisper of a million jealous stars. She took his breath away, making him reluctant to let her go.

She thanked him for his gentlemanly assistance and accepted his offer to carry her travel bags to her lodging. At the door, she extended a dainty, gloved hand.

He took her hand and gave a slight bow. When he went to open his mouth to introduce himself, he was horrified to discover that his tongue didn't work. He stood mute, heart racing, staring at the most beautiful woman he had ever seen. He was like an awkward colt taking its first steps, and chastised himself for his inability to say anything intelligent. All he managed to do was tip his hat and leave before he made an utter fool of himself.

From that first meeting he made every effort to see her, walk her to school, and escort her to church every Sunday.

Entering the jail, Blankenship was surprised to see Stanger still at his desk, but instead of working, the boy was sitting in his favorite position — leaning back in his chair, feet propped up on the desk, and a coffee mug sitting on top of the papers he was supposed to have filed. This time his eyes were closed and his chin rested on his chest. The kid was actually snoring.

Blankenship had had enough of this slacker. He marched over and kicked at the chair's leg. Stanger jerked awake. His arms flew up and he almost fell backward before catching himself. Blankenship couldn't help but laugh at the expression on his useless employee's face. The mayor should see his darling nephew now.

"Where you been?" Stanger asked and picked up his coffee mug as if nothing had happened.

Blankenship felt no need to respond to his question. He pushed aside a stack of mail to make room for the evidence report he needed to fill out. He removed the money pouch from his pocket, placed it on his desk, and then began counting.

The flapping of the bills caught Stanger's attention. "Where'd you get all that dough?" he asked, wide-eyed like a kid seeing a circus for the first time.

The question annoyed him, but he realized Stanger had every right to know. Besides, Stanger would find out sooner or later. Blankenship told him how Jarvis had discovered that Harper had been murdered and about how he and Norville found the money in Harper's house.

He didn't mention the blackmail letter found on Harper or the watch fob, however.

"You're telling me the guy was murdered and you found all that dough in his house? I don't believe it," Stanger said, his voice raised an octave.

"Keep your voice down. We don't need to tell everyone about the money," Blankenship said, motioning to the occupied cell. "And watch that coffee. You're about to spill it."

Lowering his voice, Stanger leaned closer and said, "Why, that old geezer didn't have a pot to piss in. Who'd ever think it?"

"Hey, ain't nobody gonna let me out of this stinkin' place?" Cranshaw yelled through the bars. "My old lady's gonna tear my ass apart if I ain't home to chop firewood."

"Yeah, yeah hold your horses." Taking a ring of keys from the hook on the wall, Blankenship tossed them to Stanger and then said, "Go ahead and get him out of here."

Stanger reached for the keys and spilled his coffee across Blankenship's desk.

"Watch out!" Blankenship yelled, dodging the coffee.

Stanger apologized and tried wiping at the spill, only to spread the puddle of coffee even further.

Blankenship held his tongue. He had to get away from Stanger before he lost his composure and said something he'd regret. He stuffed the bills back into the pouch, put it, along with the fob, into the large safe behind his desk, slammed the door, and spun the lock. This was one time he wished Stanger hadn't been in the office.

~ Chapter 7 ~

The clatter of dishes mingled with lively conversation greeted Blankenship as he entered the Kingsway Inn for lunch. He would have eaten lunch at his boarding house, but Mrs. Hollingsworth served cabbage stew on Tuesdays. He hated cabbage stew.

The Kingsway Inn, established nearly twenty years ago, was a regular stop for those traveling between Painesville and Cleveland. The furnishings of the inn were worn, the curtains drab, and the floor sagged in places, but the fare always delivered as promised — delicious and plentiful.

Blankenship looked around for an empty table, but didn't see one. Stuart Johnson, the town's blacksmith and livery owner, waved and motioned Blankenship to join him at his table.

"Roast beef with creamed potatoes, special of the day," the waiter said, placing a steaming cup of coffee on the table even before Blankenship had removed his hat.

"Sounds good. I'm hungry as a bear after hibernation." Turning to Johnson, Blankenship said, "Thanks for offering me a place at your table."

"It's been like this ever since I got here. People had to stand and wait for a table."

"What's going on?"

"Just good food, I guess."

Blankenship recognized most of the other patrons. Some he knew by name; others he had only a passing acquaintance. Mr. and Mrs. Lipman, sitting with their toddler, seemed to be enjoying their meal. Lipman had gained notoriety when, as a young assistant county prosecutor, he successfully brought legal action against the head bank teller who have been charged with embezzling thousands of dollars from Bert LaRue's bank. The trial made front-page news for weeks and made Lipman a household name and a very close friend of the mayor. The following year he was elected county prosecutor.

Doctors John and Charles Mathews sat casually talking. Blankenship guessed the brothers to be in their late forties. The two cut striking figures in their frock coats and top hats. Both were well-respected doctors and teachers at the medical college. Blankenship failed to see any resemblance between the two, however. John had a round face and a crop of thick blond hair that he combed straight back. He always appeared jovial. Charles, however, with his dark hair, parted in the middle, and a mustache that connected to his bushy sideburns, seemed stern and humorless. About the only likeness was their eyes; both men had steel-gray, penetrating eyes.

Blankenship didn't know much about John Mathews. His only contact with him had been during the many long hours they spent together searching for his brother's daughter. John had been stalwart in his determination to find his niece and unwavering in his compassion and strength.

Charles was another story. It could have been the devastation of losing his child or perhaps the guilt of not having watched her more closely, but Charles always kept his distance, and any time they passed on the street, Charles avoided looking him in the eye. Blankenship had always felt Charles blamed him for failing to find his daughter.

What more could he have done? Blankenship accepted his actions as those of a grief-stricken father and left it at that.

"Fascinating, those two, don't you think?" Johnson said, apparently aware that Blankenship was looking at them. "I never saw two brothers so different. John struts around town like he sprouted feathers while Charles is quiet and mysterious. Always makes me curious as to what he's up to. I just hope he's a better director of the college than old Doc Haroldson. Maybe their business will turn around now."

"Turn around? What do you mean?"

"I mean, perhaps the college will be more prompt about paying its bills now that they have a new director. I've had a devil of a time getting paid for keeping their horses at my livery. I provided the hearse for Doctor Haroldson's funeral because of what he did for my Amylee when she was sick. He never did send me a bill for all the hours he spent with her. I figured it was the last decent thing I could do for him. At least the town pays on time for boarding your horse," he said.

"That's one concession the mayor had to make."

"Bet that busted his balls," Johnson said with a snicker.

Blankenship smiled to himself. That was one victory he had over the mayor.

"So what brings you in here? Thought you'd be eating at your boarding house."

"Just needed a change today."

"Too bad about the cemetery caretaker. I wonder who will replace him?" Johnson queried.

"I don't think too many folks will line up for that job."

Their conversation ended when the waiter brought a plate piled high with the day's special. The marvelous aroma caused Blankenship's mouth to water even before he took his first bite.

As Blankenship attacked his food, two women he recognized from church came in and headed in his direction, their billowy skirts squeezing between the tables. One fluttered her eyes at him. The other whispered behind her hand and giggled. The reaction he got from women always embarrassed him.

Blankenship stiffened believing they might approach him with chitter-chatter. He nodded a polite hello when one of the ladies acknowledged him with a pleasant, "Good afternoon Mr. Blankenship." He breathed a sigh of relief when instead of stopping at his table they continued past and took a seat at a table by the window that had just been cleared.

Sitting so close, he couldn't help overhear their conversation.

"Did you see Edna Mathews strutting around in that fur stole at church last Sunday? Looked like white fox. Must have cost a fortune. She sure is nothing like her sister-in-law, Martha."

"Poor Martha. I feel so sorry for her. She hasn't been the same since her little Anna disappeared."

Blankenship's stomach tightened at mention of the child's name.

"I'm sure she can afford it. After all, her husband is rich. He's a famous doctor you know," the woman said. The feather in her hat bounced as she spoke. "Did you know they have an ice box?"

"Heavens!"

There was a slight pause before the other woman said, "Doctor, yes, but I'm not too sure about the rich part. Helen LaRue told me that her husband told her that John Mathews went to the bank and tried to borrow money, but LaRue had to turn him down."

"My. My. Do tell."

"It's all that spending Edna does."

Folks in Willoughby prided themselves on the amount of gossip they could carry in one day. If the town ever held a gossip contest, Blankenship felt these two ladies would tie for first prize.

After finishing his meal and hoping to gain insight into who Harper was, Blankenship thanked Johnson again for sharing his table, paid his tab, and then started for Ferguson's feed store. Much to Norville's disapproval, Ferguson's was the main communication center in town. If anyone wanted to know what was going on before the weekly newspaper hit the streets, or if they needed to catch up on the latest gossip, they'd stop in at the feed store.

Blankenship was about to open the door when Clay, Ramsay and Gilbert, men he knew only as loggers and who had a reputation for spreading rumors, approached him. They didn't hesitate to say what was on their minds.

"Is it true, somebody murdered that old grave digger?" Clay asked.

"A thousand dollars! Did you really find a thousand dollars in his house?" Gilbert butted in, as if the prospect were impossible.

It seemed news about Harper's murder and the money found in his house had already spread through town like a pig on fire, validating Norville's comment about not needing to publish a newspaper. Blankenship reprimanded himself for talking with Stanger in front of Cranshaw. Apparently Cranshaw had gotten mighty thirsty while cooped up in his jail cell and couldn't wait to stop in at his favorite watering hole for a drink or two on his way home and spread what he had heard about Harper to anybody who would listen. In no time the story traveled faster than the 9:05 train to Buffalo.

"Know who killed him yet, Chief?" Ramsay asked.

"It was that wife of his," Gilbert said as if it were fact. "That's who done it. She was a right cantankerous sort. Harper finally got tired of her whining and kicked her out. Why, it wouldn't surprise me if she came back and got her revenge. She claimed she'd get back at her old man someday."

Blankenship didn't have time to stand there listening to the trio speculate about who they thought killed Harper, but seeing the opportunity to obtain information, let the men rattle on.

"Revenge for what?" Blankenship asked.

"Who knows?" Gilbert answered. "Women don't need no reason to get out of sorts."

The three men exchanged their list of suspects, agreeing that most people in town hated Harper; any one of them could have reason enough for wanting him dead.

"Probably got himself mixed up with one of them black-eyed beauts at Tilly's and her boyfriend shot him," Ramsay butted in.

"Naw, Red Gundersen probably caught him messing with his wife again," Clay said.

"That could be the cause of all that whining Harper's wife's done," Gilbert added.

"Yep, Red beat her up pretty bad when he found out she was having an affair. And threatened to do worse to Harper. Think it was him?" Clay asked.

"When did Gundersen make this threat?"

Clay rubbed his chin, thinking. "Oh, six, maybe seven months ago. Wouldn't you say, Gil?"

Gilbert nodded in agreement.

"Do either of you know where this Gundersen lives?"

"Naw," all three said.

"I still say it was one of them girls' boyfriend over at Tilly's what done him in," Ramsay repeated.

"And I say that wife of his killed him," Gilbert insisted, trying to make his suggestion sound more a fact.

"Nope," Clay chimed in again. "I put my money on old Gundersen."

"Well, I know the chief here, and I bet he knows who killed him, don't ya?" Ramsay said, patting Blankenship on the back. The men waited for an answer.

"I don't know who killed him, and neither do you. You fellows aren't cooking up gossip again, are you?"

The men hung their heads like dogs having been scolded for peeing on the parlor floor. The loggers had good reason to look embarrassed. Gossip had gotten them in trouble before when they started rumors that the married preacher from the Methodist Church had had a torrid affair with a woman in Mentor. Their slanderous speculations had the girl expecting a child. The gossip got so bad the preacher couldn't go anywhere without being sneered at or having his parishioners turn their back to him when they passed on the street. Attendance at the church fell off, and the preacher was asked to leave town. The ugly rumors finally grew until they festered into tragedy. A week later his wife found him dead in the church rectory Sunday morning. He had hanged himself after writing a letter forgiving the town for their cruel and unjust assessment of him.

Red faced, the three loggers made an excuse of having something to do and rushed off. The chief watched them hurry down the street, questioning how they had time to conjure such gossip.

The sweet mix of oats, barley, and molasses filled the air of the feed store. Otis Ferguson prided himself on maintaining barrels full of feed and for having the latest in farm implements and the finest saddles and harnesses in the county.

Blankenship found Clyde Chapman and Steve Larson, two retired brakemen whom Blankenship knew from his railroad days, playing checkers near the stove when he entered. He knew the two men pretty well — well enough to know they didn't trade rumors and were a good source of information. Clyde greeted Blankenship with a wave and pulled over a stool for him.

"Who's winning?" Blankenship asked, balancing himself on the wobbly stool.

"Three out of four games so far," Steve answered.

"How's things going, Hank?" Clyde said as he took a pipe from his pocket, scraped at its bowl with his pocketknife, tapped it against the edge of the barrel, and then began stuffing it with a hickory-smelling tobacco. Satisfied the pipe was packed just right, he lit it. "You still courtin' that school teacher?" He took a long drag on his pipe, savoring the taste.

Blankenship's face grew warm. At six feet and a hundred and sixty pounds, he wore a badge and patrolled the streets of Willoughby with confidence and authority, but could be instantly turned into a flustered schoolboy by these two old gentlemen when they went to ribbing him about his manhood. Clyde in particular reminded him of his own father, not in looks, but in the way he sized him up. Both men could ride him pretty hard. They teased him something awful once when they suspected he had an eye for the woman at the telegraph office. He braved their playful jabs about that for weeks.

He didn't have a good retort, so he kept his mouth shut and ignored the question.

"Clyde, you knew Pete Harper fairly well, didn't you?" Blankenship asked, unbuttoning his coat.

"Can't say that I knew him all that well. He seemed to change a lot after the war. Why ya asking?" He blew a puff of blue smoke out the side of his mouth.

"Just checking on some information."

"Investigating his murder, huh?" Larson asked.

"Unfortunately, yes."

"All I know is Harper took to drinking and gambling after his wife left him," Clyde said. "Always hanging around Tilly's gambling away every penny he ever made, or so I heard."

Larson nodded in agreement and triumphantly double-jumped Clyde's red checker pieces.

"Know who he gambled with?" Blankenship asked.

"Never was interested enough to ask," Clyde replied.

"Did he have any enemies? Anyone you can think of who would want him dead?"

"Nope, unless one of his gambling buddies got tired of his cheating."

"Cheating? With whom?"

"Listen Hank, if you want to know about Harper and his gambling, you need to talk to Cecil Marsden. You remember him, don't you?"

He remembered Marsden all right. It would be difficult to forget a man who stood in the middle of Erie Street one night yelling his head off that those damn, rotten, yellow-bellied rebels were coming. It took three men to pin him down and haul him into the jail, and two days for him to calm down. Blankenship charged it off as having seen too much of the war and let him go once he was satisfied Marsden had returned to reality. He never had any trouble with him after that.

"He works over at the gristmill these days. Claimed he'd kill Harper if he ever saw him with a deck of cards in his hands again." Clyde stopped talking long enough to king Larson's red checker piece before continuing. "Marsden and a few others play poker regularly. But you'd have to ask him who the other players were."

"Know what Harper did that would cause his wife to want revenge?" Blankenship asked.

"Ah, you've been talking to those loggers, haven't you? That story's been floating around for quite some time. All I know is she told a few women in town that she prayed someday that he'd get what he deserved. Could be just angry woman talk. You know how they get when they're upset about something." Clyde snickered, and then added, "No, I guess a single man like yourself hasn't had that pleasure."

Blankenship let the remark slide. "Either of you know a man named Gundersen?"

"The tanner? Sure," Larson said.

"Know where he lives?"

"Has a farm someplace over in Kirtland," Larson answered.

"Yep, he's been talking to those loggers," Clyde said.

"Hank, you can't buy into everything those men say," Larson interjected.

"You think Gundersen might have had something to do with Harper's murder?" Clyde asked.

"Just want to talk to him."

"Ah, a man of mystery," Clyde said.

"I hear women like that in a man," Larson said, and gave a chuckle.

"That reminds me, did you know that Mrs. Haroldson is selling the property?" Clyde asked.

"So I heard," Blankenship said, put on his hat, and turned to leave.

"And just so you know, the mayor has his eye on the property, too," Clyde added.

Blankenship wasn't about to give these two old gentlemen anything more to ride him about. For right now, if Cecil Marsden had threatened to kill Harper, he'd ride over to the gristmill and have a talk with him. He wanted to have a talk with this Gundersen fellow, too, as soon as he found out where he lived.

He had reached the door when Ethan Grimes came in, his hands stuffed deep into his pockets and the collar of his threadbare coat hiked up around his ears. In his late teens, Ethan was far too young to look so gaunt with such dark circles under his sunken eyes.

Seeing Blankenship, Ethan stopped, opened his mouth as if to say something, but lowered his head and continued past without saying a word. The boy had the same look in his eyes that Blankenship had seen in the eyes of many frightened rebels just before they took a bullet.

~ Chapter 8 ~

Blankenship checked his watch. If he hurried, he could ride out to the gristmill, have a talk with Marsden, and be back in time to meet Katie after school and walk her home. He rushed back to the jail, saddled Mingo, and then set out for the mill.

The gristmill's old paddle wheel, turning at a lazy, hypnotic rhythm, carried water over its paddles and spilled it into the river below, churning the water into white foam. The calming sound could lull a man to sleep on a sunny, summer afternoon, but today the splashing and gurgling seemed anything but soothing; it was cold and uninviting as it slapped at the riverbank.

The mill, one of the first built in Lake County, had been destroyed by fire before the war. The lack of available men delayed it being rebuilt until five years ago. The mill's grinding stone was the only original part of the mill to remain.

Sacks of flour were stacked on the platform alongside the building ready for loading onto waiting flat wagons. On the far end, hemp bags of grain were piled six high waiting to be ground into meal. Men with their shirtsleeves rolled up worked steadily lifting and hauling the sacks to and from the wagons.

After locating the shift foreman, Blankenship asked to speak to Marsden. The foreman informed him that he hadn't been at work for the past few days.

"Probably sick again," he told Blankenship and gave him Marsden's home address. "You can look for him there."

Following the foreman's directions, Blankenship rode north past the railroad tracks to the far end of town where a small, sun-bleached saltbox stood near the edge of the cliff that dropped sharply to the river below.

He knocked and waited. Soon, a woman, whom he assumed was Mrs. Marsden, appeared at the door wearing a soiled apron covering a faded yellow dress and holding a baby wearing only a diaper. Her eyes darted from his face to the yard behind him as if looking for someone. She pulled a torn and tattered sweater across her bosom, as she struggled to hold the baby. Three small children, all in need of a good scrubbing, clung to her skirt, one crying, one chewing on a soggy cracker, the other sucking his thumb as snot ran down his face.

"You get back in there," she said and shooed the kids back inside the house before handing the baby to the oldest of her brood.

"Are you Mrs. Marsden?" Blankenship asked.

The woman nodded.

"I need to speak to your husband."

"I haven't seen him since yesterday," she politely answered and knitted her fingers together as she spoke. "He isn't in any trouble, is he?" Her voice was soft and low.

"No, ma'am. I just need to talk to him."

He thanked her and started to leave when she offered as an afterthought, "You might try looking for him down at Tilly's Tavern. He sometimes goes there."

Tilly's was located about a mile west of town. Even though the local ordinance prohibited the sale of alcohol before sundown, and forbade gambling within the town proper, Blankenship had been summoned to the tavern on several occasions because of ordinance infringements.

He had tried to shut the place down, but the mayor had the last word. Tilly's stayed open, infringements or not.

Blankenship had stopped in for a beer on occasion, but he had never been there this early in the afternoon. There were several taverns and a pool hall in town, but Tilly's was the only place where a man could find a game of chance — at least the only place Blankenship had knowledge of.

A bright red sign with gold lettering hung over the entrance. No horses or buggies stood around the building and he found the front door locked.

He went around to the back entrance marked "private," knocked several times, and waited. The door finally opened slightly and an eye peered through the crack.

"We ain't open," a woman's voice said.

"I want to talk with Tilly."

The door opened a little wider. A woman in her mid thirties stood looking at him. Seeing his uniform and badge, she said, "No liquor being sold now. It's too early."

"I'm not here about your business practices," Blankenship said and took a step forward.

The woman opened the door and stood aside to allow him in, then quickly closed it behind him. Blankenship stood blinded by the darkness of the windowless hallway.

"This way," the woman said.

He followed the sound of her voice up a flight of stairs and down a dark hallway that smelled of stale beer and cigarettes. Half way down the hall he rammed his shin into something sitting in the middle of the floor. He let out a cry of pain. Rubbing his leg and hobbling the rest of the way, he followed the woman to a room at the end of the hall. There, the woman turned up the flame on the lamp sitting on the desk and slid her eyes over the police chief before leaving him alone.

Blankenship guessed the room to be Tilly's private office. A large ornately carved desk took up most of the space. Heavy tapestry hung on the walls and two chairs, covered with the same fabric, flanked a round table. A portrait of a confederate officer hung behind the desk.

It wasn't long before Tilly appeared in the doorway. Her red hair, piled high on her head, and her wide set eyes that twinkled with mischief gave her the look of a rakish imp. The tavern owner's reputation and questionable business practices, not only for the kind of business she ran, but from the mere fact that she was a woman owning a business, brought scorn and contempt from the women in town and smiles to the faces of the men.

"I understand you had a little accident," she said. "Happens all the time. I keep meaning to put a light in, but..." She paused, walked behind the desk, opened a small box sitting on top, and took out a cigar. She rolled it between her fingers, sniffed it, and then bit off the end. Blankenship watched as Tilly struck a match and then lit the cigar. After taking several puffs and blowing the smoke into the air, she continued, "...I have to use the funds for things like license fees." She looked directly at him and raised an eyebrow. "Now, what can I do for our police chief? Would you like a beer?"

Blankenship wasn't above imbibing on occasion, but he was there on business and drinking in uniform was strictly forbidden. He waved off the offer.

"Well, then have a seat." She motioned to a nearby chair.

Preferring to maintain a dominant position, he chose to remain standing.

Tilly came around the desk, perched on the edge and crossed her legs, allowing her skirts to expose her ankle. Blankenship forced his eyes away.

"I want to know if Ceil Marsden is here."

She stared at him for a long moment, puffing on the cigar. Her dark eyes penetrated him, making him feel uncertain if she had heard what he said.

"My customers have a right to their privacy, Chief."

"Yes, ma'am, they do. But this is police business."

The woman threw her head back and blew tiny smoke-rings at the ceiling. Blankenship looked at the contradiction sitting before him a businessman in every sense of the word. Except this one was wearing a dress. It seemed the war had changed many things.

She seductively uncrossed her legs and leaned toward him.

"What kind of police business?"

"Is he here?" Blankenship said, sternly.

She must have gotten his meaning that he wasn't leaving until he talked with Marsden because she finally said, "Upstairs," and pointed to the floor above.

She went to the door, and then disappeared leaving the door ajar. The sound of a woman's laughter filtered through the thin walls. Blankenship sensed something more than honest business going on, but he ignored the impulse to see what was happening in the next room; he was there on a more important matter. Beside, he knew there would be other times to deal with Tilly's controversial business.

Marsden soon appeared in the doorway wearing his suspenders pulled up over his undershirt, looking like an unmade bed. Stubble formed a shadow on his face and his hair was mussed. Marsden, surly and rugged, seemed just the type of person to associate with a man like Harper.

"You want to talk to me?" Marsden's voice sounded like a grinding stone.

"I want to ask you a couple questions," Blankenship said and motioned for Marsden to take a seat.

"Like what?" Marsden said.

"Like what kind of a grudge you had against Pete Harper?"

"Who said I had a grudge against him?"

"I hear you hated Harper. Wanted to kill him. I want to know why."

"I don't have to tell you anything."

"Don't play games with me, Marsden. I can haul you into jail as a suspect in a murder if I choose."

"Yeah. Yeah, okay." Marsden slumped down in the chair. "Harper was a cheating, lying bastard as rotten as they come, and yeah, I threatened to kill him if he ever cheated me at poker again. Is that what you want to know?"

"And did you kill him?"

"You get straight to the point, don't ya," he said.

"Always do. You own a watch fob?"

"No, to both questions."

Blankenship didn't expect him to say otherwise. Marsden hardly looked like a man who would own such an expensive fob as the one found in Harper's house. As to him killing Harper, he didn't expect him to own up to it.

"I suppose you can account for your whereabouts when Harper was killed."

"And when was that?"

"Sometime Saturday as best Jarvis can determine."

"Hmm...let's see. Saturday..." He rubbed his stubby beard and glanced at the ceiling.

Blankenship's jaw tightened; Marsden was toying with him.

"Saturday. Right here. Yep, right here. I'm always here on Saturdays. Ask Tilly there," Marsden said, pointing to the tavern's owner standing in the doorway. The bar owner came into the room and sat down on the chair's arm next to Marsden.

"Go ahead, pretty thing, tell the man where I was on Saturday," Marsden said, touching the woman's hand and running his fingers up along her bare arm. "Tell the chief where I was all day Saturday."

Tilly flashed a saucy grin at Blankenship and said, "Of course, he was here. Good-looking is my favorite customer. Why, the place would seem empty if he wasn't around." She leaned forward just enough for her breasts to bulge above her bodice. Marsden seemed to enjoy the scenery and gave her a big grin.

Changing the tone of his questions, Blankenship asked, "Who else did Harper play cards with?"

"Hell, he'd play with anybody who had enough dough," Marsden said.

"How often did he come here?" he directed his question to Tilly.

"Most days." Then as an afterthought she added, "I never saw him around here on Saturday, though."

"How much money did Harper win at poker?"

"Plenty from what I hear, but he cheated to win most of it. He always found some new sucker to dupe," she stated.

"Any idea why he never came in on Saturdays?"

"Can't help you there."

Blankenship left the tavern with a feeling in his gut that Marsden was holding something back. His meager interview hadn't gained him much in the way of useful information, and Tilly's collaboration of Marsden's feeble alibi annoyed him. But he'd have to let it go for now. If Marsden had any dealings with Harper other than cards, he'd find out in time. Blankenship made a note to keep an eye on those two.

Blankenship rode back to town, having just enough time to get to the school and walk Katie home.

He had just reached the bridge that spanned the Chargin River when he saw two wagons in the middle, blocking traffic. Old man Sloan, a farmer who came to Willoughby once a month and a trapper, bringing his furs to town, were going at it fist to face. Sloan who could whip his weight in wildcats had the trapper in a headlock and was dragging him around in a circle. People stood on both sides of the bridge cursing and yelling for the men to move on, but their shouts fell on deaf ears.

Sloan wasn't about to give an inch and the trapper wasn't backing down. The trapper broke lose, swung at Sloan but missed. Sloan grabbed the trapper and threw him to the ground. The trapper rolled over and quickly sprung to his feet and kicked at Sloan, lost his footing, and spun himself into the wagon, dislodging its load. Barrels tumbled from the wagon, rolled across the bridge, and slammed into the railing.

Sloan gave a growl that could have caused a bear to back off and head-butted the trapper. The trapper back-peddled but caught his balance, and then went at Sloan again with balled fists. The trapper ducked but not quickly enough before Sloan landed a left hook into the trapper's gut. He grunted and flew backward, hitting the bridge. He slid down and sat slumped over in a stupor.

Blankenship had seen enough. He slipped up behind Sloan and grabbed him around his chest. Sloan broke loose, twisted around, and came at Blankenship head first, slamming him into the wagon. Both men ended up ass over teakettle on the muddy bridge, rolling around like two pigs fighting over a bucket of slop. Blankenship drew back and threw a punch, but missed when Sloan dodged the blow. Blankenship's knuckles landed on the rim of the wagon wheel. Pain shot through his hand, bringing tears to his eyes.

When Sloan suddenly realized he had just assaulted the chief of police, he went limp and offered a sheepish apology, but Blankenship wasn't buying it. He hoisted Sloan to his feet, and then arrested him on the spot for striking an officer of the law.

That would have been the end of it, but one of the barrels that had fallen from the wagon had rolled into the bridge abutment and broke open. The heavy smell of moonshine filled the air as the liquor spilled from the barrel and flowed into the river. Seems Mr. Sloan had a side business.

By the time Blankenship had cleared the congestion, hauled Sloan and the trapper into jail, and filled out all the paperwork, it was well past three o'clock. His heart sank. Not only had he missed walking Katie home from school, his hand hurt like hell.

Maybe if he hurried, he'd still have time to call on Katie before dinnertime, but noticing his mud-covered uniform, he changed his mind. What would she think of him if she saw him looking as though he had been rolling around in the mud like a pig? Then he laughed. He had been rolling in the mud like a pig.

~ Chapter 9 ~

It was still too early to walk Katie to school the next morning, so Blankenship stopped in at the newspaper office to have a talk with Norville. The editor's new apprentice, a boy about sixteen, was busy writing in a large ledger when Blankenship entered. A stack of the weekly newspapers sat in a rack by the front door along with copies of the *New York Times*.

"Adam around?"

"Back there." The boy motioned over his shoulder.

"Would you tell him I'd like to talk with him?"

"Sure thing, Chief," the boy said and disappeared behind a door leading to the pressroom.

Most days the newspaper office was filled with the noise of people coming and going, the telegraph key clicking away sending and receiving messages, and the press thumping a sluggish rhythm as it pounded out the week's news. Today, however, the room was quiet. Only the smell of ink filled the air.

A large picture of Horace Greeley, the infamous journalist and editor of the *New York Tribune*, hung conspicuously on the wall. Norville, in defiance of the town council's objections, had defended his mentor's position concerning the amnesty of the confederate leaders by hanging the portrait in the most prominent place in the office. Remembering the clamor and Norville's stubborn stand brought a smile to Blankenship's face. He liked a man who stood up for his beliefs.

Adam appeared from the pressroom wiping his hands on an ink-stained towel. Black streaks marked his cheek, making him look like an Indian in full war paint. His sleeves were rolled up to his elbows, his suspenders hung from his shoulders, and his glasses rested in his nest of hair.

"Hope you're here with news I can print. That is if I can get this damn press fixed," Norville said, with frustration showing in his eyes. "I stopped by your office twice yesterday to find out if you had anything new on Harper, but you were out."

"I've been out asking a lot of questions around town. Don't know if it's getting me anywhere, though."

"Hmm," Norville said and pulled his glasses down onto his nose.

"Why is it so quiet around here today?" Blankenship asked.

"The stupid press threw a gear last night. It will take days to get the parts to fix it. Damn machine," he mumbled. "Well, have you uncovered anything useful?"

"Just gossip."

"Is that all?"

"You sure expect a lot from a guy who has been investigating a murder for less than twenty-four hours."

"I thought you would have had Harper's murderer locked up by now."

"Now you're sounding like Bascom," Blankenship said.

"Whoops. Sorry."

"Listen, I need to know...."

Before Blankenship could continue, Edna Mathews swept into the office. Though not yet cold enough for a heavy cape, she wore a fur stole draped over her shoulders. Her ruffled skirts caught in the door as it closed behind her. She yanked at her skirts and huffed at Norville as if to say it was his fault. After untangling her skirts, she trotted to the counter, sniffing the air, and rang the bell. The tinkle brought the apprentice to his feet. Edna handed him a piece of paper, demanding that her news be printed right away. The young man read the copy, looked at the woman, and then nodded. Apparently satisfied, she turned to leave, giving Blankenship a haughty glance as she strutted past.

"Get much of that?" Blankenship asked Norville.

"Oh, that's just Edna's way of punctuating her importance," Norville replied. "She comes in here every week with her list of winners from her weekly afternoon card party. Demands that I print it. I always do." He wiped at his hands again. "You were about to say?"

"Do you know a man by the name of Red Gundersen?"

Norville opened the gate that acted as a deterrent against interlopers wishing to enter the private inner sanctum of the Fourth Estate and motioned Blankenship to take a seat. He threw the soiled towel into the corner with a frustrated sigh.

"Gundersen," Blankenship verbally nudged Norville.

"Oh, yes. Gundersen. He's one of the best tanners in the county. This is one of his leather aprons," Norville said, indicating the one he had on. "Johnson over at the livery buys aprons from him, too. Makes the best chamois around."

Snapping his fingers, he said, "I bet that's who made that money pouch you found at Harper's. Gundersen. I thought I recognized the craftsmanship."

"Gundersen? Are you sure?" Blankenship asked.

"I'd bet on it. There are several tanners around, but he's the best."

"Know where I might find him?"

Norville limped over to a large battle-scarred filing cabinet, pulled out an ink-smudged drawer, and flipped through several card files before finding the one he wanted.

"His full name is Rolf Gundersen, in case you want to know. He has a place over in Kirland." He wrote the address and directions to Red Gundersen's place on a piece of paper and handed it to Blankenship. "It's not a big place. You can't miss it."

"What's wrong with your hand?" Norville asked, apparently noticing how swollen Blankenship's hand was when he reached for the paper.

"Nothing much, just the results of taking a punch at old man Sloan. Do you have a card on everyone in town?" he asked.

"Just those who make news or who I think might have information I can use at some later date. I make note of it on these cards and file it away. It has come in handy several times," he said, taking the card from the chief. "Mr. Sloan must have a mighty hard stomach for your hand to look like that."

"I don't know about his stomach, but his wagon wheel was pretty solid." Then changing the subject, he asked, "Did you find out anything more about Harper's wife or any of the other names we saw in Harper's Bible?"

"No, I checked as soon as I got back yesterday. Nothing." He replaced the card and closed the drawer.

"How about Marsden? Have anything on him?"

"Now, him I know about. I wrote a piece on him the day he went crazy in the middle of the street. Want to see it?"

"Naw. I was there, remember?"

"Why do you want to know about Gundersen?" Norville asked.

"Just investigating what I hear. I'm finding that a lot of people didn't care much for Harper."

"Have you checked on Haroldson's property yet?"

"What makes you think I'm interested in his property?"

Norville gave Blankenship a mischievous grin. "I know more than you think, my friend. I hear it's going cheap. Forty acres. Oh, and just for your information, Bascom has inquired about the land, too."

"Yeah, so I've heard."

The mention of Haroldson's land brought thoughts of Katie to mind. He looked at the clock on the wall and realized she would have already left for school. He swore under his breath.

"I suggest you have a doctor look at that hand. You could have broken a bone."

Blankenship thanked his friend for the information and left him grousing to himself about the printing press.

Maybe he should see a doctor about his hand. He knew from tending wounded soldiers after a battle that the only method of mending a broken bone was to place the arm or leg in a wooden cast, but for a broken finger about all a doctor could do was use an adjoining finger as a splint, wrap it with cloth, and let it go at that. He would have considered doing just that, but how would it look for the chief of police to walk around with a huge bandage on his hand? He didn't want to appear infirmed.

His hand hurt like the devil, but he had been through worse. A piece of lead was still lodged in his leg from where a powder keg exploded during a battle at Fair Oaks, sending pieces of metal flying everywhere. The pain in his hand was nothing compared to that. His leg still ached sometimes when the weather turned.

Blankenship returned to the jail and saddled Mingo. Gray clouds had begun rolling in, as if ushering in an early winter. Soon summer would be only a memory. With any luck, he'd find Gundersen's place and be back before the weather turned mean.

Blankenship took the road south, riding along the river bend that cut through cliffs carved eons ago by the Chagrin River. Mingo had served him well through the years, first when he was a member of the 8th Illinois Cavalry during the war, fighting with the Army of the Potomac, and then again while he worked as a bank guard. When Blankenship slid into Mingo's saddle it was like slipping into a pair of old comfortable slippers. They moved together as one.

The ride took him the better part of an hour. A brightly painted sign announcing "Gundersen and Son, Tanner of Hides" stood by the road. Deep ruts lead to a small, well-kept farmhouse with a small barn in back. As Blankenship rode up, a man carrying a large box was walking in the direction of a shed. Blankenship knew at once he had found the tanner. The man's full, bushy red beard and bright red hair explained the reason for the tanner's nickname.

"Are you Red Gundersen?" Blankenship called as he rode up. The question was more a formality than a need for confirmation.

"Who wants to know?" Gundersen asked.

"Me. I'm Hank Blankenship, the police chief in Willoughby."

"What brings the chief of police all the way out here?"

"I need to talk to you."

"Tie up over there. We can talk inside." Gundersen pointed to a small rail at the end of the shed. Blankenship tied his horse and followed the tanner into the building. Blankenship figured the building to be Gundersen's tanning shed.

The man motioned for Blankenship to take a seat on a bale of straw in the corner and then lumbered over to a long workbench and set the box he had been carrying on the dirt floor. A workbench held an assortment of small curry and tanning tools, and several large pieces of rawhide. A shelf above the workbench held several jars, tins and small boxes.

Gundersen moved a pile of rawhide aside and rummaged through the large box until he found a clean rag. "Now talk away. Ain't got nothin' to hide from the police," he said.

"I want to ask you about Pete Harper," Blankenship said.

"What about him? What crime has he committed this time?" Gundersen picked up a bottle marked hydrochloric acid, poured a little onto the rag, and then began rubbing it over a piece of leather.

"How well did you know Harper?"

"Pete Harper? Hum. Don't know him at all. Know *of* him, of course. Guess everybody knows of him."

Blankenship didn't like the way Gundersen turned his back to him. He wanted people to look him in the eye when they talked to him.

"I heard he once had an acquaintance with your wife."

Gundersen rubbed the rag a little faster and changed his tone. "Well, yes. But that was a long time ago, you understand. I thought you were referrin' to a more recent time."

"When did you last see Harper?"

"Don't know what you're hintin' at."

Blankenship wasn't about to talk to Gundersen's back. He walked over to the workbench and stood facing him.

"Murder's what I'm talking about," Blankenship said, leaning forward just enough to see the man's face.

"Murder? Who'd Harper kill? We don't get much news around here," he said.

"Harper didn't murder anyone. He's the one who has been murdered. He was found dead in his house. "

Gundersen paused, put down the cloth, and turned to face Blankenship. "And you think I killed him? What gives ya that idea?"

It was difficult to read what was behind the man's eyes.

"Did you?"

"I hold no anger for the man."

"I understand he had an affair with your wife."

"That was long ago. I don't hate Harper for what he done. Forgot all about it."

"Are you saying you never threatened to kill Harper?" Blankenship leaned in closer.

Gundersen must have sensed Blankenship knew more than he was letting on because now he offered another slant to his tale. "Well, never's not quite right. I did tell him to stop seein' my wife, and I might've said somethin' strong about what I'd do if I ever caught him with her again. Scared him plenty cause he never came pokin' around after that."

"So you did threaten to kill Harper?"

"Like I said, what Harper done has long been forgotten. Me and the little lady get along just fine now. Just fine. What's done is done. Can't cry over what happened back then. I say turn your heart over if it shows a dark side. Love thy neighbor as the Good Book says."

Blankenship thought Gundersen offered too much affection for a man who had wronged him in a way most men would never forgive. Any man would have killed another for taking advantage of his wife.

Blankenship picked up a piece of fine leather cut into a small square and examined the workmanship. It had distinctive tooling like the pouch he found in Harper's house.

"What are you going to make with these?" Blankenship asked.

"Money pouches. I get calls for 'em all the time. Can't make 'em fast enough."

"Who buys them?"

"Just about anyone. Bankers. Businessmen mostly. Sold two just last week to a doctor at that medical school." Gundersen returned to rubbing the hide.

"Did you make one for Harper?"

"Naw, what would he need with a money pouch?"

Spying a box sitting on the shelf, he picked it up and turned the box around to read the label. A skull and crossbones was printed on front. "What's this?" Blankenship asked, opening the box. Peering inside, he found a white crystalline substance.

"That's poison — cyanide."

"What do you use this for?"

"Rats."

"Rats?"

"Yeah, rats. The cats used to control 'em, but after the heavy rains this past summer the critters took over the place. Cats weren't enough, I needed somethin' more."

"Where were you last Saturday?" Blankenship put the box back on the shelf next to boxes marked alum and salt.

"Right here."

"Can you prove that?"

"Yep, just ask my wife." The man didn't flinch. "Am I a suspect?"

"Do you own a watch fob, Mr. Gundersen?"

"Fob? Naw, why?"

Gundersen was probably stonewalling, but he saw no reason to talk to his wife. Blankenship doubted she would admit if her husband hadn't been at home on Saturday. And he knew he didn't have enough reason to haul Gundersen into jail just because he had a box of poison in his barn or because he had threatened Harper. Even though the tanner had a good reason for wanting Harper dead, he didn't appear to be in a financial position to pay off a blackmailer.

~ CHAPTER 10 ~

Late afternoon shadows had already begun snaking their way along the streets when Blankenship returned to town. Angry with himself for not getting back in time to escort Katie home after school, he used the time to ride to the cemetery. He wanted to take another look around Harper's house to see if, by chance, he had missed anything.

As he approached the house, he saw a man looking into the window. A curiosity seeker perhaps, wanting to see where someone had died? From the style of his clothing, a hat banded by a green feather, tasseled leather boots that came to his knees, and breeches and laced shirt, Blankenship figured him to be a Gypsy. In his hand he carried a large, carved walking stick.

Several yards beyond the house, a covered wagon sat along the pathway. Blankenship thought he saw movement inside.

He dismounted Mingo and walked up to him. "Are you looking for someone?" Blankenship asked.

The man turned and looked at him but didn't answer.

"I'm Hank Blankenship, chief of police. It would be wise if you told me just what your business is here."

The interloper remained silent.

"What is your name?"

When he didn't answer, Blankenship realized he was dealing with a situation that required a heavier approach. He pulled back his coat to reveal his baton.

By the man's expression, Blankenship knew he understood its meaning.

"Nagy."

"You have a first name?"

"Johan," he answered.

"What is your business here, Mr. Nagy?"

"I come do business with Mr. Harper." He spoke with a heavy foreign accent but had a fairly good command of the English language, broken as it was.

"What kind of business?"

Nagy looked back nervously at the wagon.

"Don't you think this is a strange place to conduct business?"

Nagy just shrugged, offering no further comment.

"Where are you from, Mr. Nagy?"

"Here. There. Everywhere."

"I'll ask again, what kind of business do you have with Mr. Harper?"

"Purchase merchandise from Mr. Harper."

"Just what kind of merchandise do you buy from him?"

"Things."

"What kinds of things, and please be more specific."

"Watches, rings, hair clips, pieces of gold. Anything he got to sell."

Were these the items he had found in the cigar box in Harper's house?

"How often do you come here to do business with Mr. Harper?"

"He let me know. Sometimes I come every month."

If Nagy was coming here every month, Harper must have had a good supply of items to sell. Where was he getting them? Had he stolen them? There hadn't been any reports of theft in town. Perhaps they came from gambling? Men wouldn't be too quick to admit they had lost their watch or wedding band in a poker game.

"How did Mr. Harper come by this merchandise you purchased from him?"

Nagy shifted his walking stick from one hand to the other and gave Blankenship a look of defiance.

Then the thought occurred to him. Was this the man Harper was blackmailing? Was he stealing for Nagy, and Harper wanted more money for his work?

"Come on Mr. Nagy, surely you know where he got these things. You wouldn't want me to think that the items you bought from Mr. Harper were stolen, would you?"

"Stolen? No. No, stolen."

"And you know this to be true because...?"

"I never buy stolen. Mr. Harper give his word."

From what Blankenship had heard, he doubted Harper's word meant much.

"If they weren't stolen, then where did Harper get the items he sold to you? I want the truth. Where did the they come from?" Blankenship was almost yelling at the man.

Nagy raised his hands and shrugged. "Do not know where jewelry come from, but gold is," he grinned and pointed to the gold tooth in his mouth.

How would Harper get his hands on gold from teeth? Oh good God! The thought hit him. Was Harper helping himself to the personal belongings of the deceased before he buried them? Was that what the letter meant by "doing what you wanted?" He had made a pact with the devil, stealing from the dead for a profit. The thought sickened him.

He swallowed the knot in his throat, wondering how long this had been going on, and just how many good citizens of Willoughby had been robbed? Was the watch fob one of the articles Harper had stolen?

"Perhaps talking about this in my office at the jail would help you remember where the jewelry came from," Blankenship said, and took hold of Nagy's arm. "Come along, Mr. Nagy."

"Borton! No. No, jail!"

Nagy turned and sprinted toward the wagon. The Gypsy was fast, but Blankenship was quicker. Forgetting about his injured hand, the chief tackled him and wrestled him to the ground. The man may have been wiry, but he was strong. Blankenship winched in pain as he struggled to get the Gypsy to his feet.

"This America. I have right to buy," Nagy howled.

"Buy. Yes, but buying stolen property is against the law. Especially if the person you bought the items from was murdered."

"Murdered? Who is murdered?"

"Mr. Harper."

"Mr. Harper murdered? No. No. I no kill him."

Nagy gave no further resistance while Blankenship tied his hands behind his back. As he did, he heard the sound of horse's hooves. Looking around, he saw the wagon pull out of the cemetery.

✦

Blankenship awoke to pounding on his bedroom door and his landlady calling his name. He rolled over, turned up the wick on the lantern, and checked the time on the clock on the nightstand. Three o'clock.

"This can't be good," he grumbled to himself, and padded to the door.

Mrs. Hollingsworth stood in her nightgown, nightcap askew, looking none too pleased for having been awakened in the middle of the night.

"One of your men is downstairs. Says he needs you right away." She turned with a huff and walked away.

Blankenship donned his trousers and tramped down the stairs to where Kunkle was waiting for him by the front door.

"We got trouble, Chief. Nagy escaped."

"Damn!"

Blankenship ran back upstairs, put on a shirt, and grabbed his hat and coat.

"What happened?" Blankenship asked as they set out running. Both men were out of breath by the time they reached the jail.

"Now, want to tell me what happened?"

"Don't know for certain. I just got back from Tilly's and found…"

"What in the devil were you doing there?" Blankenship questioned.

"It's not what you might think, Chief. It was a busy night. First, Mrs. Foust claimed a neighbor's dog attacked her chickens again. Found no trace of any dog anywhere, and then there was a scuffle over at the tavern. When I got back I found that Mr. Nagy was no longer in his cell."

"How did Nagy get out of the cell?"

"Sloan can tell you what happened better than I can. He saw it all," Kunkle said and pointed to the man in the cell. "Sloan, the chief's here! Tell him what you saw!" he yelled to the man lying on the cot.

Sloan sat up, swung his feet off the cot, and ran his fingers through his hair. Focusing on Blankenship he said, "I was asleep when I heard this awful racket in the outer office. They just burst in the door as if it wasn't there. Damnest thing I ever saw."

"They? They who?" Blankenship asked.

"Hell, I don't know. But there was a bunch of them. All jabbering in some strange language I never heard before. Dressed all funny. Scared the crap out of me, it did. I looked for Kunkle but he wasn't at his desk." He paused to wipe at his nose.

"Go on. Then what happened?"

"They marched over to the other cell, stood for a second talking to the man inside, and then before I knew it they were opening the door. Didn't use a key or anything. It was like they used hocus-pocus. Then they all rushed out of here. I heard their wagons roll off, and then it got quiet."

Blankenship looked to see that the cell's keys were still hanging on the peg on the wall behind his desk.

"What time was this?" Blankenship asked Sloan.

"How the hell should I know? Don't have a watch, and I can't see the clock from here, but it wasn't long after he left," Sloan said, motioning to Kunkle.

Turning to Kunkle, Blankenship asked, "What time did all this happen?"

"I signed out on the log book to see what was going on at Tilly's around one o'clock. You can check it," he said and pointed to the logbook sitting on the counter. "And I left the front door unlocked according to regulations in case there was ever a fire."

In all the time Blankenship had been the police chief, no one had ever just come into the jail in the middle of the night, unlocked a cell door, and released a prisoner. "What happened at the tavern?" Blankenship asked. "That was strange. There wasn't any disturbance when I got there. All was quiet except for the regular noise you'd expect in a place like that."

"Who told you there was a fight there?"

"Just some guy. Never saw him before. He just came in here hollering that there was a fight and I needed to go break it up."

"I smell a set up. That was just a distraction to get you out of the office."

"You know if we had an extra man on nights this wouldn't have happened."

Blankenship knew all too well the need for a stronger police force. Maybe now he had sufficient reason to request an additional man for the night shift, but getting the mayor and town council to approve the money wasn't going to happen. Not any time soon anyway. Besides that would be like locking the barn after the horse was stolen.

"Should we try and go after Nagy?"

"You bet your ass we're going after him."

What else could he do? He had allowed a thief, possibly a killer, to slip from between his fingers. An escaped prisoner was all Bascom needed to pound the final nail into his dismissal.

"But they could be anywhere by now. We'd only be chasing our tails," Kunkle said.

"Sheriffs in Geauga, Cuyahoga, and Ashtabula Counties have been keeping an eye on a band of Gypsies traveling through their areas and have sent frequent telegrams with updates as to where they were camped. The last sighting was near Gates Mills. That's just a little over six miles. If we hurry we can be there by the time the sun comes up.

"Go rouse Stanger from his beauty sleep. Tell him to hightail it over here while I get the horses. I want someone on duty here the rest of the night."

"Sure thing, Chief."

"And don't let him out of your sight until his ass is in that chair," he said, pointing to the vacant seat at Stanger's desk.

Blankenship pulled the revolver he had since the war from his desk drawer and secured it in his waist holster. He didn't think he would need it, but he always wanted to be prepared. And then, just for assurance, he took one of the Henry rifles from the gun cabinet, loaded it with a .44 round and loaded sixteen more rounds in the magazine tube, and secured the weapon in the holster attached to Mingo.

By the time he saddled Mingo and filled a canteen with water, packed an extra blanket in the saddlebag, and found a lantern, Kunkle had returned with Stanger.

Stanger, still sleepy-eyed from being hauled out of bed grumbled as he entered the office, "Why'd you get me out of bed? Kunkel wouldn't tell me anything."

"I need you to watch the jail while we're gone."

"Where are you going at this time of night?"

"To catch a man."

"Who? Why can't I go?" Stanger asked, almost pleading.

"I need you here to watch after our guest," Blankenship said, pointing to Sloan.

"Why can't Kunkle watch him? It's his shift."

"I don't have time to argue with you, Stanger," Blankenship said, giving him a stern look. "I want you to go to the telegraph office as soon as it opens in the morning and send a message to all the surrounding counties telling them to watch for a band of Gypsies, and do whatever it takes to detain them. One of their tribe escaped my jail."

Stanger's eyes grew wide. "Escaped? Why do I always miss the good stuff?"

Kunkle and Blankenship set out in the direction of Gates Mills, taking the main road south out of town. An overcast night sky covered what little light there was coming from the moon making the trip slow going, and having to guide their horses along the steep grades of the hills slowed them even further.

As Blankenship had predicted, they reached the edge of Gates Mills at sunrise and sat looking down over the small village. A fine layer of fog covered the valley, and except for a few birds flying from tree to tree and the distant bark of a dog, the valley was quiet.

Blankenship stopped and sat like a statue, looking around.

"What are you doing?" Kunkle asked.

"Listening." He turned his head to the left, and then right. "Do you hear anything?"

"No, not really. Just the early birds."

"Smell anything?" he said as he sniffed at the air.

Kunkle turned and raised his nose to the air. "Is that bacon cooking?"

"You'd make a good tracker. See that?" Blankenship pointed to a plume of smoke rising just above the trees. "Come on. That's their camp."

"Do you think they're dangerous? Will they shoot at us?" Kunkle shifted in his saddle.

"You never know."

"What do we do?"

"We go get our man. Follow my lead."

Blankenship guided Mingo along the narrow path and stopped just short of the tree line, beyond which the Gypsies were camped. The memory of a heated battle came rushing back vivid in his mind as if it were only yesterday. He, along with a company of 115 men, had encircled a rebel camp near the Chickahominy River. The Battle of Seven Pines, lasting only twenty-four hours resulted in 790 being killed, and 3,594 wounded. More than six hundred were captured and remain missing. He had lost a lot of good men and friends that day.

He shook off the image. This wasn't war, not in the traditional sense, and he didn't have fifty men behind him. Instead of flanking the camp, Blankenship chose a direct approach, and rode right into it.

Six wooden wagons were pulled in a tightly knit circle around a campfire. A line of about ten more wagons trailed along the road as if ready to pull out. Each was colorfully decorated with intricately painted designs of flowers and symbols. Steps lead up and into the body of the wagons, and thick coverings protected the doorways. Pots and pans hung along the backs and sides of each one.

A couple old men wrapped in blankets sat near the fire, cooking. He saw no women.

Dogs barked, sounding an alarm as he and Kunkle approached the Gypsies. Within seconds the men formed a line with drawn weapons.

"I don't think this is such a good idea," Kunkle whispered.

"Just keep your hands away from your gun and where they can see them."

Blankenship pasted on a big grin and rode forward as if he owned the ground.

"Good morning," Blankenship called. "I'm here to see Mr. Nagy. Anyone know where he is?"

None of the Gypsies spoke, but stood looking at the two interlopers.

"I know he is here and I need to speak to him." Blankenship dismounted, leaving his rifle in its holster on his horse. He approached the men and extended his hand.

No one moved.

A crunch of boot steps coming from behind them drew everyone's attention in the direction of the sound. An older man, with thick black hair and cold-black eyes came from behind a wagon, pulling a blanket around his shoulders. He wore a floppy felt cap and his pants were tucked into his boots.

"What is your business with us?" His low, gravelly voice suggested his age to be much older than his appearance.

"I'm Hank Blankenship, chief of police from Willows Falls." He showed them his badge.

The men tensed but didn't move.

"Mr. Nagy escaped from my jail last night. I've come to get him."

"No one here by that name," the man said.

Blankenship was well aware that Gypsies seldom told the truth, and didn't expect anyone to come forward and offer up one of their own.

"Look around, if you like." The man pulled his blanket closer to his chest, gestured to the men standing by the campfire, and then slowly walked back to his wagon. The men stepped aside, allowing Blankenship and Kunkle to pass.

Together they made their way to the wagons and searched each one, but came up with no sign of Nagy. Of course, there wasn't any sign of him. He was either long gone or they had him well hidden.

Realizing they weren't going to find Nagy, and they certainly couldn't haul the entire band back to Willoughby, Blankenship mounted Mingo, but not before offering a warning, "The police across Ohio will be looking for him. I suggest you hand him over now and save yourself a lot of grief." He might as well have been talking to the trees.

The two laymen returned to Willoughby without their man.

~ Chapter 11 ~

Around noon the next day, Blankenship and Kunkle arrived back in town exhausted and hungry. Kunkle rode with his chin against his chest and his hand holding tight to the saddle horn. Blankenship told him to go on home, he'd handle filling out all the reports. After feeding and wiping down Mingo, he opened the back door to the jail and found it clean, paperwork filed away, and Stanger sitting at his desk, awake.

"Well, I'll be damned. Miracles do happen," the chief muttered to himself.

"Moring, boss. Where's that Gypsy fellow?" Stanger asked. "Did you get him?"

"Nope."

Stanger whistled under his breath. "You let him get away?"

Blankenship had no desire to counter his accusation, and Stanger's tone only added to his frustration.

"There's a letter on your desk. Delivered just a few minutes ago."

Blankenship found the letter sitting on top of a pile of papers. He ripped open the envelope and read what it said. Seems the mayor had the town council fired up. It had taken him less than twelve hours to convince the town council to convene a special meeting. This time it sounded serious. Blankenship was to appear before the council at nine o'clock tomorrow morning, a Saturday no less, to answer to charges that he had been derelict in his duties as the chief of police.

"Derelict my ass." He slammed the letter down on his desk.

There was no doubt the mayor was behind the inquest, and had persuaded the town council to convene an emergency executive meeting to oust Blankenship from his job. If Harper's murder wasn't bad enough, now he had an escaped prisoner to answer for. This was going to be the final blow to his career, if it could be called that. He knew the mayor wasn't going to let the escape of a prisoner pass without notice and would demand his dismissal. He'd personally see to it that the council had him escorted to the depot and put on the first train heading south to go live with those "damn secessionists" as the mayor liked to call them.

"Mr. Norville has been in a couple times looking for you. Told me to tell you he wants to know what happened."

Blankenship wasn't in the mood to answer Norville's questions. All he wanted to do was go back to his boarding house, crawl into bed, and pull the covers over his head.

"Hey, do I get extra pay for the extra time I spent here doing Kunkle's job?"

Blankenship was just too tired to get into it with him. His irritation was on the edge of exploding but he held his tongue. Instead, he told Stanger to go get lunch, go do anything, but get out of the office.

Stanger was up and out of his chair before Blankenship could finish the sentence.

The chief sat at his desk for the next hour writing reports about the escape and the attempt to capture the escapee. He filled out the expense forms and cleaned his weapon, although it hadn't been fired. Old habits carried over from the military. The clock ticking it constant rhythm could have easily lulled him to sleep sitting in his chair, but he needed to go back to Harper's house and retrieve the box containing what he believed to be items taken from the folks Harper buried. It was now evidence. He sluggishly pulled himself up and had almost made it to the coat tree when the back door opened and Kunkle came in.

"What are you doing here? Thought you'd be curled up in bed by now," the chief said.

"Couldn't sleep from all the excitement of chasing after that Gypsy, so I thought I'd come in and see if you needed me to do anything around here." He pulled out a chair and asked, "Where's Stanger?"

"I sent him home, or wherever it is he goes. That kid is like a gnat buzzing around my head. He can really get on my nerves."

"I know what you mean. I think he means well, though. He just needs to learn how to be more responsible."

"Believe me I'm working on it."

Wanting to take another look at the watch fob, Blankenship spun the dial on the safe. As he took out the fob, it slipped from his fingers, fell to the floor, and rolled under Kunkle's feet, spinning like a top until it came to rest on its side.

"Where did you get this?" Kunkle asked, picking up the fob to examine it.

"It was in Harper's house. I'm keeping it as evidence."

"No kidding. How did Doc Mathews' fob get there I wonder?" he asked, flipping it as if it were a coin.

"What do you mean Doc Mathews' fob? How do you know that it belongs to him?"

"I saw it hundreds of times attached to the gold chain on his pocket watch. He comes into my wife's bakery every morning on his way to the college. I'd be there just getting off work. Whenever he'd pay for his purchase, he pulled back his coat, and there it would be, all bright and shiny."

"This fob belongs to Charles Mathews? Are you certain?"

"Oh no, not Charles, his brother, John."

Blankenship wasted no time heading for the medical college where a young man in the administration office told him that Doctor Mathews didn't work on Fridays and that he'd most likely find him at home.

Prestigious old homes along Dobson Street, belonging to the more prominent citizens of Willoughby, were mostly dark red brick with large front porches and porticoes. John Mathews' home was no exception. Blankenship found the architecture to be similar to the plantation homes he had seen in the south. A waist-high iron fence surrounded the property. A lightning rod adorned the high-pitched roof of the round turret and two large, white pillars at the entrance of the front porch gave the house a stately appearance. Leaves had been raked and the shrubs trimmed to perfection. Baskets of fall flowers hung from the porch, giving it color.

Blankenship followed the brick-lined walkway and climbed the wide steps to the porch. Just as he reached the top step, Bert LaRue came charging out of the house, slamming the door behind him, and almost rammed into the chief. He halfheartedly tipped his bowler in recognition before hurrying down the walkway. Odd. LaRue was always a friendly sort, and it was unlike him to be rude. He watched as LaRue climbed into his carriage and rode off without looking back.

Blankenship raised the heavy lion's-head doorknocker and let it fall back against the brass plate, making a rich resounding clap. Before he raised the knocker a second time, a black man wearing a white jacket opened the door.

"May I help you?" he asked as if Blankenship were a customer in a department store.

"I'd like to speak with Doctor Mathews."

The man stepped aside allowing the chief to enter.

The amber light from the crystal chandelier in the foyer dispensed a warm welcoming glow. Blankenship took off his hat and followed the servant into the parlor.

"Wait here, please," the man said.

The chief knew, or figured, John Mathews had money, but from the looks of his home, he was filthy rich. A sofa with elegantly carved arms sat in front of a heavily draped window, and a round single-pedestal table with a marble-top held a lamp with a hand-painted globe. Fringed silk scarves covered a beautiful mahogany pianoforte. Across the room, a large curio cabinet filled with the kind of porcelain figurines that ladies like to collect stood against the wall. Seems Edna Mathews had collected quite a few knick-knacks over the years. The massive mantel above the brick fireplace held an ornately framed painting of Doctor and Mrs. Mathews and their two children. All the walls were covered with wallpaper depicting a scenic landscape.

According to Norville, Mathews' father and grandfather had made their fortunes in the railroad business back east. Blankenship wondered how much of that money made its way to Willoughby and how much of what he saw came from the practice of medicine.

"I see you were admiring my wife's art pieces," John Mathews said, appearing in the doorway wearing a waistcoat. Standing more than six feet tall, Mathews cut a striking figure. His hair was combed to perfection and a small scar above his lip creased his mustache.

"My wife has excellent taste. Won't you agree? She brought many of her favorite pieces from England when she came to this country. She especially favors early Baroque furniture. Isn't the marquetry on the secretary magnificent? The ivory elephant is one of a kind. From Africa, you know."

"I'm afraid I wouldn't know African ivory from store-bought soap," Blankenship replied.

"How may I help you?" Mathews asked.

"I need to talk to you, Doctor Mathews."

"Do you have a fever? Seems everyone is coming down with the grippe this time of year," Mathews said, taking out his stethoscope and directing him into his private office.

Like the parlor, it displayed expensive fabric and highly polished cherry wood furniture. Rows of medical books with leather bindings lined the shelves and a glass-front cabinet containing medicine bottles of various sizes, each with a printed label, stood along the far wall. A crystal inkwell sat next to a dark green leather stationery box. Both were placed squarely in the middle of a blotting pad trimmed with the same dark green leather.

"I'm not here for medical reasons, doctor. I need to ask you about..." He fumbled in his pocket. "...about this." He showed him the fob. "Is this yours?"

"Why, I should think not," Mathews said, and with a gesture fitting an actor on stage, pulled back his morning coat to reveal an identical watch fob dangling from its chain attached to a button on his vest.

"You might want to talk to my brother, however. Ask him if he has his. We have identical fobs. When Charles and I graduated from medical college at Fairhaven in New York, our father gave each of us an engraved watch with the date of our graduation. See, mine says May 10, 1855. Charles graduated two years later. He's my younger brother, you understand. Then our grandfather gave us each a watch fob with the family crest as a symbol of our family's heritage." Reaching for the fob he continued, "If you like I can return it to my brother. Seems as if he has been a little careless."

"That won't be necessary. I'll return it."

Blankenship thanked the doctor and left with his head spinning. Two watch fobs — both identical. He hadn't counted on that. Clearly, if this watch fob didn't belong to John, then it must belong to his brother, Charles.

❦

Enclosed by a white picket fence, the modest two-story, wood-framed house on River Street stood in stark contrast to John Mathew's elegant brick mansion. The gate squeaked when Blankenship pushed it opened. An arrow painted on a small gray sign inscribed "Dr. Charles B. Mathews, M.D." pointed to the side entrance.

The police chief took each step slowly, remembering the last time, some four months ago, when he had come to this house and knocked on the front door; the time that he carried the news that he had to discontinue the search for their child. The child that should have been inside, warm and secure, playing in front of a cozy fire with her dolls.

Mrs. Mathews opened the door wearing a black mourning dress. The grief of having lost her child was carved in her face, making her look old and withered. Her eyes, rimmed with dark circles, widened when she saw him as if begging him to tell her he had found her daughter.

Blankenship stood with his hat in his hands, wishing he could bring her good news. Believing that would never happen, he was grateful that she didn't ask. He cleared his throat and said, "Morning, Mrs. Mathews. I'd like to see the doctor, please."

"I'm sorry, he's gone to deliver Mrs. Spurlock's baby. I don't know when he'll return." Her voice sounded flat and distant. She offered no further comment.

"Please tell the doctor that I'll call again another time."

She nodded as if she understood, but from her vacant expression, he doubted that she would remember to deliver the message.

~ CHAPTER 12 ~

By the time he awoke the next morning, Mrs. Hollingsworth had closed her kitchen for the day, and no matter how much Blankenship tried to sweet talk her into making him a fried egg, she wouldn't budge. She had her house rules as she had told him on many occasions. She did, however, give him a telegram that had been delivered only moments before he came downstairs.

Blankenship read the telegram and smiled. Not all telegrams brought bad news it seemed. He tucked the paper into his shirt pocket and left his boardinghouse.

He stopped at the bakery and bought a sweet roll before continuing to the town hall to face his lynching. He was coming out of the bakery when Norville rode by.

"Need a ride?"

The editor had that look in his eyes that told Blankenship he wanted every detail of Nagy's escape. The chief was grateful for the ride and climbed aboard anyway, knowing Norville would drill him for information.

"Where are you headed this early on a Saturday?"

"I was summoned to appear before the town council. Bascom is at it again, or should I say, still at it, trying to get me fired. Guess you want every detail."

"That's what I had in mind. Stopped by your office several times yesterday."

"I've never known anyone to be so annoying," Blankenship said, looking at his friend.

"And I can't recall anyone ever escaping from the jail before either. This is news and I've got…"

"…a responsibility to print it. Yes, I know," Blankenship finished his sentence.

The chief filled him in on how the Gypsy had escaped, the ride to Gates Mills, and how he and Kunkle had chased after him with no success.

"What did you bring him in for in the first place?"

Blankenship hesitated then turned to his friend and said, "Norville, you've got to keep this out of the paper. Promise you won't report what I'm about to tell you. At least not until I get to the bottom of it and sort things out. It could have dire consequences if the citizens of this town found out."

"This sounds serious."

"It is. Will you promise?"

"Alright."

"Remember the box of jewelry we found in Harper's house?"

Norville nodded.

"That stuff didn't come from gambling and it wasn't family heirlooms like we first thought. I believe Harper was robbing the corpses before he buried them."

"Holy mackeral!"

"Harper was stealing from the dead, and that Gypsy was buying the personal effects he stole. Harper got greedy, wanted more money, and tried blackmailing him. The letter said he had done what he wanted and indicated that he wanted more for his trouble."

"And you believe that Gypsy killed him?"

"That's another story. The guy just didn't seem to be a killer. A thief and rascal, yes, but a killer, no. He was genuinely surprised when I told him Harper had been murdered."

"Could have been a good act."

"True. But I have a pretty good sense when someone is lying to me."

Blankenship could see the newspaperman's instincts were itching to start writing, and he would have if he hadn't been holding onto the reins.

"No story, remember. You promised," Blankenship said.

Norville frowned and said, "So, what are you going to do about it?"

"What can I do? The man is dead. Can't hang a dead man. Not sure what to do with the jewelry in the box, though. If I try to find the owner's family and return the items it would cause them great distress, not to mention the trouble it would create. That kind of news would tear the town apart."

"You've got that right."

They arrived at the town hall before Blankenship could tell Norville about discovering to whom the watch fob belonged. He'd just have to save that piece of information for another time.

Norville reined in the horse and brought the carriage to a halt in front of the town hall.

⚜

A blue-gray haze from Bascom's cigar had already filled the room when Blankenship walked into the council chamber. The chief could feel the heat of the mayor's stare as it followed him to his seat. Blankenship removed his hat and took the chair at the table indicated by the council president.

In any other town there were legal procedures to follow required by law in order to call a special council meeting on such short notice. This meeting, scheduled on a Saturday, emergency or not, was highly irregular. But then the mayor had a lot of clout.

As Blankenship expected, Norville followed him into the council chamber and took a seat in the back of the room and waited for the proceeding to begin. He nodded and gave his friend a pencil salute as if to wish him luck.

The council president no sooner called the meeting to order when Bascom jumped up from his seat and began listing the charges he had brought against Blankenship.

"You can kiss your job goodbye right now," the mayor said to Blankenship. The mayor had a long list of grievances. First, there was the little boy who drowned, and then Anna Mathews disappeared. The mayor even brought up Marsden's episode in the middle of the street, as if it were his fault. Now, he was facing charges for allowing a prisoner to escape. This just could be strike three.

"Blankenship is incompetent. He has a total disrespect for the law. He refuses to wear a regulation hat, insisting to wear that thing." He pointed to the cavalry hat sitting on the table in front of Blankenship. "He's guilty of dereliction of duty, and has allowed a murder suspect to escape his jail. He should be fired," Bascom said and pounded his fist on the table.

"Please take your seat, Mr. Mayor," the president of the council demanded.

"He isn't fit to wear that badge," Bascom continued.

The council president cautioned the mayor again.

"Chief Blankenship, as you know charges have been brought against you regarding your ability to manage the police department. This meeting has been called only to determine if your actions warrant a formal hearing. Do you understand?"

"Yes."

"Is this true, Chief Blankenship that you allowed a prisoner, a murder suspect, to escape from your jail?" the council president asked.

"Not entirely. First, Mr. Nagy, the man in question, wasn't a murder suspect. He was being held on an unrelated charge. Second, he escaped with the help of his people, during the night, after they created a diversion that drew Officer Kunkle away from the jail."

The city council listened, nodding occasionally, while members took notes.

"You say they created a diversion? How so?"

"Officer Kunkle has explained the event in the police log. In it he states that a man came into the jail and told him that there was a fight at Tilly's Tavern. Of course, Officer Kunkle responded."

"He left the jail unattended," Bascom barked.

"If we had a full workforce, we would have had two men watching the jail. As you know, we can't leave the jail unattended in case there is a fire. My request for additional men has been ignored."

It felt good to rub that issue in the mayor's face. But he was unable to counter the mayor's remark. Kunkle had left the jail unattended. He had done what was necessary under the circumstances and he followed regulations. Blankenship would like to have mentioned that Bascom's fair-haired boy had left the jail unattended many times, but held his comment.

"Tell us, Chief Blankenship, what exactly did happen that night?"

"Officer Kunkle came to my boarding house to get me the instant he discovered the man had escaped. That was around three o'clock. The man in the other holding cell, a Mr. Sloan, told how a band of Gypsies had burst into the jail and freed the detainee."

"Then what did you do?" a council member asked.

"Relying on reports from the Cuyahoga County sheriff's office that said a band of Gypsies was last seen around Gates Mills, Kunkle and I set out after him."

A murmur rose from the five council members.

"Did you find him?

"We found the camp, but Mr. Nagy wasn't to be seen. I suspect he either had taken off before we got there or they had him well hidden."

"You didn't even try," the mayor yelled. "He shouldn't have allowed the man to escape in the first place."

"I received a telegram this morning," Blankenship pulled the telegram from his pocket and handed it to the council president, "saying that the band of Gypsies were caught in Cuyahoga County. The sheriff is holding three of them for stealing a horse. One of the men matches the description of Johan Nagy. The telegraph goes on to say that after they are finished with them, if they haven't hung them for horse stealing, they will release them to us."

"That seems to clear up this issue," the council president said.

"That man is incompetent! He should be stripped of that badge," Bascom said, pointing to Blankenship.

"We'll take that under advisement, Mayor. For now, council is dismissed. We will advise you of our decision within a few days, Chief."

~ Chapter 13 ~

Blankenship had looked forward all week to a day without gossip, innuendo and speculation about the murder of Pete Harper, but mostly he was looking forward to spending Sunday afternoon with Katie at the church social. He hadn't seen her all week and today was to be special. Although he had been courting Katie for several months, he always felt like a schoolboy every time he thought about seeing her again.

Blankenship polished his boots to a high gloss. After inspecting his chin for any stray stubble and rechecking his sideburns to make sure they were even, he made one last attempt to straighten his tie that always seemed to ride up on one side. He wanted to look his very best today.

If he wished to believe Mrs. Hollingsworth's assessment of him, he still turned women's heads. No lines creased his face, and he still had all his hair — unruly as it was. Gray streaked his temples though he was only thirty-two years old. Knowing that his father had grayed prematurely, he accepted his fate as a fact of life. His waist size remained the same as it had been before the war. He chuckled, recalling how Mrs. Hollingsworth chided him about his shirts being too large for her ironing board. He had to remember to thank his landlady for pressing his Sunday suit.

He arrived at Katie's front door at exactly nine thirty as promised. Katie opened the door on his first knock, looking like a china doll just taken out of its wrapping on Christmas morning. Her dress, a subtle shade of blue, trimmed with white lace, hugged the curve of her tiny waist. Her hair, always pinned back in a bun on school days, now cascaded in ringlets, and a bonnet with blue ribbons crowned her head.

He quickly removed his hat and said, "You look lovely." He wanted to tell her how much he loved the way her eyes sparkled and how much he loved the way a dimple dented her cheek when she smiled. He wanted to tell her that she smelled like honeysuckle after a gentle rain. There were so many things he wanted to tell her but held his tongue for fear he'd sound like an ignoramus.

"Thank you," she said as her cheeks flushed. "I hoped you would like it."

Of course he liked her dress; he liked everything about her. "Beautiful," he said. She invited him into the parlor only long enough to help with her cape. A soft, sweet smelling curl brushed against his fingers as he placed the cape over her shoulders. He hoped she wouldn't notice how his hands trembled.

"What's this?" Spying a cloth-covered basket.

"My donation for the potluck social."

He snuck a peek. In the basket was a dozen golden brown buns. Beautiful and a good cook, too, he thought. The potluck social was a big event and always included a special program planned by the ladies auxiliary, but the highlight of the day remained the meal.

"Where is your aunt?"

"She's a bit under the weather today and won't be attending church."

Blankenship almost leaped with joy, but said, "Oh, I'm sorry. I hope she isn't sick."

"Nothing serious. Just a little head cold."

The short walk to the church was quite pleasant despite an overcast sky that held the sun at bay. Being with Katie today, strolling casually along together, was very different from the first time he had accompanied her to the primary school.

It was at the beginning of the school year when he met Katie at her front door and offered to carry her tablets and books. They walked to Erie Street in silence and turned onto Center Street in the direction of the school. *Come on, Hank, ask her. You only have a few more steps to go.* He was the chief of police and had fought in a war for God's sake. Why couldn't he talk to this beautiful lady? They were nearing the school when he finally blurted out, "Miss Wilson..." he gulped, "...would you do me the great honor of accompanying me on a picnic in the park this coming Sunday?"

She slowed her pace slightly, but didn't answer. Did she hear his question? Once, he thought he caught her glance his way, or was it just wishful thinking.

At the school, he followed her to the door. She retrieved her books, lowered her eyes and said, "Thank you, Mr. Blankenship." That was all she said. His heart plummeted. It had taken all the courage he could muster to ask her to a picnic and now she wasn't going to answer.

Disappointed, he turned to walk away when he heard her say, "Yes, I would like very much to accompany you to the picnic. And you may call me Katie."

Katie. What a beautiful name. The sidewalk melted under his feet. The most beautiful woman he had ever met had consented to his company on Sunday.

That Sunday, as they sat relaxing under an oak tree eating the delicious lunch Katie had prepared and listening to the band play in the gazebo, that he learned her full name was Kathleen Marie Wilson. Her family was from Lancaster, Pennsylvania. She had been educated at the Lake Erie Female Seminary and loved teaching children. After her parents died aboard the passenger steamer, *G. P. Griffith*, when it caught fire on Lake Erie, she had come to live with her aunt. She spoke without the pretense and flirtatious coyness he found annoying in most women.

Since that first Sunday, they had spent many Sunday afternoons together. Being with her had become as comfortable and natural as the rain in spring, and he soon discovered he no longer stumbled over his words when he was with her. It wasn't long before he knew he was falling in love.

The church was almost full by the time they dropped off the buns at the social hall and entered the church. They squeezed into the only remaining unoccupied pew. Sitting so close to her made his heart pound.

Blankenship went through the motions of standing to sing hymns, bowing his head during prayer, and doing what was expected of him in church, but it was difficult to pay attention to Reverend Watkins' sermon with Katie sitting so close.

Between the sermon and communion his mind wandered to the murder of Pete Harper. Knowing that someone in the congregation could very well be a murderer didn't set well with him. Would a murderer even come to church? Blankenship speculated he would if wanting to keep up appearances, pretending to be a God-fearing Christian, all the while sitting in the house of God with blood on his hands.

Blankenship looked around the sanctuary. He had come to know many members of the congregation. Doctor and Mrs. John Mathews, along with their two boys, Dilbert and Harland, sat in the front pew marked by a plaque with their name. Charles Mathews sat alone; his wife wasn't in attendance. Calvin Lacy, the pharmacist, and his wife attended church services every Sunday, but always sat near the back of the church. Bert La Rue was in his regular seat near the side door. Also in attendance were shopkeepers and tradesmen, professional men, as well as laborers. All were good folks, hard working and caring. It was hard to imagine any one of them committing murder.

When the minister raised his hands, the pump organ wheezed a few sour chords, and on cue, everybody stood to sing the hymn on page forty-three of their hymnals. When the last chord sounded and the long "amen" in chorus reverberated through the rafters, the congregation sat down, and Reverend Watkins made the weekly announcements. The Ladies Auxiliary would hold a baked goods sale next Saturday to raise money for a new pulpit; a preacher from another town would be visiting next month; a young couple announced their marriage bans. Blankenship wondered if someday the minister would be announcing his and Katie's wedding bans.

※

Blankenship couldn't remember ever being so glad to see a church service end. As everyone began filing into the aisle, he took Katie's arm and guided her from the sanctuary into the social hall. The ladies of the auxiliary had decorated the room with brightly colored streamers, and placed vases of flowers on each table. Clusters of women chatted among themselves, while men eyed the food table, and the boys ran around laughing and pulling girl's pigtails. From the amount of food piled on the table an entire cavalry regiment could survive for days on the fried chicken, baked ham, roasted potatoes, vegetables, breads and pies.

The Reverend and Mrs. Watkins stood at the door welcoming the congregation. The Mathews family sat at a table marked "Reserved." Mayor Bascom, with his wife's hand draped over his arm, strutted around the room, shaking hands and smiling at everyone as if it were Election Day. He never missed an opportunity.

Once everyone had gathered, Reverend Watkins gave the blessing and folks quickly formed a line at the food table. He and Katie walked through the line filling their plates. Blankenship piled his high and took an extra biscuit that Katie had made for the social, and then looked for a place for them to sit. Blankenship spied an unoccupied table on the far side of the hall and headed to it, but before they reached the table, he heard someone call to him. When he turned to look, he saw Mrs. Douglas elbowing her way through the crowd pulling a young lady along behind her.

Unable to navigate around chairs quickly enough, he and Katie were trapped with nowhere to go and no way to avoid her. Mrs. Douglas was on them like fleas on a dog.

"Yooo hooo, Chief Blankenship," she called again.

"Oh, Chief Blankenship, I'm so happy I saw you there. I want you to meet my niece, Charlotte. She arrived in town yesterday and I just couldn't wait for you to meet her," Mrs. Douglas said, pushing her niece at him.

The girl, looking like a sheep being lead to slaughter, extended her hand and lowered her eyes. With both hands full, carrying his and Katie's plates, all he could do was nod and say, "Pleased to meet you."

"You two have a lot in common. She's a good cook and likes cats." Turning to her niece she said, "Chief Blankenship has a cat in the jail. Oh silly me, I don't mean he has the cat locked up in the jail. Of course, he wouldn't do that. The cat lives there," she babbled.

"Mrs. Douglas, this is Miss Katie Wilson...." Blankenship started to say, but Mrs. Douglas interrupted, took hold of the chief's arm, and turned him toward her niece. "Now, I have a lovely supper planned for this evening and you're invited. I just know you two will get along."

"Ah, Mrs. Douglas, I...." Blankenship attempted again.

"Mrs. Douglas," Katie interrupted, stepping between Blankenship and Charlotte, "Chief Blankenship is having supper with me this evening.

I'm sorry but he is unavailable. Now, if you will please excuse us, our food is getting cold."

Mrs. Douglas stood, mouth gaping, red-faced and sputtering as Katie turned and Blankenship hurried to the table.

"I owe you one," Blankenship said.

"I plan to collect," Katie said and squeezed his arm.

Near the end of the meal, the minister stood and called for silence by tapping his knife against his water glass. He thanked the Lady's Auxiliary for the magnificent food and for decorating the hall. "And now I want to recognize a member of our flock. As you know Doctor Charles Mathews has been named the new director of the Willoughby Medical College, and I want to personally take this opportunity to congratulate him and ask God to bless him in his new position."

The Reverend motioned for Mathews to stand. Charles stood reluctantly, took a small bow and mouthed a "thank you" before sitting back down. The mayor, not to be outdone, stood and added his two cents by saying the school was in good hands and would certainly move forward under the leadership of Dr. Mathews. His comments brought nods and murmurs of agreement.

"And now ladies and gentleman," the minister continued, "we have a musical treat for you. A marvelously talented member of our congregation has graciously consented to play the piano for us today. Miss Kathleen Wilson is not only a gifted teacher, but also an accomplished pianist. She will play..." he read from his notes, "she will play a selection of pieces by Chopin; first the Polonaise in B-flat major, then a mazurka in A minor, opus 17, number 4."

The audience shifted in their seats with anticipation as Katie made her way to the piano and sat down. After everyone quieted, Katie raised her hands and with a delicate flair, placed her slender fingers on the keyboard. The piano came alive as she began to play. Members of the congregation sat spellbound holding their breath as music filled the room. Even children, who normally couldn't sit still, sat quietly mesmerized by the music.

Blankenship's chest swelled with pride as he sat listening. He had no idea Katie could play the piano. He realized how little he knew about her.

After she played the final chord, Katie stood, curtsied to the applause, and returned to her seat, a slight pink covering her cheeks.

"I'm glad that's over," she whispered to Blankenship with an expression of relief.

"You were wonderful," he said and patted her hand.

The social came to an end when the minister gave the benediction. Blankenship wasted no time getting Katie's cape and quickly ushered her out of the hall.

They had gotten as far as the fence gate when Mayor Bascom came rushing at them, his Bible clinched in his hand and a frown on his face. He started to say something, but seeing Katie, he scowled, made a half-hearted gesture at tipping his hat to her, and then stormed off.

"What was that all about," Katie asked. "He looked as though he wanted to have a serious talk with you."

"The murder of Pete Harper has him upset."

He didn't tell her how the mayor had been on his back ever since he took office and how the major would like nothing more than to see Blankenship lose his badge. He knew it wasn't prudent to say anything about the town council's meeting called to investigate his running of the police department. He didn't wish to worry her.

Not wanting their time together to end so soon, Blankenship suggested they take a stroll through the park. The cool morning air and gray overcast had given way to a bright sunny afternoon. Light, fluffy clouds floated overhead teasing the sun and making the park a pleasant place for folks to take a leisurely walk.

"I didn't know you played the piano," Blankenship said.

"My father was a violinist and my mother played the piano. I grew up with music in our home. Guess it just comes naturally. Do you play a musical instrument?"

"No, but I had a great uncle who played Chopin on the kazoo," he teased.

They soon reached the park that rested along the Chagrin River and covered more than fifteen acres. It was the perfect place for Sunday picnics, playing sports, and for holding political rallies, and when the pond froze over in the winter, children and adults enjoyed ice-skating.

The grass and weeds stayed trampled most of the summer with children playing tag, hide and seek, or hoop and stick. Most Sundays you could find men, sleeves rolled up, in a game of horseshoes, but today a group was playing ball. The game had grown in popularity around the country with professional teams forming in major cities. Here in Willoughby the game had become a favorite pastime on Sundays and holidays and today was probably the last Sunday for men to get in a game before winter weather set in.

Blankenship and Katie made their way along the macadam walkway to the gazebo, passing other couples walking arm in arm. Ladies waved a hello and men tipped their hats to them as they passed. Some folks carrying picnic baskets and blankets, called out to their children who ran along ahead of their parents. Katie stopped to speak to a woman pushing a baby carriage. Blankenship's imagination leaped to visions of him and Katie someday walking through the park, her holding a parasol while he proudly showed off their child.

His thoughts were brought back to reality when one of the ball players ran up to him. "Chief, we need another man for our side. Would you play?"

Blankenship had no desire to get into a game of sport. He was in his Sunday suit and if he got it dirty Mrs. Hollingsworth would have a few words for him–most of them unpleasant. Without giving a reason, he politely declined.

The man had turned to leave when Katie placed her hand on his arm and said, "It would be fun to watch you play. I bet you are a fine ball player."

He had played ball during his time in the army. He wasn't great at connecting with a ball, but he had a good arm and could throw the ball quite a distance, but his best skill was running.

"Oh, I forgot about your hand. Does it still hurt?"

Even though his hand ached as if hammered by a mallet, and he still had difficulty bending his fingers, he forced a smile and said, "Sure I can play. My hand doesn't hurt at all." Besides he still had one good hand. Catching the ball in his left shouldn't be a problem. Gripping the bat might be another issue, however.

About the only activity Katie had ever seen him do was walk her to and from school. He wasn't one to show off and didn't feel the need to prove himself, but playing ball did provide an opportunity to display his manly prowess.

They walked to the playing field where a man was in the process of pacing off the distance between the bases and placing a flour sack filled with straw at the designated spot.

The chief recognized most of the players as workers from the mill. He didn't see Marsden among them, though. A couple players belonged to his church and one man he had never met had volunteered to be the umpire.

"Good luck," Katie said and smiled up at him when he removed his coat and spread it on the ground for her.

Blankenship trotted to the field where the umpire announced the rules. They would play seven innings, or longer if the game didn't run into supper hour. "There is to be no more throwing the ball at the runner," the umpire told them. Blankenship remembered last year when a ball coldcocked a player and knocked him out. Holding the ball, he said, "It's a mush ball, fellows," and allowed each team member to handle the ball.

Blankenship found a position on the field in view of Katie and loosened up by doing a few deep knee bends and twisting from side to side. He glanced in Katie's direction to see if she was watching.

The pitcher, a lankly fellow, circled his arms over his head and threw a practice pitch to the catcher. The ball hit the dirt, sending dust flying. The catcher retrieved the ball, threw it back and waited for the umpire to start the game.

The first batter swung at the first pitch and missed. He also missed the second and third throw. When he took a swipe at the forth ball, corkscrewing himself around, someone yelled, "Hey, Nelson. You swatting at bugs?" The umpire called the batter out.

The next two hitters did no better, but the forth made it to second base before the last batter struck out.

By the time Blankenship's team came to bat, a small group of people had gathered to watch. The first batter popped up to the man standing at the first base. As the ball came at him, he pulled off his cap and caught the ball in it. The umpire called the hitter out and people cheered.

As Blankenship picked up the bat, someone yelled, "Hey everybody, the police chief is playing ball." It didn't take long before the small group of people turned into a large crowd. Blankenship was self-conscious enough playing in front of Katie, now it seemed the entire town was watching.

He winced as he wrapped his hand around the bat, hoping the pain didn't show on his face. He hiked up his suspenders and waited for the ball.

From watching his first teammate at bat, he knew the pitcher had a good arm. The ball flew at Blankenship much faster than he had anticipated. The chief swung and missed. The second throw came in a little slower and Blankenship socked the ball to the right. The man standing near the first base was too slow and missed the ball. It landed behind him and rolled under a carriage. Blankenship took off running but only got to third base before he was tagged out.

With the next two players doing no better, Blankenship's team took to the field again. After playing seven innings the score stood at fifteen to fourteen. The opposing team was ahead with one man on second base. As the batter stepped up, Blankenship noticed two men standing off near the tree line toe to toe in an animated conversation. By their angry expressions, he knew they weren't engaged in polite social talk. Blankenship recognized one of the men as John Mathews; he wasn't familiar with the other man. Mathews held the other man's arm as he waved a piece of paper in his face and emphasized each word by jerking on his coat sleeve. The man looked at the paper, shook his head, and then scowled.

What was so important that these two would choose this public place on a Sunday to engage in such a heated discussion? The man broke free of Mathews' grip and stalked away. Mathews stood motionless, staring after him.

"Heads up," someone called. Blankenship looked up, but too late. The ball was sailing toward him. Forgetting his injured hand, he reached up and caught it. Pain shot up his arm all the way to his shoulder. Stars floated before his eyes. Not wanting Katie to see him wincing in pain, he turned away, clutching his hand to his chest. By the time he regained his composure and threw the ball, the runner had made it around all three bags and was heading home.

All Blankenship could do was hang his head. He had cost his team the game.

Their walk back to Katie's house was subdued despite Katie's attempt to cheer him up. "You were wonderful. I didn't know you could play so well."

He knew her praise wasn't earned, but at least he hadn't embarrassed himself too much.

As they reach her Aunt's house Katie said, "Hank, may I ask a favor of you?"

I'd do anything for you. Anything.

He would ride a horse to the moon and bring back a star to pin in her hair if she asked.

"I was wondering if you would come to school and speak to my students tomorrow?"

Anything but that.

He had handled rattlesnakes, disorderly drunks, and even a yellow-bellied rebel, but speaking in front of a group, even if it were just kids, made him break out in a sweat.

"Speak to your class? Whatever for?"

"I know it's not an ordinary subject, but I thought it important for the children to have an understanding of how our government works. Hearing about the police department would not only answer their questions but help them appreciate what you do."

He swallowed hard. "Of course, I'd be honored to speak to the children. What should I talk about?"

"Just tell them what you do. How you help the citizens." She squeezed his arm and gave him one of her disarming smiles. He gave a half-hearted smile in return.

Sadly, it wasn't long before they were once again standing at Katie's front door. He wanted to kiss the delicate white softness of her throat, hold her in his arms and feel the warmth of her body next to his. Despite the fact that every fiber in his body urged him to do just that, he tamed his emotions and gently kissed her hand instead. She responded by standing on her tiptoes and kissing his cheek.

Blankenship felt like skipping down the front porch steps and turning cartwheels in the street. The afterglow of the wonderful afternoon had wrapped itself around him, warming him like a bottle of fifty-year-old scotch.

~ CHAPTER 14 ~

Blankenship awoke Monday morning still wrapped in the warm glow of having spent Sunday afternoon with Katie. He would have given anything to stay curled up under the blankets. The only thing that would have been better would be if Katie were under the covers with him. He banished the picture in his mind, he had a murder to solve.

Believing now that the jewelry and pieces of gold he had found in the box in Harper's house were possibly tied to his murder, Blankenship returned to the cemetery. The contents of the box were now evidence in a crime, and he needed to secure it. He entered the former caretakers house and found the box still where he had left it in the drawer under the lace. Nothing in the room seemed to have been disturbed, but then how could he tell?

With the box securely tucked inside his coat and remembering that Nagy had indicated the gold had come from teeth, he went to the one person he hoped could identify the gold pieces that he now suspected were from teeth of the deceased.

He climbed the stairs to Doctor Fenway's dental office on the second floor. The waiting room was empty and the door to the examination room was closed. The sound of grunts and groans from beyond left no doubt the doctor was with a patient.

When the door finally opened, a man came out holding the left side of his swollen cheek, looking pale and none too happy for having just experienced Doctor's Fenway's dentistry technique. "Keep the packing in place for the next two days, Mr. Krane," the dentist instructed. "Contact me should you have any bleeding after that time. And don't forget to use that powder I gave you."

The man mumbled something that sounded like, "Ank ooh" and left.

Seeing the police chief standing in the outer office, Doctor Fenway straightened himself to stand a little taller and asked, "Tooth bothering you, Chief?"

The dentist looked to be in his late forties and was well respected for not over charging his patients.

"No, nothing like that," he said, pulling a piece of gold from the box. "Can you identify this?" he said and handed it to him.

"It's gold filling from teeth," Doctor Fenway said examining the piece of gold. "See how the ridges are formed here," he said and pointed to the ridge.

"How many people get gold fillings?"

"Just about everyone these days."

"Is there any way you can tell who this might have belonged to?"

"No, these pieces all look pretty much alike."

Blankenship was beginning to believe finding Harper's killer was going to take more investigative skills than he possessed. Maybe Bascom was right; he wasn't cut out to be the police chief. He had to find the "why" like Norville said.

He had just sat down behind his desk when the newspaper editor came hobbling through the door.

"Wind's picking up," Norville said, going straight to the stove for a cup of coffee.

"How does that newspaper of yours ever get printed if you're not there to publish it?"

Norville ignored the jibe and helped himself to the chair beside of Blankenship's desk.

"So, what's on your mind?" Blankenship asked.

"Wanted to tell you what I found out about Harper's wife."

"You work fast."

"I discovered that Catherine Harper is living in Fairport. She lives there with a friend."

Cleopatra, hearing Norville's voice, came slinking out from her cozy spot behind the stove and rubbed against his leg.

"She couldn't have killed Harper, if that's what you've been thinking. In fact, she couldn't have killed anyone, at least not recently. From what I heard, she's in bad shape. Bedridden. Can't talk without catching her breath between every word. She has consumption and is coughing up a lot of blood. She isn't going to last very long."

"Where'd you hear all this?"

"From Joshua Garrett, Harper's brother-in-law. Harper had a sister, Nora. That's the Nora Garrett we saw listed in the Bible. Tracked him down from a source I found in my card file."

"Ah yes, your card file."

"According to Garrett, Harper and his family grew up dirt poor. Garrett fell in love with Nora, married her before the war and brought her here to Willoughby. He claims Harper always carried a grudge against him for some reason. Who knows why? Garrett didn't elaborate. Harper didn't need a reason to dislike someone.

"Anyway, Nora passed on in '65. Garrett kept in touch with his sister after she left Harper. He never remarried. Other than Garrett, there aren't any living relatives as far as I can find."

"Did he tell you why she left?" Blankenship asked.

"Garrett was tight lipped about that. Only offered that they had some kind of disagreement."

"What kind of disagreement would cause her to leave? When I spoke with Clay at the feed store he claimed she talked about getting revenge, and Clyde Chapman mentioned that Harper's wife had said something about him getting what he deserved. Think there could be anything to that?"

"Like I said, Josh told me she's pretty sick. Even if she had reason enough to kill him, I don't think she was able to get out of bed to do it. I doubt Josh would lie. He's a reliable sort."

"That kind of news deserves a cup of coffee," Blankenship said.

"Is that all you can offer a fellow who has trekked through mud and muck to get information for you?"

"Can't offer you anything else unless you want a swig from one of old man Sloan's moonshine jugs." He pointed to the corner where three barrels of Sloan's liquid harvest sat waiting for Kunkle to haul off for disposal.

"I can see the headline now. *Police Impropriety,*" Norville said, making a wide sweeping motion across the air.

"I can see the headline if I don't solve this murder."

"Have you heard from the town council yet?" Norville asked.

"No, and I've got to confess, it has me worried. The mayor pulls a lot of weight in this town. Their decision could be the end of my job."

Cleopatra gave Norville a loud "Meow" and stretched her front paws up on his leg as if wanting in his lap.

"That bastard came into my office the other day wanting to know if I intended to report that Harper was involved with the college in some way," the editor said.

"Why did he ask that?"

"It was news to me," he said. Cleopatra, not waiting for an invitation, jumped onto Norville's lap.

"What did you tell him?"

"I didn't tell him anything. What was there to tell? Thought it was a strange question, though."

"Hum," Blankenship said under his breath.

"Do you have anything new on the investigation?" Norville asked, finally getting to the reason for his visit.

"As a matter of fact I do have some news for you to chew on." Blankenship paused, taking his time, toying with his friend.

"Well?"

"I discovered who the fob belongs to."

The editor's eyes widened as he readied his pen.

Blankenship told him about Kunkle identifying the fob as belonging to John Mathews.

"You've been busy," Norville said.

"I talked with John. He had his fob securely attached to his watch, and said that this fob belonged to his brother," Blankenship said.

"But surely you don't think Charlie had anything to do with this? Come on Hank, Charlie a murderer? No, I can't believe that. He's hardly the sort."

"Murderers don't go around wearing a sign."

"We still don't know who the blackmail letter was meant for. What if it was meant for Charles Mathews?"

"I think you are stretching your theory there. You're way off track with this."

"The fob points to him."

"What did Charles say when you talked to him?"

"I haven't had a chance to speak with him yet."

Norville fell silent for a moment, lifted Cleo off his lap, and got up. When he reached the door, he turned and asked, "Have you given any thought to Haroldson's property?"

"Why's everybody so fired up about me buying Doc's property?"

"Maybe because a few of us would like for you to stay in Willoughby," Norville said as he opened the door.

Before Blankenship could say anything more, the door closed behind his friend.

Perhaps sticking around Willoughby wasn't such a bad idea. Maybe he would check into buying the property. Then as quickly as the thought came, it dissolved away. He had nowhere near enough money to buy the property and getting a loan from LaRue would be near impossible. He had no collateral, and was certain the money he had managed to save wasn't nearly enough for even a down payment. Blankenship sighed. If he didn't find out who killed Harper, it wouldn't matter anyway. Bascom would make sure he was out of a job, leaving him with no hope of ever getting enough money to buy the property.

Blankenship pulled a sheet of paper from a drawer and printed the word SUSPECTS across the top. He thought for a moment and then wrote the names Ceil Marsden, Red Gundersen, Catherine Harper and Johan Nagy. From what Norville had told him, it was unlikely that Catherine killed her husband if she was bedridden, but that didn't preclude her from hiring someone else to do the job. Nagy was most likely a dupe and had no idea what Harper had been up to, but if Nagy were responsible for Harper's murder, he'd have to wait until Cuyahoga County was finished with him. Marsden and Gundersen were his prime suspects. Both had reasons for wanting Harper dead. Marsden had motive. Gundersen had means, remembering the bottle of cyanide in his shed, and both men had opportunity to kill him. His interview with them hadn't netted much information, but he'd keep a close eye on them, even though neither owned a watch fob.

He started to fold the paper, then stopped and added Charles Mathews' to the list, and then underlined it.

~ Chapter 15 ~

After lunch, Blankenship took time to comb his hair and make sure no mud stuck to his boots. He checked his tie and straightened his badge. He wanted to look his best for Katie and her students.

It hadn't taken much for Katie to convince him to talk to her students. All she had to do was look at him with her big brown eyes, and he was under her spell. Besides, he loved kids. How hard could it be to talk to them? He just hoped he wouldn't look like a donkey as he had done the first time he tried to speak to her.

He hadn't thought much about what he was going to say. Katie had given him several options, but stressed that he should keep his talk lighthearted. No gory details.

The two-room schoolhouse on Browning Road sat behind a white fence, with steps leading to the door. Blankenship stood at the front door with buzzards flapping around in his stomach. He took in a deep breath and entered the building, wondering what he had gotten himself into.

As many times as he had walked Katie to school, he had never been inside and suddenly realized he had no idea which room she taught in. He took a chance and stood listening at the door on the right. When he heard her sweet voice drift from beyond it, he knocked softly.

Katie greeted him at the door and showed him where to hang his hat. The room was much larger than the schoolroom he remembered sitting in so many years ago. The teacher was prettier, too. A blackboard covered the wall in front of the room and a small American flag hung to the left of it by the window. The children sat on benches, four abreast, with a long table for a desk. Along the back wall were hooks where the children could hang their coats. A stove like the one in his office sat off to the side of the room.

Katie introduced him to the children who sat in anticipation, waiting for him to speak. "Class, Chief Blankenship is here today to tell us about what he does as a policeman. I know many of you think the only job of the police is to arrest bad people, but that's not all they do. They have a very important job in keeping us safe. Now, I expect you to be on your best behavior and pay attention."

Blankenship watched the children sit up straight and fold their hands in front of them, waiting. He knew many of the students by name. Most were good kids. He recognized one in particular who had a first-hand acquaintance with the law when Blankenship caught him stealing a loaf of bread from the general store. Theodore Mathews, brother of the child who disappeared a little more than four months ago, sat in the front row of seats.

He was thankful when Katie asked him a leading question to get the process started because he had no idea where to begin.

"Chief Blankenship, would you tell the class how you became a policeman?"

Blankenship began with what it was like working for the Pinkerton Detective Agency. Once he got started he discovered that talking to the children wasn't as difficult as he had anticipated.

A hand flew up in the front row. He turned to Katie for guidance.

"Yes, what is it, Zachary?"

"Have you ever shot someone?" the boy asked.

How could he answer that? War was a murderous business. He had shot and killed many men during the war, but he couldn't tell them that. Many of their family members had been killed in battle and lay buried in the cemetery. He thought it best not to mention the bloody side of war. Katie had asked him to keep his remarks light, so his answered with, "Being a policeman isn't always about shooting people. It's more about protecting the citizens."

The boy's expression showed disappointment.

Another hand went up.

"Yes, Benjamin?" Katie acknowledged.

Benjamin was one of the Taylor twins who had found Harper and came racing to his office to tell him about it. He sat beside his brother in the back of the room. The boys were identical in every aspect; hair, eyes, even their missing-tooth-grin was the same.

"Do you know who killed Mr. Harper? My pa says that man was bad."

That was the last question Blankenship expected. "No, not yet." And then quickly added, "But we will."

"You know he was all covered with blood from head to foot," Benjamin said.

"Now, Benjamin. You can't know that," Katie said.

"But we do. We saw him."

The children turned to look at the twins.

Kids sure could stretch the truth, he mused. Apparently they had added a few embellishments to their story about finding Harper's body.

"Yeah, covered with blood," the other twin repeated.

"Now, Leonard, you didn't see him," Katie said.

"Yes we did. Tell her, Mr. Blankenship. Tell her how we found old man Harper dead."

"That's true. Benjamin and Leonard did find Mr. Harper."

A collective murmur filled the room.

"We saw Mr. Marsden, too," one of the twins said.

Katie started to admonish the boy, but Blankenship held up his hand to stop her.

"Let's hear what the boys have to say, Miss Wilson." Then to the boys, he said, "Go ahead. What did Mr. Marsden do?"

"Mr. Marsden was there, hiding in the bushes, but he never saw us."

"Yeah, the bushes." Benjamin affirmed.

Why would they add that man into their tale? Was that just another embellishment? But what if Marsden had been hiding in the bushes? If he had killed Harper surely he wouldn't stay around and take the chance of being seen? Maybe he hadn't killed him yet. Maybe he went back for the money. Blankenship wasn't quite satisfied with Marsden's alibi for where he had been while Harper sat drinking cyanide-laced whiskey. Maybe there was more to Marsden's story than he was telling. That was a lot of maybes.

"What's this you were saying about Mr. Marsden hiding in the bushes?" Blankenship asked the twins.

They didn't miss a beat telling how they saw a man hiding in the bushes when they went to Harper's house.

"How do you know it was Mr. Marsden?

The boys looked at each other then back at Blankenship. They shrugged and in unison said, "Cause we saw him."

This information added fire to an already hot cauldron. Even though he knew relying on the twins' story wasn't good police practice, he couldn't ignore what they said either. He wanted to have another talk with Marsden.

"You boys did right by coming to me and reporting what you saw. And that goes for all of you. If you know of a crime that has been committed, or if you think something is wrong, you must report it to the police. That's what good citizens do. Understand?"

The students nodded.

Blankenship wrapped up his talk, and Katie walked him to the door and thanked him for coming to talk to her class. "I hope you weren't put off by the twins interrupting. They do have quite an imagination."

"No, what they said was true and they provided pertinent information that I plan to follow up on."

Katie looked surprised but didn't pursue the topic.

˜

As soon as he had finished speaking to Katie's class, he returned to the jail's stable, saddled Mingo, and rode out to the gristmill once again. The shift foreman directed Blankenship to the far end of the mill where Marsden, hands and face covered with a fine layer of flour dust, labored at the large grinding stone.

"I need to talk to you, Marsden," Blankenship shouted over the noise within the mill.

Marsden acknowledged Blankenship with a scowl. "Now what? I thought you had your talk the other day," he yelled back.

A fine haze floated in the air as a young man squeezed in between the two men, untied the full sack at the end of the chute, and replaced it with an empty one. He moved liked a well-oiled machine.

"I want to talk to you. And I want to talk now," he said, motioning for Marsden to leave the grinding wheel and meet him outside.

Blankenship stood on the landing and blew his nose to get rid of the dust while he waited. It was several minutes before Marsden appeared, charging out the door like an angry bull.

"Just what's so damned important that you come here? You're going to get me fired if my boss sees the police coming around asking questions — questions I already answered. Make this fast. It's cold out here."

"There are a couple questions you haven't answered. I want to know why you were hanging around Pete Harper's house the night he was killed." Blankenship watched Marsden's face for any sign that he might lie.

Marsden scratched his head. "What makes you think I was hanging around Harper's house?"

"Somebody saw you."

"Nobody saw me do anything."

"My source says otherwise," he said, knowing his two witnesses were about as reliable as gunpowder in a rainstorm.

Marsden dropped his shoulders, leaned against the wall, and pulled a pouch of tobacco from his pocket. He sprinkled the tobacco into a small piece of paper and rolled each end. Cupping his hands around the flame of a match, he lit the cigarette, and then took a long drag before he spoke. "Okay, so somebody saw me at Harper's. So what? That doesn't mean I killed him. Not that I didn't want to. Would've felt good to strangle the bastard and watch his eyes pop out, but somebody beat me to it."

Interesting that Marsden would mention strangling Harper. Was that a slip of the tongue? The fact that Harper had been strangled hadn't been mentioned to anyone and Norville hadn't printed it in his newspaper. He doubted that Jarvis would have given out that information. With a broad chest and arm muscles that swelled beneath his shirt, there was little doubt that the miller was strong enough to strangle someone.

"You were seen hiding in the bushes. Why?"

Marsden took another long drag, inhaling deeply. "I went to see Harper. The bastard owed me a hundred dollars from a gambling debt. He said he would pay me but never did, so I went to collect."

"You told me you were at Tilly's Saturday night?"

"I was there, just later," Marsden said and coughed.

"What time were you at Harper's house?"

"About five o'clock. It was just starting to get dark."

"Then what did you do?"

"When I got there I found Harper lying on the floor, dead. I tried looking for the money, but my God, how that place stunk. I started to get the hell out of there and got as far as the side of the house when that Grimes fellow came along, so I hid in the bushes. I stayed there until I heard him leave."

"What was Grimes doing there?"

Marsden shrugged. "How the hell should I know?"

"What did Grimes do?"

"Nothing. He just knocked on the door and stood there. Of course, Harper didn't answer."

"Did he go in?"

"Nope." Marsden glanced back at the mill.

"And that's all you did? You went there to get your money and left?"

"Yep."

"Did you see anyone else?"

"Nope."

Marsden's one-word answers were beginning to annoy him. "Why didn't you tell me about this before?"

"Why should I?" He took a long puff on the cigarette that had burned to a stub, and then smashed the butt into the ground with the toe of his boot. Was Marsden shivering from the chilly air or was something else making his hand tremble? He turned to go back inside, then asked, "Hey, who saw me there? I bet it was that damn Grimes kid, wasn't it? I'll teach him to keep his yap shut."

Blankenship rode back to his office dissatisfied with Marsden's story, and he was even more displeased with the idea that Ethan Grimes might be mixed up with Harper. He made a mental note to have a talk with the boy.

~ CHAPTER 16 ~

Even after a day spent with rowdy children, Katie looked as fresh in the afternoon as she had that morning when he escorted her to school.

They walked in silence for several blocks. Always with a pleasant disposition, Katie would often talk about the children in her class, how well they were doing and about her hope for their future, but this afternoon she seemed preoccupied, lost in thought. When she didn't say anything, he asked, "Something on your mind? I wasn't that bad was I?"

"Bad? Bad, how?"

"My talk. Did I fail your class?"

"Oh no. You were marvelous with the children today. After you left they wouldn't stop asking questions. Several of the boys claimed they wanted to be a policeman. Even one of the girls said she did also. Of course, I had to tell her that police work could only be done by a man." She placed her hand around his arm as they walked along. Her touch sent a chill through him.

"Then why so glum?"

"I couldn't burden you with my problems."

"Try me. I have a pretty good ear. I might be able to help."

She waited until they had crossed the street before she said, "I was thinking about one of my students, Theodore Mathews."

"What about him?"

"He's very smart, very studious. In fact, I'd have to say he is my best student."

"So what's the problem?"

"Lately, he has been inattentive in class. I've caught him daydreaming."

"He seemed to pay attention to me when I was talking," Blankenship said.

"I had cautioned the class that they were to listen to you."

"Gee. And I thought it was my charm and that they were truly interested in what I had to say. I didn't know you had threatened them within an inch of their lives if they didn't pay attention."

"No. Nothing like that, silly." She giggled. "It's just that he seems distracted lately." She paused long enough to wave to a woman she knew, and then continued. "Now, today he failed an arithmetic test. He's my best student. It's just not like him."

"Maybe he's got his eye on a cute little girl."

"Oh, I doubt that. He's much too young to be thinking of girls."

"He could still be upset about his sister. I'm sure that was tragic for everyone in the family."

"That must have been dreadful for poor, dear Mrs. Mathews to lose a child like that, and not know what happened to her."

Blankenship didn't want to talk about the boy or the missing child. He wanted to ask if she liked horses. He wanted to ask her so many questions.

"Do you know his father very well?" Katie asked unexpectedly.

"Not really, but I did spend a lot of time with him while searching for his daughter. He never offered much in the way of conversation. The doctor kept his feelings to himself. Could have just been the circumstance at the time," Blankenship said. He wasn't going to tell her that he suspected Mathews was somehow involved with Harper's murder.

They had covered several blocks when she said, "Considering his behavior, I sent Doctor Mathews a letter requesting a conference, but he hasn't responded."

Blankenship also wanted to speak with Doctor Mathews, but for a very different reason.

"Probably busy with his new job. Being the new director of the medical college must take up a lot of his time," he said.

"Still, his recent action is contrary to his normal approach to the child's education. He and Martha have always attended conferences when I set them, and showed quite a concern about their son's studies. I wish more parents were as involved with their children's education. If I don't hear from him today, I'll have to call on him at the college. I feel something is wrong and it can't be ignored much longer. The boy's grades are beginning to suffer. Maybe talking with his father will shed light on Theodore's behavior. I'm afraid there's a deeper problem."

When they reached the front gate Katie said, "Oh, I almost forgot, Aunt Ruth wanted me to ask you in for a moment if you have time. I think she wants to ask you something."

Unlike the first time he had met Katie's aunt, his knees no longer turned to jelly at the mention of her name. She had turned their first meeting into an inquisition, drilling him for what seemed hours about his family — what he did for a living, did he drink, and did he believe in God — before determining that he was suitable enough for her niece. Good thing she approved, because he intended to continue seeing her with or without her aunt's consent.

Ruth Jenkins, widowed since the war, was still a jolly woman with a youthful exuberance and energy. Blankenship estimated her to be in her fifties. She had the same delicate features as her niece and the same twinkle in her eyes. The family resemblance was remarkable. Good looks must run in the family.

Ruth ushered them into the parlor and waited for Blankenship to help Katie with her coat. "Now, you two love birds sit over there on the sofa and chat while I get tea. You would like a cup of tea wouldn't you?"

Without waiting for a reply, she said, "Of course you would. It's getting colder than a miner's rear end out there. Tea will be ready shortly." She hurried off into the kitchen.

"Your aunt certainly speaks her mind," Blankenship said.

Katie laughed. "I remember my mother cautioning her many times to hold her tongue. Didn't do much good."

Katie's aunt's house was warm and inviting with comfortable furnishings. Lace doilies covered the back of each chair, and the smell of polishing wax filled the air. The centerpiece of the room was a piano. He wondered if her aunt also played.

In the corner was a strange box about waist high sitting on a table. Wondering what it was, he stood and ambled over to the box. "Is this new?" He ran his hand along the top. "I don't recall seeing it before. What is it?" he asked, taking a closer look.

"That's a stereoscopic viewer. Auntie takes great pride in owning one. Not many people can afford them. Would you like to see how it works?"

Not waiting for an answer, Katie opened a lid on the top of the box, slid in what looked like a photograph on a card, and turned the knob on the side. "Look through here," she directed, pointing to the two lenses in front.

Blankenship was amazed to see a photograph of a family seated together in front of a large drape. Katie flipped the knob again and another photograph appeared showing a lovely young girl.

"That's my auntie when she was much younger."

Katie inserted several more photographs, mostly scenic views. "Now, here's one of me when I was in school." But before she could insert the picture, Aunt Ruth came in carrying a tray with a small teapot, cups, and a plate of muffins, and set the tray on a tea table. "I hope you like the tea. It's my special blend."

As she handed him a cup she asked, "How is your hand? I understand you injured it."

"Right as new, thank you. I can bend my fingers now and the swelling is gone." He demonstrated by gingerly taking the teacup. Truth was his hand still hurt if he bumped it into something, but he'd never admit it.

After pouring tea, Aunt Ruth wasted no time getting to the point. "I need to know if you are going to arrest Catherine Harper for the murder of her husband."

The statement caught him off guard. He wasn't sure how to answer. "What makes you ask?" He took a sip of the tea that tasted like cinnamon.

"I've heard stories that you have been asking about her."

"He can't talk about that, Auntie. That's official police business," Katie said.

"Nonsense. The whole town's talking about it."

Blankenship knew that to be fact.

"I can't image what Catherine must be thinking right now," Ruth said.

"You know her?" Blankenship asked as he bit into a muffin.

"We're friends. She used to come into the millinery store where I worked to buy cloth and thread. One day the storeowner offered her a job minding the counter a couple days a week, and later hired her to sew. She made a good stitch. We became friends, and I got to know her fairly well. She worked there until she got on the outs with Harper."

"On the outs? How?"

"I know word got around that he kicked her out, but it wasn't like that." She gathered her thoughts before continuing. "When I heard she was ill, I paid her a visit. She looks like she's on death's door. Poor dear. Her friend is taking care of her the best she can."

That confirmed what Norville had told him.

"She told me that Harper had caught her helping those black folks come north. He refused to abide it. They fought. She believed God made everyone alike inside."

Ruth paused to take a sip of tea. "She has a good heart, Catherine does, but Harper believed Negroes were put on this earth for only one purpose. I can't repeat the words she told me he said about them. Catherine said she wasn't about to stay in a house with a man who went against God. She's the one who left. They used to have a nice home on Grove Avenue. Lived there for quite a few years. After Catherine left, Harper got that job in the cemetery and moved into that shack on the property. Awful place. Catherine did well to rid herself of him, if you ask me."

That certainly put another angle to the story. Feeling that Ruth wasn't one to add her own color to rumors, he took her information as valid.

He thanked Ruth for the delicious muffins and tea, and told Katie he'd stop by in the morning to walk her to school. He felt certain now that Catherine Harper had no reason to murder her husband simply because they disagreed on a moral issue. He mentally marked her name off his suspect list.

~ Chapter 17 ~

Blankenship walked with Katie to school the next morning then crossed River Road. He was on his was to the library to see if he could find a translation of the Latin engraved on the fob, when Theodore Matthews came running up to him.

"Mr. Blankenship, can I talk to you?" the boy called. His face was flushed and he was breathing hard.

"Shouldn't you be on your way to school?" Blankenship asked.

"Yes. I'm on my way, but I need to talk…I mean…I have something to tell you about…"

Theodore appeared genuinely disturbed about something. And remembering what Katie had told him about the boy's behavior, he asked, "What's on your mind?"

"Remember what you said about telling you if we knew that something was wrong?"

Before the boy could say anything more, Blankenship heard shouting coming from the center of town. He couldn't make out the words, but by the frantic sound of the voices, the problem was something more than just a wagon blocking the road.

Leaving the boy standing in the middle of the street, Blankenship set out running toward the commotion, his boots pounding the planked walkway. He had reached Erie Street when a whirling mass of black fabric rounded the corner, coming in his direction.

Nuns, one pounding a drum, another holding a bucket, marched toward him.

The Charity March! Was that today? He had forgotten all about it.

The nuns had the look in their eyes that could only be interpreted as one thing – they were on a mission from God. A herd of children in shabby clothing followed close behind, singing a hymn at the top of their lungs. The nuns and their charges filled the narrow walkway, preventing him from moving past.

The disturbance coming from down the street grew louder and he saw people running toward Second Street. He had to find out what was going on.

Blankenship looked for a way around the nuns. Darting into the muddy street was the only way around them, but the omnibus, drawn by a team of horses, was making its hourly run and took up most of the road. Not wanting to be trampled, and with nowhere to go, Blankenship pressed his back against the building to allow the parade to pass, but they didn't.

The nuns stopped and stood in front of him. One looked at his badge, then at his hat, and then directly into his eyes and said, "Give to the orphanage." She had a voice that could cut wood. He didn't know if he should nod, kneel, or pray.

He tried looking over their heads, but their long flowing habits and veils blocked his view.

The nun holding the bucket prompted, "Give to the children." It didn't sound like a request. One of the children tugged on his trouser leg and looked up at him with big, sad, begging eyes. The children's hungry faces made his heart ache. Blankenship wondered when they had last eaten.

Blankenship dug into his trousers and pulled out a quarter and dropped it into the bucket. The nun looked at the coin, and then peered up at him. Her scowl told him he had better cough up more. He had heard stories about how nuns could squeeze milk from a stone. Now he knew how they did it. He wasn't about to tangle with this woman of God. He dug deeper and came up with a matching twenty-five cents — the last of his lunch money — and dropped it into the bucket.

"Bless you," the nun said and motioned for the procession to continue down the street.

Blankenship let out the breath he had been holding and took off down the street. By the time he reached the disturbance a crowd had gathered in front of the bakery. A man standing at the front door motioned to Blankenship. "Over here," he yelled. "Come quick!"

"What's wrong?" Blankenship asked, as he pushed his way through to the front of the store.

"It's awful. Just awful," the man said.

Entering the bakery, he saw Mrs. Kunkle, slumped in a chair, pale and shaken, looking like she had just seen a ghost. A young woman stood holding her hand while two others hovered around, cooing and consoling her.

"Mrs. Kunkle, what's wrong? Have you been hurt?"

He saw no evidence she had been burnt. It had happened before when the oven overheated and caught fire. He prayed there was no fire.

"Not her. She'll be all right. It's back here. You need to see this," the man urged, pulling Blankenship by the sleeve to the back door.

The chief followed him to the back of the store, then out into the alley where a cluster of people stood staring at something on the ground. Finally getting close enough, he saw Andy Jarvis lying alongside of the building, wedged between a garbage can and a large stack of metal trays. His head was tilted oddly to one side and his tongue protruded between blue lips. His eyes were glassed over, a familiar sight Blankenship had witnessed many times on the battlefield. Jarvis' pant legs were muddy and the sleeve of his coat was torn. His hair was mussed as if he had just gotten out of bed.

Had he fallen and hit his head? Blankenship wondered as he checked for a head wound, but found no blood.

"You there," Blankenship pointed to a man standing nearby, "run to the college and get a doctor." Then motioning to another man, he said,

"Go to the jail and get Deputy Stanger. Tell him to come immediately." *This was one time that he better be in the office or his majesty, the mayor, would get an ear full about the incompetency of his fair-haired nephew.*

While waiting for the doctor, the police chief dispersed the crowd, and then took notice of the surroundings. Jarvis' house doubled as a mortuary, and his family lived upstairs, facing Spaulding Street. The back of the building bordered the alley. A fence surrounded a small backyard, and a path lead to a small gate that opened onto the muddy alleyway. The gate was open. Except for clothesline poles that took up space to the side, the yard was empty.

He found an old apron in the bakery and covered the body. What was Jarvis doing in the alley? Taking out the garbage, perhaps.

It wasn't long before he heard John Mathews' booming voice. "Someone said you needed me. What happened here?" he asked, coming closer.

"It's Andy Jarvis, doctor. You need to take a look at him." Blankenship knew the man was dead, but it was formality for a doctor to pronounce the fact.

Mathews went to Jarvis, put his fingers on his neck, felt for a pulse, and then looked into Jarvis' eyes. "Looks like a heart attack." The doctor turned and walked away as if he were taking a Sunday afternoon stroll.

Minutes later, Blankenship heard Stanger's voice. "Stand back and let me through." He pushed through the spectators that had collected once again and gasped when he saw Jarvis lying on the ground. "What happened?"

"Get these people out of here," Blankenship ordered. "And then watch over the body until the hearse arrives."

Stanger, taking on an air of authority, began herding the curious crowd out of the alleyway.

Returning inside the bakery he saw that Mrs. Kunkle, still pale, had regained her composure somewhat and sat wiping at her eyes. Blankenship shooed the gawkers and locked the door.

Careful not to upset Mrs. Kunkle any more than she already was, Blankenship asked her if she could tell him what happened.

She sniffed a few times before answering. "I went out back to put the morning trash in the garbage pail. I had just lifted the lid," she said, kneading the handkerchief in her trembling hands, "when I saw him. I... I just froze."

"What time was that?"

"Just a few minutes ago. Couldn't have been more than fifteen."

"Was anyone else in the alley?"

"I didn't see anyone, but I couldn't look at anything but him."

"Did you hear any strange noise prior to going outside?" She thought for a moment and then said, "Just the garbage can being tossed about. Animals are always getting into the cans. I didn't pay much attention to it."

"Do you have any idea why Mr. Jarvis would be in the alley?"

She took a deep breath and said, "He comes in by the back door every morning around this time to get a sweet roll. He eats it standing right there," she pointed to the counter. "He's been doing that ever since I opened the bakery five years ago. Jarvis and his sweet tooth got to be a joke around town. He was such a nice man." With that she broke into tears again. Blankenship, realizing the trauma the woman had just experienced, didn't push for more information. The man had just died of a heart attack, nothing more to it.

When the hearse from Jarvis' own funeral parlor finally arrived to carry his body away, Blankenship realized the irony of the situation. Jarvis' assistant would have to work on his own boss.

Blankenship thanked Mrs. Kunkle and then prepared himself for the job he hated most — notifying Jarvis' family.

There was no delicate way to tell a woman that her husband was dead and his awkward attempt didn't make the task any easier. He had dealt with men's angry outbursts. He had even withstood the cries of his men when they were cut down by cannon fire, but when a woman wailed, as Mrs. Jarvis did, his knees went limp and a lump caught in his throat. He gave Mrs. Jarvis his condolences. What more could he say or do?

~ CHAPTER 18 ~

Blankenship tried to push Mrs. Jarvis' stricken expression from his mind, but it clung to him like a bad dream. Putting his trip to the library on hold, Blankenship headed back to his office. He needed to write up the incident report about Jarvis dying in the alley first.

Norville caught up to him just as he was about to enter the jail. How did that man manage to always know when something happened? The publisher had that look in his eyes that told him he wanted every detail.

"So what happened to Andy Jarvis?" Norville inquired.

Blankenship didn't care to stand in the middle of the street discussing it, so he suggested they go inside. He could fill out the report while he answered what he knew would be an endless stream of questions.

"Mrs. Kunkle found him dead behind the bakery this morning. Doc Mathews says it looked like a heart attack."

"I'll have my boy get information from the family for his obituary. Where's Cleo?" he asked.

"She's around here somewhere." He pulled a file folder from the cabinet containing blank incident report papers. "You have an obsession for that cat don't you? You know, you and that cat are a lot alike."

"How's that?"

"You both love chasing down your prey." He picked up a pencil and began to write.

"Watch and learn," he said, and then changed the subject. "Anything new on Harper?"

"Katie's aunt cleared up the possibility of Harper's wife having killed him. She didn't have a motive, and as you told me, she's bad off. So far all I have is the fob and the blackmail letter. I'm pretty sure the fob belongs to Charles Mathews, but the letter still hasn't fallen into place."

"May I see that paper again?" Norville asked.

Blankenship swung his chair around and took the letter from the safe and handed it over.

Norville adjusted his eyeglasses, took them off and wiped them with his handkerchief, held them up to the light, squinted through the thick lenses, and then replaced them on his nose. After reading the letter, he handed the paper back to him. "Something's wrong here," he mumbled and rushed out the door, leaving the police chief scratching his head.

&

Ms. Benning, the librarian, suggested he try *Aids to Writing Latin Prose Composition* by George Granville Bradley after Blankenship described what he needed.

"Are you wanting to study Latin?" she asked.

"No. I need to find a translation on something."

"Come this way." She wove her way through the rows of shelves until she came to the section marked Languages. She pulled the book from the shelf, handed it to him, and then stood nearby as if waiting for him to ask her for help.

He perused the contents of the book for a few minutes before it became obvious he didn't understand what he was looking at. The book, with its tiny print, gave page after page of verbs, grammar, and usage, but nowhere did it list the phrase he was hoping to find. He needed someone to put the words together so they made sense.

"Need some assistance?" the librarian asked as if reading his mind.

"Who would study this stuff?"

"Doctors, of course," she prompted.

Why hadn't he thought of that? Of course, doctors used Latin for just about everything. He returned the book to its place on the shelf and then headed to the medical college. He found the secretary in the administration office busy typing. The young man was polite but couldn't give him the answer he was looking for, but suggested he ask Doctor Carlton who had just come into the office.

Blankenship introduced himself and handed him the fob. The young doctor turned it over in his hand several times, examining the engraving. "The phrase can be translated several ways," he said. "But the essence of it is, through difficulties to honor. It could also mean through trial to triumph, though. Does that help?"

It didn't, but Blankenship thanked him and asked to speak with Charles Mathews. The young doctor told him that the director was in a staff meeting and wasn't to be disturbed. The chief left word with the secretary that he needed to talk with Doctor Mathews as soon as he was available.

∞

After hanging up his hat and coat, he placed the table scraps commandeered from Mrs. Hollingsworth's breakfast table near the stove for Cleo. She was a good mouser but a few treats from time to time wouldn't hurt. He poured himself a cup of coffee, took the fob and blackmail letter from the safe, and sat studying them as if they would impart a great secret. He turned the fob over and rubbed his thumb over the engraved words. The translation Doctor Carlton gave him didn't reveal much. The letter, indicating Harper was blackmailing someone presented another challenge. Why was the letter still in Harper's pocket? If Harper had intended to extort money, why hadn't he delivered it? Maybe he was going to when he was murdered. At this point he was almost ready to ask Madam Olga to look into her crystal ball.

"Morning boss," Stanger said, coming in the back door, carrying an armload of firewood.

"Let me mark my calendar before I faint," Blankenship said, seeing Stanger actually working.

"Huh?" His lips formed the word around a stick of licorice.

"Never mind."

As Stanger placed the logs by the stove, one slipped from his grasp and clattered to the floor, scaring the cat which, in turn, startled Stanger, who jumped and dropped the remaining logs, sending them flying in all directions. With all the commotion, Blankenship considered it a miracle that he noticed Charles Mathews riding down the street in his carriage. He rushed to the door, leaving Stanger picking up the logs.

"Doctor Mathews. Stop! I need to talk to you," the chief called.

Mathews turned and looked at Blankenship, but kept going at a steady pace.

He called again. When Mathews didn't respond, Blankenship set out in a run. He raced down the muddy street dodging puddles and horses, leaving people scurrying to get out of his way.

Thankful he had stayed in good physical condition since the war, he caught up with the doctor at the bridge. Running alongside the carriage, Blankenship called, "I need to speak with you, doctor."

Mathews reined in the horse, bringing it to a halt.

"Can this wait? I'm on my way to visit a patient. I don't have time to chat." The horse danced sideways, jerking the carriage

"You're a difficult man to track down. Did you get my message?"

"Yes. Martha told me, but babies have their own time schedule."

"So I've discovered. I left a word at the college, too."

"I've had other important business to attend to. What do you want?"

"I'd like to know where you were last Saturday."

"I really must go." Mathews snapped the reins, but Blankenship seized them, stopping the carriage from moving.

"Are you deliberately trying to avoid me?" He held the horse in place.

Mathews sat back and loosened the reins. "Just what is it you want to talk to me about?"

"I need to talk to you about Pete Harper."

"What about him?"

Blankenship wanted to ask him about the blackmail letter and the watch fob but wasn't about to discuss the subject of murder standing in the middle of the bridge. And he wasn't going to allow the doctor to ask the questions.

"I need you to come to my office today."

"Make an appointment with my secretary. Now, excuse me. I'm in a hurry." He snapped the reins, and the horse took off.

"My office as soon as you return," Blankenship called to Mathews as he drove away.

Blankenship didn't know if the doctor heard him or not, but he did expect the doctor wasn't going to cooperate. Displeased with the results of his encounter, he jogged back to the jail. The doctor was definitely hiding something. He retrieved the fob and letter from his desk and was about to return them to the safe when he noticed the corner of an envelope sticking out from under a newspaper. On the envelope the words, To Police Chief Blankenship, were written in a personal hand and underlined. He ripped it open and read the contents.

"I have to talk to you. I know who killed Mr. Harper

and I know what happened to the little girl.

She's next to heaven."

It was signed, Ethan Grimes.

"Damn! Why didn't you come directly to me if you knew who killed Harper?" Blankenship mumbled to himself. Why send a note, and what could he possibly know about the little girl, and what did he know about Harper's murder? Marsden had said he saw Grimes at Harper's house the night he went to get his money, confirming that Grimes could somehow be involved.

133

~ CHAPTER 19 ~

Blankenship cut through the alley to the blacksmith shop where Ethan Grimes worked as a Smithy, making and fitting horseshoes. Entering, he saw no sign of the young man. The smell of raw iron, smoke, and sweat filled the shop. A soot-covered leather apron lay on the workbench next to a wagon axle. A cross pein hammer, tongs, and iron file sat next to an anvil. Several pieces of iron lay beside the forge ready to be heated and pounded into shoes.

Thinking that Grimes may have stepped out, Blankenship sat and waited for him to return. When Grimes didn't appear after five minutes, Blankenship walked around to the livery stable next door and found Stuart Johnson busy honing an ax — a sideline income when the livery business was slow.

Blankenship rapped on the open door. Johnson looked up, but kept working. Johnson's ham-size arms and barrel chest strained the buttons on his shirt, testament to his many years of pounding raw metal into horseshoes, wagon rims, and barrel hoops. Blankenship had seen him practically lift a horse off its hind legs when the stubborn animal refused to cooperate as he was shoeing it.

"Chief, what can I do for you? Did your horse throw a shoe again?"

"Nope. I'm looking for Ethan Grimes. He doesn't seem to be around."

"He didn't come to work this morning," Johnson said, as he ran his thumb along the blade of the ax. He stopped long enough to wipe his forehead on the sleeve of his grease-streaked shirt.

"Any idea where he is?"

"No, and I have three horses that need new shoes. It's unlike him to not show up. He's a good worker. Always prompt," Johnson said.

"When was the last time you saw him?"

"Last evening. I sent him to the firehouse to shoe one of their horses. He left here around five. Didn't come back. Since it was so late, I figure he went on home."

"Please let me know if he comes in. It's important that I talk to him."

Johnson put down the ax and followed Blankenship to the door. "Does this have anything to do with Harper?"

"Why do you ask that?" Blankenship turned to look at Johnson.

The blacksmith hesitated, and then offered, "It's probably nothing, but just the other day he said something that didn't make much sense. Strange, in fact, coming from him."

"Strange? Like what?"

"I don't know if I should say. I mean he's a good kid. I could have misunderstood."

"I have reason to believe that Grimes may have information about Harper's murder. I'd appreciate knowing what he said."

Johnson looked out beyond the door as if making sure no one was within earshot. "The other day he said he should have been the one to kill Harper. I asked him what he meant, but he didn't answer. He was heating a piece of iron in the forge at the time and the flames lit up his face. He had murder in his eyes."

"Did he say anything else?"

"No. That's all. I didn't think too much about it at the time. Let's face it Harper wasn't the best-loved person in this town. There are a lot of folks who would have liked to see him dead. Still, I thought that was a strange comment for him to make."

Blankenship didn't like the story Johnson offered about Grimes but thanked him anyway. Wanting to talk with the boy, he started down Vine Street to where he lived with his parents. Perhaps Grimes was sick and couldn't get word to Johnson.

Aside from a broken shutter and the boards needing a fresh coat of paint, Grimes' house appeared neat and clean. A flock of chickens pecked at the ground in the front yard and a shaggy dog lay with his nose poked between the porch rails. The hound raised his head as Blankenship approached, but made no effort to get up.

Earl Grimes stood about five-foot six and his clothes hung on his thin frame like a flour sack draped on a broom handle. His wrinkled face revealed years of hard work and worry, and although his smile seemed somewhat hesitant, he managed a warm welcome and extended a rough and callused hand to Blankenship.

"Good afternoon, Mr. Grimes. Is Ethan at home?"

"Something's wrong, isn't it?"

"I don't know. I was hoping you could tell me. He isn't at work. Stuart Johnson said he hadn't been in all morning, and I need to talk with him."

"I knew something was wrong when he never came home for supper last night. Ethan hasn't been home since he left for work yesterday morning. He's never stayed away from home this long before."

"Could he have gone to visit a friend?" Blankenship asked.

"He doesn't have many friends, and he'd never go off without telling me or his ma where he was going. That boy is much too considerate to worry her."

"Do you know where he is, Mr. Blankenship?" Mrs. Grimes asked, appearing at the door.

"No ma'am," he said, tipping his hat.

"I just know something's wrong. I have his supper still warming for him. He never misses supper." Her worried expression showed the concern that only a mother can have.

Blankenship assured them that if he saw or heard from their son, he would contact them right away.

Blankenship made his way back along Erie Street asking each proprietor if they had seen Ethan Grimes. At each store, he got the same negative reply; no one had seen him. Johnson said he sent him to the firehouse. Maybe someone there had seen him.

The firehouse stood on Clark Street. A service barn behind the building housed the horse-drawn ladder wagon, its horses, and hand pumper. On the roof was a large tower that housed the alarm bell. Thankfully, the bell didn't ring often, but when it did, it meant disaster. If any one of the many homes or businesses caught fire, most of the town would burn to the ground before volunteers could be mustered. Although the firehouse was constructed of brick, that wouldn't prevent its destruction, should a fire ever break out.

Blankenship entered the building and found Guy McDonald polishing the brass on the pumper. Guy was a salty old dog and as gruff as they come, but the chief never had any problems with him.

Guy looked up when he saw the chief and extended his hand. "Well Lordy be, if it isn't our illustrious police chief. And what might I do for ye?"

"Were you here last night?" Blankenship asked.

"Certainly was. My week to ring the bell," he said quite proud of the fact.

"Did you see Ethan Grimes?"

"The lad was here, yes. Came to shoe one of the horses, he did. Right professional about his business, too."

"How long was he here?"

"Not long. Went right to work. Done his do'n and left."

"Did you see him leave?"

The fireman pushed his cap back and paused as if thinking. "Well, no, but I heard him drive off."

"You mean in a wagon?" Blankenship questioned.

"Of course, what else?"

Someone had given the boy a ride, but who? Blankenship thanked McDonald for the information and left the fireman to his polishing.

He ran various possibilities through his mind as to where Grimes might be. Not knowing much about the lad left him without much to go on. One possibility was Tilly's Tavern. Grimes didn't appear to be the type to frequent that kind of establishment, but he'd inquire anyway.

He checked his watch. Damn! It was way past time to walk Katie home. What was she going to think? He feared she might come to believe he was irresponsible, or worse, avoiding her. Hopefully, she would understand he had a murder to solve.

He went to the stable, saddled Mingo, and rode out to the tavern once again to inquire if anyone there had seen Grimes.

Horses, tied to the rail, lined the front of the building. It wasn't quite five o'clock, yet the tavern bustled with customers coming and going. Inside, Blankenship squinted through the smoke-filled room. Except for two gaslights above the bar and a lamp hanging from the ceiling, the tavern had little illumination. Many men frequented the tavern on their way home after work. Most went home after having a quick beer, but a few pickled relics, who had nothing better to do, sat hunkered over their brew, attempting to drown their miseries. Several men stood at the bar with beer in hand–he recognized Marsden as one of them. Others roosted at gaming tables tempting their luck. Women with too much face paint and too little clothing walked around, talking to customers and making sure their beer glasses stayed filled.

Heads turned and eyes follow him through the thick haze as he strode over to the bar. During the past week, the murder of Harper had become the main topic of conversation, and the tempo of conjecture about who had killed him had risen to a fevered pitch.

"Hey, Chief, caught any criminals lately?" came a voice through the din.

Blankenship ignored the question. It came as no surprise to see Marsden and two other men standing at the bar sucking on beers. Blankenship watched Marsden pat a full-bosomed redhead on her bottom as she passed by. The woman giggled, leaned over, and tweaked his cheek. Blankenship couldn't hear their conversation, but by Marsden's expression and the woman's husky laugh, he knew they weren't talking about the weather.

Blankenship waited until the woman found another customer to amuse, then walked over to Tilly who was busy pouring drinks.

"You're getting to be a regular around here, Chief. Want a beer?" Tilly said.

"Some other time. Has Ethan Grimes been in today?"

"Don't recognized the name," Tilly said. "I know just about everyone who comes in."

Blankenship walked through the room questioning customers about Grimes and got the same answer. Nobody had seen him.

He started to leave when Jack Barnes, a bully and trouble maker, began spouting off.

"There's something mighty peculiar goin' on over at that medical school if you ask me," Barnes said loud enough for everyone to hear.

Blankenship suspected the comment was made for his benefit.

"Yeah, I heard that Harper made a few midnight stops at that place," a man wearing a red shirt offered.

"Fred Simpson told me he saw Harper carryin' something along the back alley of the school that looked a lot like a body," another man added.

"Fred Simpson is so cross-eyed he wouldn't know a body from a fishing pole," a man sitting with Barnes butted in.

"My brother-in-law works down at the Ohio Penitentiary in Columbus and he told me there ain't been no one died there in months, and he'd know because he's the one who takes care of seeing that bodies nobody wants are brought up here to that college."

"So, I want to know, where do those corpses come from if it ain't from no prison?" Barnes said.

"Maybe they ain't from no proper place," the man said.

"I always knew there was something fishy going on over there," red-shirt piped up, and then added, "But I'd keep my mouth shut even if it was true."

"You're getting all excited over nothing. My cousin Ben's boy went to that school and so did Officer Stanger," the man next to Barnes said.

That brought a few snickers from the group, especially after the man reminded them how Stanger had been kicked out of the medical college because he spent more time drinking and playing billiards than studying.

"Yeah, maybe we just ought to go over to that college and take a look around for ourselves," Barnes threatened. "We'll get some answers about where those bodies come from."

"Yeah," two men at the table agreed, "let's go over to that school."

The men grunted in agreement and started to get up. Blankenship could see that the amount of liquor consumed over the past few hours was doing the talking. Barnes was whipping up trouble again and Blankenship intended to squelch any notion of it getting past the front door.

Blankenship sauntered over to Barnes' table and looked him in the eyes. "I don't think starting a stink over at the college is a good idea. You're going to get a lot of people fired up and cause a lot of trouble, and then I'll have to come over and clean up the mess you've started, and believe me, you really don't want me to have to do that." He paused long enough for his comment to sink in.

Barnes' comrades looked at each other and taking the hint, sat back down. Besides, it was nice and warm in the tavern.

Blankenship left Tilly's with the feeling he hadn't heard the last of Jack Barnes.

ஐ

"What are you doing here so late? You sure look busy."

Blankenship looked up from the paperwork to see Norville standing at the railing watching him.

"Sorry, I didn't hear you come in."

"I was just passing by and saw you through the window sitting at your desk. Where's Kunkle?"

"He's making his rounds."

"You look like a man in deep thought. What's on your mind besides that school teacher and finding out who killed Harper?" Norville said.

He had been deep in thought, but it wasn't about Katie this time. He was thinking about what Barnes had said, and if true, what he was going to do about it.

"I'm afraid there's a new wrinkle." Blankenship showed his friend the note from Grimes.

"He knows who killed Harper and the little girl?" Norville's voice raised an octave. "Did you talk to him? What did he say?"

"The kid's missing. I've looked all over town for him, but the boy hasn't been seen since late yesterday. I don't have a good feeling about this."

"Hum," Norville said, and then taking off his hat he continued, "He'll show up. You know how young boys are. They get their mind on one thing and before you know it something else takes hold of their interest. He's probably off courting some young lady."

"I hope you're right, but from what his father said, I have my doubts about that."

"So, what else is on your mind?"

"I just came from Tilly's Tavern. I don't like what I heard there," Blankenship said.

Norville waited like a kid expecting an ice cream cone.

"It seems Jack Barnes is trying to cause trouble again."

"What was his yammering about this time?"

"He and a few other drunks are pointing fingers at the college, saying that bodies are going in the back door."

"What's so unusual about that? Aren't they supposed to have cadavers to practice on? It's a teaching college. That's what they do."

"Yes, but it's the way Barnes put it that has me worried." Blankenship leaned back in his chair. "So, what did you stop by for? Come to see Cleo?"

Norville ignored the question, adjusted his glasses, and then said, "There could be some truth to the story floating around over there. I was going through a stack of old newspapers and came across this article. You might want to take a look at it." He handed Blankenship a newspaper article, yellowed with age, from a small town in New York dated some fifteen years earlier.

Blankenship read the headline. "Despicable Practice." The story told about a local doctor being dismissed after a citizen discovered that the Fairhaven Medical College used bodies from a local cemetery for clinical dissection."

"What does this have to do with Harper?"

"That's the same school Charles and John Mathews graduated from and worked at before coming to Willoughby," Norville said. "The doctor was discredited and died about two years later of a heart attack. Now, I'm not suggesting that Charlie has anything to do with Harper's murder but it seems strange to me that Harper just happened to dig graves for a living and is now somehow connected to Mathews by way of the fob. Maybe Harper was doing more than stealing; maybe he took bodies out of graves as well as put them in. And maybe Charles Mathews initiated the request, and maybe that's who Harper was blackmailing."

Blankenship didn't want to believe what the men at Tilly's said could be true but they had put together quite a compelling set of inventions about where the cadavers used at the college might have come from. Just how much of their story came from a seed of truth or how much came from the alcohol? Even though he knew their claims were unwashed rumor, but now with Norville's revelation, he began to question if there was a connection between Charles Mathews and Harper.

He definitely had more questions for the good doctor.

❦

That night in his room, Blankenship sat pondering what he knew about Harper's murder. If the tales told at the tavern, coupled with the story in the newspaper were true, Harper could have been doing double duty in the graveyard. Harper needed money to support his assorted vices. Gambling, the jewelry, and the gold that Harper sold to Nagy could have been the source of some of the money, but apparently that wasn't enough for him. He stole bodies and sold them, too. Harper must have figured he deserved more than what he was getting paid and elected to blackmail whomever it was that hired him. The money and letter served as hard evidence to support Blankenship's theory.

But why blackmail? Harper would surely have implicated himself in the scheme. That didn't make sense. Like Norville, he also wasn't fully convinced that Charles Mathews, the director of the medical college, was involved. But Mathews had opportunity. It would have been easy for him to sneak through the cemetery to Harper's secluded house unobserved — and Mathews, being a doctor, certainly had easy access to cyanide and he had knowledge of how to administer a lethal dose. Finding a watch fob identified as Charles Mathews' added to evidence against him.

The doctor had made a great effort to avoid answering his questions, and when Blankenship did finally chase him down he was uncooperative.

Blankenship rocked back in his chair, thinking. The letter said he wanted more money, indicating he had been paid for his services before. If Mathews were involved in paying off a blackmailer, he would have known Harper had money. Why hadn't he taken it from the house? But as Norville had said, perhaps he didn't know the money was still there. Maybe Mathews figured Harper had spent the money, or maybe he had searched for it, but couldn't find it, or maybe his nose couldn't stand the stink. Maybe someone like Grimes or Marsden interrupted him. There were too many maybes for his liking.

He stood, stretched his back, and shook a kink from his leg. He crossed to the window that looked out over Willoughby. The town, with only a hint of light from the moon, was resting, but beneath its peaceful facade hid a murderer.

Returning to his chair, he picked up a book but put it back down. The news article Norville had shown him threw suspicion on the doctor. But why would Charles Mathews kill Harper? Even though he had opportunity and easy access to poison, what was his motive? The only reasoning Blankenship could come up with was the doctor needed bodies for medical practice, but that didn't make sense. They should have gotten the cadavers they needed from any hospital across Ohio — unless they didn't want to pay their price.

Accusing the trusted head of the medical college of murder was bad enough, but to discover that the remains of loved ones were being dug up and used for medical science would rip the town apart. None of this was going to sit well with the citizens of Willoughby, especially the mayor, but he had no other choice. He knew what he had to do.

~ CHAPTER 20 ~

The clock in the church tower had just struck eight o'clock the next morning when Blankenship knocked on the door of Charles Mathews' home. He hoped the doctor was in this time. He didn't want to get a warrant and have him hunted down and brought in like a common criminal.

Mrs. Mathews answered the door on his first knock. She said her husband was at home and invited him in.

Charles Mathews' house was very different from his brother's. The reception room contained only the most modest of furnishings. No heavy draperies with matching upholstered chairs decorated the room; no highly polished mirrors hung on the walls. A deacon's bench and three Windsor chairs and a table were the only furniture filling the small room. Apparently the brothers lived very different lives.

It didn't take long before the door to the clinic opened. Seeing the police chief, Doctor Mathews' expression quickly changed from one of recognition to what Blankenship could only interpret as annoyance.

"What may I do for you?" Mathews said sourly, his hands resting on his hips.

"As you most likely know, I'm investigating the murder of Pete Harper."

145

"And just what does that have to do with me?" he asked.

"I need to know where you were Saturday about two weeks ago."

Mathews hesitated for a moment before answering. "I really can't say. I can't be expected to remember everything I do and when."

Seeing that Mathews was hell bent on not answering that question, he moved on.

"How well did you know Pete Harper?"

"I've never had any dealings with Mr. Harper," Mathews said, his tone rigid as steel.

"I have information that proves otherwise."

"And just what does that have to do with me?"

"Do you own a watch fob, doctor?"

"Of course, I do."

"Care to show it to me?"

Mathews hesitated. "I'm afraid I can't do that."

"And the reason would be?"

"I no longer have it."

"Then is this yours?" he asked, taking the watch fob from his pocket and holding it for the doctor to see.

The doctor stared at it, his eyes wide, before answering. "Yes, it's mine. Where did you find it?" He reached for the fob. Blankenship quickly pulled it back.

"I found this fob in Harper's house. You admit it belongs to you. You offered no alibi for where you were on Saturday when Harper was murdered, and since your brother has his fob and you don't have yours and no one else in town has one like this with the Mathews' family crest on it, I can come to only one conclusion, doctor. You were at Harper's house and lost your fob while you sat watching him drink the whiskey you poisoned."

"Preposterous. I most certainly was not at his house. I did not kill the man, and I resent the implication. Just what is your purpose here?"

"My purpose, Doctor Mathews, is to get to the bottom of Harper's murder. Right now you're my prime suspect."

"As I said, I hardly knew him. I see no reason why I should be subjected to this inquisition. Now, if you'll excuse me, I have office hours and I'm expecting a patient any minute. I'll have to ask you to leave."

"And I'll have to ask you to get your coat, doctor, and come with me to the jail."

"I certainly will not."

"I'm afraid your patients will have to find another doctor today. You're under arrest."

Mathews scowled. "You're arresting me? On what charge, losing my watch fob?"

"No. Murder."

∽

Charles Mathews sat locked in the holding cell with his hands folded in his lap and a bewildered expression on his face while Blankenship sorted through the morning mail. Charging Mathews with murder shouldn't be difficult with all the evidence he had. But the fact that his main suspect was a prominent doctor and the director of the medical college called for delicate handling. Few people in town, if any, would like the idea of Charles Mathews being arrested for murder. Since Anna's disappearance, Mathews and his family had gained the town's sympathy. Arresting him would certainly cause quite a stir. The mayor, town council, and every citizen of Willoughby would want Blankenship's hide for arresting the finest doctor in town.

Blankenship had finished filing reports when he heard the front door open and then slam shut. He looked up to see Bascom marching into his office. The chief wasn't surprised. Word must have spread that the police chief had sent Stanger to the county prosecutor's office for an arrest warrant charging Charles Mathews with murder. Norville liked to say that in a small town like Willoughby when one person gets gas the whole town farts. The mayor, snorting like a wounded bull, shoved open the swinging counter gate and stomped over to Blankenship's desk.

"I just received a telegram from the prosecutor's office that my nephew... Deputy Stanger is there with paperwork claiming you're holding Charlie on some trumped up charge of murder. Murder! That's ridiculous! I want an explanation."

"I had an idea you would." The arrest of the new director had definitely gotten him in a fury.

"You've gone too far this time, Blankenship. I want him released immediately," he shouted and pointed to Charles sitting in the cell.

"Sorry, I can't do that. He's the prime suspect in the murder of Harper."

"Murder of a derelict like Pete Harper? Have you lost your senses?" Bascom said and raised his fist at Blankenship.

Blankenship knew the mayor would want every last detail. He also knew he had no obligation to tell him anything, but he would extend the courtesy anyway. It wasn't going to be a long story. Blankenship opened the safe and took out the envelope containing the blackmail letter and handed it to the mayor.

"Here read this."

Bascom took the paper holding it between his thumb and index finger as if touching it would contaminate him.

"Go ahead read it."

He just stood there glaring at Blankenship without saying a word as smoke belched from his cigar like a stovepipe.

"Just read the damn letter," Blankenship almost shouted.

The mayor looked surprised that someone had the nerve to yell at him. He picked up the paper and mouthed the words as he read: *What you gave me wasn't enough. If you want my services you'll have to pay me more or I'll tell.*

"So this is the blackmail letter my nephew told me about. This is all you have? You call this evidence? Proof? There's no name on it. This could have been meant for anyone and for this you arrest Charlie?" He tossed the paper onto Blankenship's desk. Purple veins wove furrows across the mayor's forehead and disappeared into his receding hairline. "I repeat. You've gone too far this time."

"The letter and the fact that Mathews has no alibi for the time of Harper's murder, plus the fact that the doctor had means and opportunity gives me good reason to suspect him. Finding Charles' watch fob in Harper's house adds to the evidence against him. That gives me all I need."

He let that soak in before continuing. "I'm just holding him for now, but I will arrest him as soon as Stanger gets back with an indictment."

The mayor scowled as he paced around the office. Blankenship enjoyed seeing him agitated.

"This is a serious matter." The mayor shook his wrinkled, liver-spotted hand in his face.

It was serious all right. Blankenship knew the mayor didn't want anything to happen to his prime supporter in the next election, and doctors at the medical school carried a lot of votes.

The mayor stood speechless, fuming unable to counter Blankenship's accusations.

Blankenship had done his job. Now, all he had to do was to wait for the warrant.

⁂

Later that afternoon, Blankenship wrapped his hand around the cell's bars and shook them. For an instant he imagined the strangle hold was around the mayor's neck — the prosecutor's too. Stanger had returned from the county prosecutor's office with the news that Lipman didn't buy it. He had deemed Blankenship's report and all his evidence insufficient to charge Charles Mathews with murder. It seemed the mayor had strong ties in political circles and his influence spread beyond the town of Willoughby. Doctor Mathews wouldn't be indicted for murder and wasn't going to stay locked up in a drafty jail cell.

~ CHAPTER 21 ~

Blankenship trudged alongside Katie, head bent and his shoulders sagging. Arresting Doctor Mathews was a big mistake. His job was now in serious jeopardy. This last mistake was sure to get him fired. With any luck, after the city council got through with him he'd be allowed to ride out of town with only the clothes on his back. And waiting for the town council's decision was nerve racking. What more evidence did the prosecutor need? The mayor was probably gloating right now, smiling from ear to ear.

Katie must have sensed his mood. "You seem lost in your thoughts. Is something bothering you? Want to talk about it?" she asked, placing her hand on his arm.

He didn't feel comfortable talking about his problems with a woman, and murder wasn't fit conversation for a lady, but her gentle touch was all it took for him to melt under her charm. "This whole business with Harper's murder has taken an ugly turn. Guess it's gotten under my skin," he confessed.

"I may not understand the workings of the police but I do know the workings of the heart and I can tell yours is very heavy right now. Sometimes talking about it helps."

Before he knew it, he had told her about the blackmail letter and how he found the watch fob that pointed a finger at Charles Mathews and how he unsuccessfully tried to arrest him.

She listened attentively.

"To top everything off, Andy Jarvis up and dies of a heart attack."

"Yes, I heard about Mr. Jarvis. One of his children is in my class. I'm truly sorry to hear about his passing. He seemed like a nice man. I'll call on his wife this afternoon."

She walked on silently for a few minutes then asked.

"When did you say Mr. Harper died?"

"As best Jarvis could figure, it would have been sometime Saturday almost two weeks ago."

Katie thought for a moment, wrinkled her brow, and then said, "It would have been impossible for Doctor Mathews to have killed Mr. Harper on that particular Saturday."

"What makes you say that?"

"Considering Theodore's behavior I sent a note home with the boy requesting a conference with his parents for that Saturday. It is difficult to meet with his father during the week. He's always so busy. Martha sent me a note stating that the doctor was out of town and wouldn't be back until Sunday evening on the last train."

Blankenship caught himself before he swore in front of Katie. How could he have missed that? He had never asked the doctor where he was at the time Harper was murdered. Then he remembered, yes, he had asked him — twice. But Mathews had ignored the question both times.

"I know this business has you upset. You will find the answers you're looking for. It may take a little time, but you will. I have confidence in you."

They reached her aunt's house sooner than Blankenship wanted. He would have liked nothing better than to spend the rest of the afternoon talking with her, looking into her beautiful eyes, and smelling the sweet scent of her. He wanted to wrap his arms around her and kiss her right

151

there on the sidewalk, and would have but thought it inappropriate. Instead, he tipped his hat and backed away before the urge to take her in his arms overwhelmed him.

Back in his office, he thought about what Katie had just told him. Why hadn't Charles Mathews cleared his name when he had the opportunity? If he wasn't in town the night Harper died, that surely cleared him of any suspicion, but why the devil didn't he say something? He had a perfect alibi.

Blankenship sorted though the daily correspondence, answered some, and filed others all the while wondering where Stanger was and why he wasn't in the office again.

He had to do something about him. His lack of respect for the law and his duty as an officer of the law proved he wasn't cut out for the job. The chief had made up his mind. He was going to have a long talk with the kid–that is if and when he came to work. Stanger would straighten up and start doing the job he was getting paid for or he'd find himself without a job.

Among the mail he found a wanted poster declaring that a man from two counties east of Willoughby was wanted for robbing the post office there. Blankenship pinned the poster next to the others on the bulletin board. It didn't make him feel any better knowing that other police officers had problems also.

He had reached the bottom of the papers when Theodore Mathews came in, stopped at the counter, and cleared his throat before he spoke. "Mr. Blankenship, please can I talk to you?"

This was the second time Theodore had asked to speak to him. The first was just before he found Jarvis dead. The boy stood nervously twisting his cap in his hand, but that wasn't unusual. Most children seemed uncomfortable around him. Perhaps that was the reason Katie had asked him to speak to her class. Let them see that a lawman was just an ordinary guy, but by the expression on this child's face, he had failed miserably.

"Come on around here and have a seat." Blankenship opened the swinging gate and motioned for Theodore to take the chair by his desk. The boy sat looking around the jail. His gaze stopped at the cells that took up the back half of the jail where his father had been held the day before.

"How is your mother?"

"She's well, sir."

"Just what did you want to talk about, Theodore?" Blankenship sat back, folded his hands in front of him and waited.

Theodore gulped as if trying to work the words out of his mouth. "I...need to tell you something, and...well...I...." His voice was barely above a whisper.

"Speak up, Theodore. What's on your mind?"

"You told us in class that if we knew about something that was wrong we should tell you about it."

"That's right. I did."

"Well...I...I did a terrible thing. You have to search the graveyard for my sister." He twisted his cap in his hands.

"You know we searched the cemetery. We searched everywhere we possibly could. I'm very sorry, son, but she wasn't in the graveyard."

"But she is! I know she is. I know it." The boy was almost shouting.

"What makes you think she's there?"

"Because I told her to go there."

"You told your sister to go to the graveyard? Why?"

"I told her that golden pumpkins were growing in the graveyard and that if she got one she could get money from it, and then she disappeared."

Blankenship had tried many times to erase the memory of those many long hours searching for the little girl. Being reminded of the child's disappearance caused the biting burn to grab at his stomach again.

Theodore had twisted his cap until it begun to look like a wad of cloth.

"When was this?'

"The day before she disappeared." A tear welled up in the boy's eyes.

A pang of sorrow spread through Blankenship. He knew the parents had gone through a terrible time with the loss of their child, but he never stopped to consider how the brother might have felt.

He wanted to offer other suggestions as to where the girl could be, but instantly changed his mind. There was no need to scare him with stories of little girls being abducted and murdered, which is what he had come to believe had happened to the boy's sister.

"I'm afraid I can't help you. This is something for your parents to handle. Why haven't you talked to them about this?"

Theodore hung his head. "No. No. I can't tell them. You don't understand. I mean...it would upset my mother something terrible, and my father would...I just can't. Please, you have to check the graveyard again. I know she's there," the boy pleaded.

"Just what makes you so certain that your sister went to look for a golden pumpkin in the graveyard?"

"I...I know things. My Ma says I had a special connection with my sister. We were twins, you know. She sometimes talks to me in my head."

The boy was obviously not thinking right. He needed help. Theodore's story was far outside the realm of police business. The child couldn't possibly know where his sister was.

"There's more." Theodore paused again and shifted in his seat. "She said she's next to heaven and to look for gray mud on his boots."

"What?" Blankenship just about jumped out of the chair. Where had he heard that before? He hurried to the filing cabinet and took out the letter Ethan had left for him. I know what happened to the little girl. She's next to heaven, it read. Blankenship swallowed the lump in his throat. How did this boy know what was in the letter, and how did he know about the gray mud he had seen on Harper's boots? Mud around town was brown. The only place, for some reason, for that color mud was the graveyard, and he hadn't mentioned the mud to anyone. In fact, he had forgotten all about it. It hadn't seemed important at the time, but now he was beginning to think otherwise.

He was about to ask him how he knew this when Kunkle rushed in, breathing hard. "Hank, come quick! Hunters just found a body hanging in Latham's Woods."

Blankenship had told Theodore to go home and talk to his parents. The story the boy told him was far beyond the range of his job and personal experience. He hated leaving the kid like that without giving him some direction, but there wasn't anything he could do for the boy at the moment.

Blankenship had no choice but to lock the jail. Stanger hadn't shown up. The chief saddled Mingo, and with Kunkle by his side, the men headed west toward the woods. Once beyond the town, it didn't take long before the two policemen reached the edge of the Latham's Wood where a hunter stood waiting.

"Follow me," he called.

The two lawmen followed the hunter along a path that lead into the depths of the woods. Sunlight barely penetrated the thick canopy of the trees, making it difficult to make out details in the shadows. Off in the distance Blankenship heard the mournful baying of hounds.

Blankenship's heart sank when he recognized Ethan Grimes hanging like a limp rag from a withered oak branch. The boy's head was pitched forward at an odd angle and a piece of paper was pinned to his coat. Three hounds were howling and jumping at the tree trying to reach the body.

Both hunters, seeing the police chief, started talking at the same time.

"Whoa, slow down. You," Blankenship point to one of the men, "want to tell me what happened?"

"We were running our dogs when Carlos, that's my Bluetick here, began howling and took off like the devil himself was on its tail. We followed the dogs and found the body hanging from a tree. I sent my boy back into town to tell you."

"That's right." Kunkle nodded. "I was just about to begin lighting the gas lamps on Erie Street before coming to work when the boy came running up to me," he said, confirming the man's story.

Blankenship cautioned the men to stay back. He dismounted Mingo and tied him to a nearby tree while Kunkle, reaching from his mount, cut Grimes free. Blankenship carefully caught Grimes' body as Kunkle lowered it to the ground. He knelt and closed the young man's eyes, and then loosened the rope from around his neck. As he did he noticed that underneath, where a rope burn should have been, were marks the shape and size of a man's fingers.

He removed the paper. On it was a message: *I just can't live with this any longer. I am Sorry.* There was no signature.

Blankenship rubbed the paper between his fingers. Where had he seen this kind of paper before?

"That's odd," Kunkle spoke up.

"What's that?" Blankenship asked.

"How did he hang himself from this tree? There isn't anything around here to stand on," Kunkle said.

Blankenship scrutinized the surrounding woods. Kunkle was right. Grimes couldn't have hung himself unless he had a horse to spur out from underneath him. Ethan's father hadn't said anything about his son taking their horse. Johnson, nor anyone else, reported one missing. So how did he do it? There was no tree stump close by to have jumped from.

"Maybe he climbed the tree and jumped," one of the hunters said.

Blankenship considered the idea but quickly dismissed it. "Don't think so. I don't see how anybody could climb that tree. He'd have to be part bear." There just wasn't any apparent way he could have done it by himself, but Blankenship kept his thoughts to himself.

"Hey, look at his," one of the hunters called to the chief from several yards away and pointed to the ground.

A sack with a hammer and shoeing nails inside lay thrown in the bushes. Blankenship recognized the tools as belonging to the blacksmith.

Now, for the second time in a week he had the unpleasant duty of notifying a family that a loved one had died. Willoughby was no longer the sleepy little town he had come to love. It had become a breeding ground for death.

~ Chapter 22 ~

Blankenship instructed Kunkle to follow him. The first stop they made after seeing that Ethan's body was properly attended to was Ceil Marsden's house. Remembering Marsden's threat, "I'll teach Grimes to keep his yap shut," made him a prime suspect in what the chief believed to be murder. Although Marsden was probably no more than a scoundrel, and Blankenship doubted he was capable of murder, but he had made the threat.

They reined in their horses about fifty yards from Marsden's house. Blankenship instructed Kunkle to cover the back entrance while he went to the front door.

As before, Marsden's wife answered his knock, and the same dirty urchin clung onto her dress. A baby squalled from within. The woman didn't ask what he wanted, but stood waiting for the police chief to speak. A purplish bruise circled the edge of her eye and her bottom lip was red and puffy.

"I need to talk to your husband."

She didn't reply but cast her gaze to the ground and wrapped her arms around her waist.

"Mrs. Marsden, I must speak with your husband."

"He didn't come home last night," was all she said as tears formed in her eyes.

"Do you know where he might be?"

She stood silent for a moment before offering, "He's probably at *that* place again."

"Do you mean Tilly's?"

She nodded, turned, and slowly went back inside.

Blankenship called to Kunkle and together they rode to the tavern. The place was buzzing with activity when they entered. Tilly was at her usual place behind the bar talking to customers. Seeing Blankenship, she waved a big hello and motioned him over.

"I see you brought a friend with you." She gave Kunkle a come-hither look.

"Have you seen Marsden?" Blankenship wasted no time with small talk.

"Not today, but he was here last night."

"What time did he come in?"

"Don't remember exactly, but I had just opened. That would have been at five o'clock."

"When did he leave?"

"He took off with one of my girls early this morning. From the satchel she was carrying, I doubt she'll be back. Good riddance to them both, I say." She busied herself by wiping at a spill on the bar. "How about a beer for you two? On the house," she said, handing him a glass filled to the brim.

Blankenship refused the offer. Kunkle following the chief's lead, also declined.

"Are you certain he was here all night?"

"Look, I don't go around checking on people's private business. He comes to see Sally every week, if you know what I mean," she said and winked.

"Did Sally say where they were going?"

"Never said anything to me."

Suspecting that Tilly might not be telling him the whole story, he needed confirmation.

"I want to see her room."

"I'm rather busy at the moment as you can see."

Blankenship placed his hand, ever so lightly, on Tilly's, causing her to stop wiping the bar and look up. "I want to see her room now," he said, leaving no doubt that he meant business.

"And I've told you before my guests have a right to their privacy."

"Not when they are a suspect in a crime, they don't."

"Crime? What crime?"

Blankenship chose not to answer, but said, "Now, the room."

Tilly reluctantly stopped what she was doing, called one of the other attendants to the bar, and then led the two men upstairs and down a narrow hall. She stopped at the last door on the right and pointed to it.

"Open it, please," Blankenship said.

Tilly knocked. Getting no answer, she turned the doorknob and pushed the door aside.

"Please stay here," Blankenship ordered when Tilly attempted to follow them into the room.

The room was small and sparsely furnished with a bed, chair, and nightstand. A wardrobe stood against one wall, its door open and the inside empty. A purple bedspread covered the bed and the scent of perfume failed to cover the smell of stale tobacco smoke. He pulled out the drawers in the dresser. Both were empty. Sally had left nothing behind that gave a hint as to where the two had gone.

Hearing what sounded like laughter coming from another room, Blankenship started down the hall. Tilly tried to protest, but Blankenship told her to go on about her business. He knocked on the door where the sound was coming from.

Blankenship was shocked to see a girl, probably no more that sixteen open the door. She stood looking at him. The chief introduced himself, and then asked if she knew Sally and where she might be.

"Of course, I know her. We work together. No, I don't know where she is." The girl seemed genuinely surprised that Sally was gone.

"Did she ever talk about her relatives?"

"Not to me she didn't. Sally kept to herself most of the time."

Blankenship thanked her and, seeing no reason for further questions, returned downstairs to the bar.

"Did Marsden have a horse?" Blankenship interrupted Tilly, who was now talking to a customer.

"Never knew him to have one, but we weren't very close."

He doubted that statement, but let it slide. Once again Blankenship left Tilly's feeling the bar owner knew more than she was saying. Was she covering for him?

"So, you think Marsden killed Grimes?" Kunkle asked as they returned to their horses.

"Anything is possible, but from the looks of the body when we cut him down, he had been dead around twenty-four hours. Guy McDonald at the firehouse said he last saw Grimes around five o'clock yesterday. Tilly said Marsden came in about that time. That doesn't leave him much time to ride out all the way to Latham's Woods and string the kid up and then get back here."

"So what are you going to do?" Kunkle asked as he mounted his horse.

"There's no reason to track him down just because he ran off with some woman, or because he beat his wife. I will, however, send a telegram around to the surrounding counties to watch for him. He has to land somewhere."

Once back in town, Kunkle went about lighting the streetlamps and Blankenship returned to the jail to once again plow through the paperwork. The chief had barely removed his coat before Norville showed up, flopped down in a nearby chair, and pulled a pencil from his pocket.

"Heard someone hung himself in Latham's Woods. Any truth to that?"

"Yes, unfortunately, it's true. We found Ethan Grimes hanging from a tree with a note pinned to his coat confessing to murdering Harper."

Norville couldn't write fast enough. He wanted every detail and asked question after question in an attempt to find the how, when, and what. He already knew the who and where. The why was something Blankenship couldn't answer.

Blankenship watched as his friend scribbled on his notepad. From time to time Norville would stop, lick the end of the pencil, and then adjust his glasses before continuing. The chief had never seen him so intent in his work. Once Norville had finished his notes, he stuck the pencil in his nest of hair, folded the paper and put it in his pocket, and then let out a long, slow sigh as if the task had exhausted him.

"Are you all right?" he said, looking up at Blankenship. "You look like you could chew nails."

"Not really. I have a murdered cemetery caretaker who I believe was stealing from the dead, an escaped prisoner, Andy Jarvis up and dies, and then Ethan Grimes possibly committed suicide. I arrested a man who had an alibi but didn't give it, and a boy telling me strange tales. I have a misfit for a deputy who takes off every time I leave him alone. And then there's the mayor who watches every move I make trying to get me fired. Other than that, everything's fine. How are things with you?"

His friend lost his reporter face and said, "I'm really sorry, Hank."

"Yeah, me too." The chief's voice fell flat.

Norville rose, hobbled to the stove, and stood as if in deep thought. He suddenly spun around. "What do you mean *possibly committed suicide?* A man hangs himself in the woods and leaves a note confessing to the murder of Harper and..." He looked directly at Blankenship. "You don't believe it was suicide, do you? Come on, Hank, what do you know about this?"

"Adam, I can't and won't say anything about what I suspect because I don't know yet. I'm asking you nicely. Please, don't play with this."

He wasn't about to tell his friend he suspected that Grimes hadn't hung himself. The marks on his neck suggested otherwise. This time he was keeping his cards close to his coat buttons. The note he found on Grimes' body — the one written on paper suspiciously similar to the blackmail letter Jarvis found in Harper's pocket — would stay a secret for now.

"Well, all right, but...."

"I know. I know. You want everything when this is over."

"So what's this about a boy telling you strange stories?" Norville asked.

"I have no idea what that's all about, but he claims his sister is in the graveyard."

Norville scratched his head, and then walked back to his chair and flopped down. "Speaking of that blackmail letter. Something's been bothering me, Hank. Couldn't remember what it was at first but then it came to me. The letter you showed me — the one that Harper supposedly wrote to blackmail Mathews..." He paused, took off his glasses and wiped them on his handkerchief. "Harper couldn't write. I remember some years back, on one of those rare occasions when he was in the feed store buying something. I can't remember what, but that's not important. Old man Ferguson asked him to sign for his purchase, but Harper wouldn't sign his name. I remember because Ferguson made a fuss. You know how he is about his bookkeeping; he wanted Harper to sign the receipt but Harper couldn't."

Blankenship blew out a long breath, put his elbows on his desk, and rested his head in his hands.

"That's what has been bothering me, Hank. How could Harper have written that letter if he was unable to sign his name? Plus the writing was too perfect. That man had a third grade education at best. That's also why there weren't any newspapers lying around Harper's house. I don't think he could read. I didn't make the connection at first. I usually notice when it involves the newspaper. Somebody wrote that letter trying to make it look as though Harper had written it. And come to think of it, I never saw any stationery like the one the letter was written on in his house, either."

Blankenship had felt all along that something wasn't right — things were too neat, but couldn't put his finger on it. This piece of information suggested another, more alarming possibility — one he didn't like at all. Somebody was trying to frame Charles Mathews, but who, and why?

"Adam, if what you're saying is true, this means I've fallen for the oldest game in the book. I was sent on a wild goose chase. If the letter was planted, that means someone purposely put it in Harper's pocket, knowing that Jarvis or somebody would find it. Who would hold that kind of grudge?"

"What about the money?" Norville asked. "Do you think that was planted, too?"

"I doubt it. I suspect some of the money came from gambling and the rest from the personal possessions he stole."

"That makes more sense."

Blankenship got up and paced back and forth mumbling to himself. All the questions he had about why Charles Mathews killed Harper were now turned around to why somebody was framing him. Then there was Grimes. How did he fit into the picture?

"Think you better sit down, Hank, you're making me dizzy pacing back and forth like that."

"Sorry, just thinking." After a long pause he said, "There's still a piece of the puzzle missing. Adam, everything fits except the watch fob. How did Charles Mathews' fob get into Harper's house?"

"If someone planted the letter, they could have planted the fob, too."

Norville's revelation about Harper not being able to read nor write put a new wrinkle in the works. His friend was definitely on to something about the watch fob. Perhaps another talk with Charles was in order.

Blankenship was on his way out the door when Stanger came rushing in. "Wait till you hear what I just found out," he said, grinning from ear to ear.

"I have no time now, Stanger, but when I get back you and I are going to have a talk, and by God you better be here! Do you understand? Don't leave this building until I get back."

~ Chapter 23 ~

Once again, Blankenship stood at the door of Charles Mathews' house. Trying to talk with the man he had held for murder wasn't going to be easy. In justification, he told himself that if Mathews were innocent he should have tried to clear himself. Why didn't he offer an alibi? Mathews gave no explanation for the evidence that pointed at him. Why hadn't Mathews tried to carve a defense for himself? As the director of the medical college, being above suspicion of any wrong-doing should have been paramount. His reputation in the community and medical society was at stake.

"What is it this time?" Mathews said, opening the door.

"Good evening, Doctor Mathews. I'm sorry to be calling on you again, but may I speak with you?"

"I thought you understood you have no evidence against me for the murder of Pete Harper. Wasn't that enough or have you come to arrest me for tying my horse to the wrong post?"

"Doctor Mathews, you're right and I'm sorry for that. At the time, I had strong evidence against you. I know now that I was wrong and for that I apologize. As you know, however, this affair isn't finished. It won't be until I've caught whoever murdered Harper. I must talk to you."

"And what does that have to do with me?" Mathews stood holding the door.

"It's the watch fob, doctor. There is something that doesn't quite hit the mark on this. I was hoping you could clear it up."

"I've answered all your questions. I don't see why you feel you need to come to my home and continue this matter." He started to close the door, but Blankenship placed his hand on the door, stopping him.

"As I said doctor, the watch fob — the one you're missing and the one that was found in Harper's house. You never answered me while in my office. I must know. How did your fob get into Harper's house?"

"You seemed quite satisfied before to assume I dropped it while I sat watching Harper drink poison. And now you have doubts. Is that it? Perhaps you should have thought about that before you hauled me into your...ah...office."

Blankenship accepted the sarcasm without offense. The evidence leading to the arrest of Mathews was a ruse and he had fallen for it. He wasn't going to make that mistake again.

"Doctor Mathews, all the evidence I had suggested that you murdered Harper. Everything pointed to you. I now believe you were framed. Someone tried to make it look as though you murdered him."

Blankenship paused before continuing. "You never answered me when I asked about the fob. Once again, how did your watch fob get into Harper's house?"

Mathews didn't answer immediately but stood as if thinking over the question, and then opened the door, allowing the police chief to enter his home.

"Perhaps we should talk in private."

Mathews showed Blankenship into his office and offered him a chair next to a scarred writing table while he chose to remain standing.

"I can't tell you how my fob got into Harper's house because I don't know. What I can tell you is that my fob was stolen."

"Stolen? By whom? When did this happen?"

"Just before spring break. I recall checking my watch because I was running late for class. I seldom run late. When I checked my watch, the fob and watch were attached to its chain." Mathews paused and sat down behind his desk.

"And?" Blankenship prompted.

"It was an anatomy class, as I recall. I took off my coat and placed it over the back of my chair. I detached my fob from the chain and placed it in the pocket because it gets in the way when I am teaching dissection. Then I proceeded to class. When I returned to my office after class, I noticed someone had rummaged through my desk. I checked my pocket, the fob was gone."

"What did you do? Why didn't you report it missing?"

"Aside from looking around my office, I did nothing. What was there to do? Should I have gone around asking who stole my fob and making wild accusations?"

"Who had access to your office?"

"Any number of people."

"Any one in particular?"

"Yes."

"It's difficult for me to believe that you knew who might have stolen your fob and that you did nothing."

"That's true. I did have a suspicion."

"Who did you suspect?" Blankenship prodded.

Mathews paused as if deciding how to answer, and then he said, "Your deputy, Stanger. I remembered him asking to be excused during class. He wasn't the...well, shall we say, he wasn't the best or brightest of students. He frequently missed class, and I often detected the odor of liquor on his breath. He was hardly a reputable candidate to become a doctor. He was the only student to leave the room. When I discovered my fob missing I confronted him. He tried to deny it, but I sensed he was lying, so I gave him an ultimatum, either return the fob — with no questions — or face the humiliation of being dismissed. He chose the latter."

Blankenship's head was spinning. First, everything pointed to Charles Mathews as the killer; then the evidence pointed to somebody framing the doctor, now the question was what did Stanger have to do with all of this?

Stanger had lied about school. He wasn't expelled because of poor grades, but left under suspicious circumstances, and now thinking back, the mayor said that Stanger had told him about the blackmail letter. How did Stanger know about it before he showed it to the mayor? Nobody knew about the letter except Norville and Jarvis. Just what else was Stanger guilty of?

◈

Blankenship couldn't get back to the jail fast enough. He wanted to talk with Stanger immediately. He intended to find out just what Stanger's involvement was in all of this, and he had better be in the office.

When Blankenship arrived at the jail, Stanger was sitting in his favorite position, reading a newspaper. The chief made no attempt to stop the door from slamming behind him.

Stanger looked up in surprise. "Hey, do I get paid overtime for working late? Kunckle is out somewhere."

Blankenship stormed to Stanger's desk, yanked the newspaper out of his hands, and slammed it down on the desk in front of him. "Just who told you that there was any question of blackmail?"

"Huh?" Stanger sat up, startled. "What are you talking about?"

"Blackmail. How did you know about the blackmail letter? Norville and Jarvis were the only two people who knew about the letter until I showed it to your uncle. How did you know about it?"

"I read it." Stanger looked like a cat caught with bird feathers in its whiskers.

"You what?" Blankenship leaned in, his nose only inches from Stanger's.

Stanger backed away, his eyes wide with surprise. "Oh, come on, Chief! The letter was on your desk. Remember the other day I came in carrying firewood and dropped a log? For some reason you ran out of here like a dog chasing a rabbit. Either the noise of the logs hitting the floor or you blowing out of here scared that cat. She jumped up on your desk and knocked over your coffee cup. Made one hell of a mess. When I went to clean up, I saw the letter. It was just sitting there for anyone to see, so I read it."

Blankenship was sure he had put the letter in the safe. He was too careful to leave something as important as a piece of evidence lying around. Maybe he was getting forgetful. Then he remembered. He had gotten a cup of coffee before taking the letter and the fob out of the safe to examine it, and like Stanger said, after seeing Mathews pass by, he had rushed out, leaving everything on his desk.

Not offering an apology, but changing the subject he continued, "I just came from speaking with Doctor Mathews — Charles Mathews. He told me why you were expelled from the medical college. Why did you lie to me about it?"

"I didn't lie about it," Stanger said, sounding hurt and offended at the same time. "You assumed, like everybody else, that I flunked out because I couldn't make the grade. After the incident with the fob, Uncle Frank didn't want it to get out that I... I was kicked out because I was suspected of being a thief. Mathews gave me a choice and I took it. My uncle softened the truth a little, that's all."

"And the fob, did you take it?"

Stanger sprang from his chair as if his pants were on fire. "I went though hell with my uncle over that damn fob and was called to answer to his inquisition. I don't see why I should answer to you."

"You'll answer and give me some straight answers or find yourself with a not so softened truth spread all over this town. Now, sit back down!"

Stanger sat. "No, I didn't steal his fob," he said, looking his boss directly in the eye. "I know when it came up missing, it looked bad for me. I couldn't prove I didn't take it, but Doctor Mathews assumed I did." His voice sounded strained.

"Did you leave his class the day the fob disappeared?"

"Yes. But not for the reason he thinks. It was the day after a night at Tilly's and I wasn't feeling so good. I asked to be excused. I went to the privy and came right back. That's all. Doctor Mathews is a powerful man. I told him I didn't take his fob, but he didn't believe me. I couldn't buck him. I went to Uncle Frank and told him what had happened. He said he would see that everything was kept quiet and get me a job here in Willoughby so I wouldn't have to go back home in disgrace. He was none too happy about it, but everything seemed to be working out."

Not only had the mayor given him a misfit for an officer and entrusted him with the safety of the citizens of the town, he was also flaunting his disregard for the police chief and the entire police department.

"What's this all about anyway? Why are you questioning me as if I killed Harper?"

"Did you?"

Stanger no longer looked like a carefree kid still wet behind the ears.

"No! I didn't kill him or anybody else who might have dropped dead within the last twenty-four hours. And if you hadn't rushed out of here so fast earlier, I could have told you what I found out when I went over to the college to talk with an old buddy about what Harper might have had on Doc Mathews. For your information, I've been doing a little detective work of my own."

Blankenship blew out a long breath and sat down on the edge of Stanger's desk. "Go on, I'm listening."

Stanger paused before speaking as if unsure how to begin. "While I was a student at the medical college, I became good friends with a guy by the name of Razzy Leggett."

"Razzy? What kind of a name is that?"

"Don't ask. It's a long story. Anyway, Razzy and I got to be friends and when we weren't in class or studying — I did study in spite of what people think — we would, on occasion, go to Tilly's for a drink and to relax." Stanger paused as if thinking. "We never drank much, but one night we were feeling...a little more relaxed than usual after drinking several pints and thought it would be fun to go back to the laboratory and do a little work. We wanted to see who could make the straightest incision in the thoracic cavity, but we never got that far. As we came up behind the college we saw Pete Harper unloading something from a wagon that looked like a body. Harper knocked on the back door. The door opened and he carried the body inside. We never saw who opened the door to let him in. Harper came out a few minutes later. We changed our minds about testing our skills and didn't go in that night, but the next day there was a new body waiting for us when we got to class."

"You actually saw Harper carry a body into the college? Are you sure it wasn't a bag of something?"

"A bag of something doesn't have arms and legs. I know what I saw."

"Are you sure it was Harper?"

"Yes, I'm sure."

Stanger's tale substantiated Jack Barnes' story that Fred Simpson also saw somebody carrying what looked like a body in the back door of the college.

"Why would you think that was strange? Doesn't the school use bodies for study?"

"Sure, but they always come during the day. Me and Razzy had to help carry a body in one time. The courier wouldn't be driving at night, and besides a doctor has to be there to sign for the body and the doctors don't work at night, not that late anyway."

That sounded reasonable, Blankenship thought. "Then what happened?"

"Nothing really. We didn't say anything, not at first, but to be honest with you it bothered me. So one day I asked Doctor Mathews about it. The next day he claimed his fob was missing and accused me of stealing it and you know the rest."

Blankenship leaned forward and rubbed the back of his neck. Would he ever put the pieces together?

"I went over to the college this morning to have a talk with Razzy," Stanger continued. "He stayed on after he graduated. He works as Doctor Kibby's assistant. I asked him if he ever found out anything more about the body we saw that night. He was very reluctant to talk at first, but then seemed relieved to get it off his chest."

Stanger returned to his desk and sat. He took his time before continuing. "Seems that all the bodies we were dissecting during anatomy class didn't come from the prison like we were told. Those bodies cost too much and were often too slow in coming. He told me that he suspected the college was in financial trouble. He didn't say why, but somehow he found out that someone at the college considered it was cheaper and faster just to go to a local graveyard and dig up a fresh corpse whenever needed." He paused again, unbuttoned the top button on his shirt before continuing.

"I guess everything was working out pretty well until Razzy and I came along that night and saw Harper with that body. I was foolish enough to ask Doctor Mathews about it. Mathews found a way to shut me up with the threat of exposing me as a thief."

"Why didn't you say something about this before?"

"How could I prove it without getting a whole lot of people worked up? Mathews never knew about Razzy's involvement. He made me promise to leave him out of it. I gave him my word, Hank. He's a good doctor and besides we can't undo what's already been done."

Blankenship tried to make sense of what Stanger just told him. Something fishy going on at the medical school, isn't that what the men at Tilly's had said? Bodies were being dug up and used for medical studies. Good God! And there was Mathews again, right back in the middle of it, but if everything was going so well, why kill Harper and mess up a good deal?

"Are you telling me that you dissected bodies taken from our local cemetery and you never recognized the person as someone from our community?"

"I came here a little more than two years ago, if you remember — about the same time as you. I don't know everyone in town. Besides the bodies were unrecognizable. Jarvis may have been a fine man but his skills at preparing a body for viewing weren't the best. The faces were drawn and withered. I wouldn't have recognized my own mother if she were lying on the autopsy table."

Some of it made sense; the rest was just a bundle of questions. He had to get to the bottom of this before the town discovered bodies of their dearly departed friends and loved ones were being dug up and used for anatomical studies at the college.

The question now was how to prove it? He couldn't just march into the college and ask to see the bodies, or make accusations without proof. And Stanger's story wasn't going to stand up anywhere; not with the stigma he carried for having been kicked out.

171

"How much of this does your uncle know and believe?"

"I told him everything, but I don't know what he believes. You'd have to ask him."

The mayor knew what was going on at the college but did nothing. Charles was told about the bodies and did nothing. Just what in the hell were they hiding?

~ Chapter 24 ~

Blankenship paced the floor of his room that night mulling over what Stanger and Charles Mathews had told him. By two o'clock in the morning he still didn't have the two conflicting stories straight. All he knew so far was that somebody had murdered Pete Harper and made it look as though Charles Mathews had committed the crime. But why Charles? And where did Ethan Grimes fit into all this? That's one question regrettably he might never find the answer to.

That wasn't his only problem. Yesterday, thanks to Jack Barnes and a few diehard drunks over at Tilly's, rumors about bodies being dug up from the cemetery had gotten around town and angry threats began surfacing. He knew he had to squelch such talk before it started or he would have a great deal of trouble on his hands.

Blankenship wrestled for hours over what he should do. The threats made him edgy. He had no real proof of anything. All he had were rumors, and rumors had caused enough trouble in the past. Spreading tales wasn't a reason to arrest someone. If it were, he'd have most of the town locked up.

The story told at Tilly's, coupled with Stanger's confession, fit the puzzle, and the evidence connecting Harper to the college matched, but the fob still didn't fit into the mystery anywhere. The familiar burn in his stomach returned.

Grave Secrets

He needed all the pieces to come up with a complete picture, and right now too many pieces were still missing. Unfortunately, the parts of the puzzle he did have indicated a more sinister plot, and he didn't know how to prove any of it. Not yet.

A lot of talk seemed to point toward the cemetery and the medical school. Blankenship considered the possibility of a conspiracy. That thought made the matter even worse than it already was. He needed proof–real proof, not planted. He knew all too well the evidence he had on Charles Mathews made the doctor seem guilty. He had to be careful if he were to prove that despicable deeds had transpired at the medical school. Another finger pointed in the wrong direction would certainly cost him his job — if he hadn't lost it already. Allowing a prisoner to escape was a court martial offence in the military. He didn't know what the charges would be in a civilian court if they found him incompetent, and derelict of duty as Bascom charged. He still hadn't heard from the town council and with each passing day, his concern for his job increased.

For right now he was still the police chief and had a job to do. Maybe a trip to the medical school was in order. He'd go there and poke around and see if he could find evidence that might shed light on who killed Harper.

The light of a gray dawn seeping in through the window matched his mood. Looking into the mirror, he saw that without much sleep or a shave, he looked no better than Harper did the night he found him lying on the floor of his house. The water in the pitcher had turned cold, and not wanting to make more work for his land lady he made the decision to get a shave at Ned's barber shop before going to the college.

The six-foot red, white, and blue striped barber pole could be seen from four blocks away. Ned had opened the barbershop after his wife started nagging him about the hair clippings and aroma of after-shave in her kitchen. She told him to stop cluttering her house with his cutting and shaving tools, so he took his scissors, combs, and razors and set up shop on Second Street. Blankenship figured the golden knob on top of the extra large barber pole signaled Ned's independence. The barber pole and the grand opening were the talk of the town for weeks.

A tiny bell hanging over the door jingled when he entered the barbershop.

"Morning, Chief. You're in mighty early this morning," Ned said, looking up to greet him. "From the looks of you, I'd say you never went to bed."

"Just a shave today, Ned."

A large collection of personalized shaving mugs belonging to each of Ned's regular customers were displayed on a pigeonhole shelf along one wall, advertising his success. The mayor's cup slightly larger than the others, sat on the top shelf. A towel steamer sat hissing next to the coffee pot on the stove in the corner. Stacks of clean white towels, bottles of after-shave, and various powders took up space on a shelf behind the barber chair. Ned's cash register sat prominently on the counter in front of the large mirror that made the fifteen by twenty room appear larger than it really was. A glass-eyed moose head looked down at customers from its place above the back door.

Normally, several men sat in the barbershop either waiting their turn or just passing the time of day. This morning, however, the chairs were empty. Too early for tale spinning he guessed.

"On second thought, I could use a little trim, too," Blankenship said.

Ned went right to work trimming his hair and passing along the latest gossip.

"Heard about that Gypsy fellow escaping and about you arresting Doc Mathews. Do you really think he killed the caretaker?" Before Blankenship could answer, Ned continued. "I could've told you Doc Mathews could never kill anyone. Why he and his brother are the salt of the earth."

Blankenship watched in the mirror as Ned pulled strands of his hair between his fingers, and then snipped off the growth. He parted the chief's hair down the middle and then rubbed oil into his scalp. When he finished cutting his hair, Ned tilted the chair back.

Taking a hot towel from the steamer, he jostled it from hand to hand before unfolding and wrapping it around Blankenship's face. The warmth of the towel felt good. Blankenship sat back and let the heat penetrate and relax him. He listened as Ned took the mug with the police badge painted on the front from the shelf and began whipping lather into it.

"You know, you might never find out who killed Harper," Ned said.

That possibility disturbed him. Allowing a killer to run free didn't sit well with Blankenship. He had a duty to the citizens of Willoughby to keep them safe.

As Ned slapped his razor blade against the leather strop hanging on the side of the chair, two men dashed in, both talking at once. Blankenship peeked through the opening in the towel and recognized Clark and Grant Talbot, brothers and partners in a building company.

"Mornin' men," Ned said. "Come on in and sit a spell."

"Mornin'," Grant returned the greeting.

"It sure is a cryin' shame about that Grimes kid, though," Grant said, continuing the conversation the two had apparently started before entering the barbershop.

"Can't understand it. No, can't understand it at all," Clark said.

"It's definitely strange that a boy like Grimes would kill himself when his family is having such hard times," Grant said.

"I've known him ever since he was a knee-high sprout. You did, too, didn't you Ned," Clark said.

"That's right," the barber replied.

"His pa is a real right sort. Two sons killed in the war and now this. That family has had nothing but bad luck," Clark continued. "Yep, real strange. And sad, too."

Blankenship thought the same thing, but had other reasons for being upset about Grimes' death. He hadn't told anyone of his suspicions, not even Norville with all his probing, that he believed Grimes had been murdered. But he wouldn't be surprised if Norville came to the same conclusion. As far as Blankenship could tell, Grimes couldn't have committed suicide. Nobody hangs himself from a ten-foot-high tree branch the way Grimes supposedly did without assistance. There hadn't been anything high enough near the tree for Grimes to jump from. He couldn't have used a horse. According to talk, old man Grimes had sold the family horse last summer and none were missing from the livery. The scene just didn't look like suicide.

Plus the marks on the young man's neck when he cut him down suggested strangulation by hand before the cord was wrapped around it. Furthermore, the position of the rope didn't line up with the bruises. No, he wasn't about to allow information to get out about how Grimes died. He was more careful this time.

Ned removed the towel, brushed lather over his face; and then proceeded to slide the blade skillfully down the side of his jowl.

"Hello, Chief," Clark said, finally noticing him.

"Morning," Blankenship muttered, careful not to move.

"Did you know the boy, Chief?" Ned asked.

"Not really."

"That lad worked all the time to help support his family when his pa went to ailing. I saw him many times putting up hay and chopping wood for different folks. Why I even saw him over at Calhoon's helping that niggra feller fix his roof," Grant added. Ned turned Blankenship's chin and glided the razor along the other side of his cheek. Ned worked swiftly and confidently without mishap. Blankenship never knew Ned to nick anyone.

"Came around our company asking for work not long ago," Clark said. "Sure wish I'd known how bad things were for the boy. Business has been slow. We just didn't have any work for him."

Silence hung over the room for a long time before Clark asked the chief if he knew yet who killed Harper. It was the way Clark said the word yet that gave Blankenship a spark of hope that he would solve the murder, but for now he was no closer to finding out the killer's identity than the day Jarvis told him that Harper had died from drinking cyanide.

The bell jingled again. "Burr. It's colder than my mother-in-law's heart," Morris Colburn said, blowing on his hands as he entered the barbershop. "Looks like we're in for an early winter."

"Morning Morris. Come to sit a spell?" Ned said, continuing his work.

Did anybody ever come to Ned's for anything other than to sit a spell, Blankenship wondered? Morris' balding head indicated that he was there for conversation only.

"Morning," Morris said, eyeing the coffee pot. He helped himself to a cup and then took a chair by the stove. Morris was about the only person in town who could drink Ned's coffee.

It didn't take long for the conversation to turn to the topic of the day.

177

"I wonder what will happen to the medical college now?" Morris said.

"Charles will do a good job as the new director. He's a mighty fine doctor," Ned offered.

"It takes more than being a good doctor to run a whole school. You have to have a head for business, too," one of the brothers said.

"That Kibby fellow was in here the other day talking like he wanted the job," Ned interjected.

"Guess a lot of doctors wouldn't mind running the place," Morris said.

"I sure hope the school is run better now," Ned said.

"What do you mean by that?" Blankenship asked.

"Don't get me wrong, but I've heard the school's finances weren't in the best shape."

"Pooh," Morris scoffed.

The men stopped talking when John Mathews came in.

"Morning, Doc. Come to sit a spell?"

"No, just my usual shave today, Ned."

The doctor strutted to the clothes rack, removed his coat with a dramatic flair and then pulled off his calfskin gloves, delicately tugging on each finger one at a time. He carefully placed his gloves over his top hat and removed his white silk scarf, before taking the empty chair next to the door. Blankenship noticed John Mathews still wore his fob.

"How's everything at that school now that your brother is director?" Morris asked.

"Everyone is pitching in and doing double duty to make a smooth transition. Even the janitor seems to be working extra hard. The atmosphere is solemn, but we must carry on. The school first, you understand."

"Sure was a shame about old Doc Haroldson. He looked peaked those last few weeks now that I think back."

"Yes, very sad," Mathews said.

"You two were good friends, weren't you?" Morris asked.

"I knew him for a long time. Attended to him frequently while he was ill."

"Your brother has a big job ahead of him with running that college and all."

"A director should love the work and the college," Mathews said, crossing his legs.

"Well, your brother certainly fits those two categories," Morris said. "Never saw anybody who cared more for that school than him, or you for that matter." Turning to the others, he said, "Doc Mathews here raised the money for the new laboratory equipment last year all by himself. Isn't that right, doc?"

Mathews grinned with pride at the recognition of his accomplishments, and then said, "The passing of Doctor Haroldson is a great loss to us all. My sympathy goes to his dear wife."

Ned finished his last stroke under Blankenship's chin and put down the blade. He wiped off the remaining spots of lather, sprinkled bay rum into the palms of his hands and slapped it on the chief's face. The after-shave stung, but was refreshing. As a final touch, Ned dusted talcum powder on his neck.

Blankenship thanked Ned and handed over ten cents. The cash register gave a tinny ring when Ned pushed a button and dropped the money into the tray.

~ CHAPTER 25 ~

The chief changed his mind about going to the medical school; nobody would be there this early. He'd visit the school later.

Entering his office, he found an official looking letter on his desk. Across the front were the words *Willoughby Trustees*. Blankenship's heartbeat quickened as he picked up the envelope. He knew that whatever was inside would seal his fate. Had the town council exonerated him or would he be sent packing? With shaky hands, he slit open the envelope, and read the letter.

To: Police Chief Hank Blankenship

We, the Willoughby Trustees, deem your actions as the chief of police of Willoughby to be in accordance with policy standards set by the town council and find the charges brought against you to be unfounded. There will not be a formal hearing.

Regards,

Russell Craig

Trustee President

It was short and to the point.

Blankenship pictured Bascom spitting and sputtering and stomping around his office when he got the news that his accusations hadn't held water. The chief couldn't stop the smile from spreading across his face. His job was safe for the time being.

After clearing his desk of the daily reports, and with Stanger at his desk, trying to look busy, Blankenship set out to Vine Street to have another talk with Ethan's father. He didn't know much about Ethan Grimes, just that he was a skinny kid with a hungry look in his eyes and a dark secret in his soul. Maybe his father might be able to shed some light on what his son had been up to before he died. But more importantly, maybe he would discover Grimes' connection to Harper, if any.

For the third time as the chief of police, Blankenship had the dreadful duty of having to speak to the parents who had just lost a child. He was beginning to dislike this job.

Blankenship stood in the street in front of Grimes' home for a few minutes thinking of what he would say to the man who had just lost his child. Everything he came up with sounded trite. He stepped to the door with his hat in his hand. A black ribbon hung limp and motionless on a grapevine wreath attached to the front door indicating a house in mourning. No sound came from inside. He tapped twice and waited.

Mr. Grimes answered the door. His stooped shoulders and haggard, grief-stricken face left little doubt about his most recent tragedy.

"Mr. Grimes, I'm sorry to bother you at a time like this, but I would like to speak with you."

Grimes nodded and asked Blankenship to please wait. He returned shortly wearing a long black coat frayed thin at the cuffs.

"I would ask you in, but if this is about Ethan, I don't want to upset the Misses any more than she is already."

"I understand."

Grimes walked like a man carrying a thousand ancient sorrows in his heart, slowed even more by his age. They lumbered along in silence for several minutes before Blankenship finally spoke. "Mr. Grimes, I have been hearing rumors about Ethan that I hope you can clear up for me."

Grimes looked at him with haunted, questioning eyes.

"I'd like to know more about your son."

"He was a good boy. I can't believe he would go and..." Grimes' voice cracked. He wiped at his eyes and then continued. "After my other two boys were killed in the war, Ethan grew up fast. You know he was the last of my sons. Those yellow-belly rebels." He bowed his head and sighed. "Ethan was all we had left. Now, all my children are gone. It ain't natural for children to die before their parents. His mama's heartsick."

Blankenship knew about the loss of Grimes' sons in the war. A tombstone marked a grave for each of them in the cemetery.

"What did Ethan do in his spare time?"

"Spare time? What spare time? He worked practically every minute he was awake. After I got sick, he found extra jobs to help earn enough money to keep the family alive. Without my other boys and the rain coming on like it did last summer, it was all we could do to hold everything together. That son of mine was a good boy, I tell you. He worked hard. Never gave me no trouble. No sir. Now he's gone, too," he said, sniffing and wiping a wet spot from his cheek with the back of his hand.

"You say he took on extra jobs. Can you tell me what kind?"

"He worked for a while down at the sawmill — that was on Saturdays during the heavy time. He helped me out at the blacksmith shop, and when my back went out, he took over. He was good with that hammer. A good striker, too."

"Can you think of any other work he had?"

"Well, I don't know for sure, but he would come home for supper, eat, and then rush right back out again. That went on for about two months. I remember he'd come home all dirty. His mama would get after him for tracking mud into the house. Got so she would stop him at the door and make him take off his boots."

"Do you have any idea why he would want to kill himself? Was he in any trouble?"

Mr. Grimes lowered his head. "It just ain't right. I don't understand why he went and...." His voice broke into a sob.

They had walked to the end of Vine Street where the railroad track crossed before heading back. Blankenship figured he had gotten about all the information he was going to get. Reaching the house, he thanked Mr. Grimes and again offered his sympathies to him and his wife. That's when he noticed a pair of boots sitting by the porch railing covered with the same gray mud he'd seen on Harper's boots.

Could one of Grimes' extra jobs have been working with Harper in the cemetery?

If Grimes did work at the cemetery he might have known about Harper taking personal belongings from the bodies he buried. He might have also known that the medical school was using corpses stolen from the cemetery for medical practice, if in fact that had actually occurred. Maybe that's the reason someone killed him and made it look like suicide. That would confirm his suspicion. It made more sense than a young boy killing himself just because he knew something about the Mathews child and Harper's killer.

He was convinced now more than ever that a talk with someone at the college was in order. Blankenship cut through back streets and had just crossed Maple Street on his way to the medical school when he heard someone call to him. He turned to see Doctor Carlton, the young doctor who had translated the Latin phrase on the watch fob, standing next to the dry goods store. The doctor had an expression similar to that of a frightened colt being saddled for the first time. Carlton motioned for Blankenship to come closer.

"May I talk to you?" he asked, glancing over his shoulder.

"Sure, go ahead."

"Not here. Not in the street. Wait a few minutes and meet me in the library. I'll be in the biology section," he said, and then hurried away.

What was that all about?

Blankenship watched the young man disappear down the street, never looking back.

Before he could follow the doctor, Anna May Clark, the postmistress, trotted up to him, waving a letter.

"Good, I found you. I've been trying to track you down all morning. Don't you ever stay in your office?"

He half expected her to shake a finger at him and say he had been a bad boy.

"I can't do my job sitting in a stuffy old office. Criminals aren't going to come to me, you know."

"Well," she said, "this came for you this morning." She handed him an envelope with the return address, *Knoll & Knoll Attorneys at Law, Lansing, Michigan*, typed in bold letters at the top.

Anna May stood with her arms folded as if he were supposed to read its contents to her. When he didn't, she turned with a huff and went on about her business.

Blankenship slid his finger along the fold of the envelope, breaking the seal. The letter inside was typewritten on fine stationery. The formality of it surprised him at first: *"Dear Mr. Henry Carson Blankenship"* it began. Nobody in Willoughby knew his full Christian name. Blankenship read the letter twice, then a third time, unable to believe its content.

"Well, I'll be damned. Two letters in one week, both with good news," he muttered to himself, tucking the envelope inside his coat pocket. He took the letters as a positive sign. Maybe his life was beginning to turn around.

He hurried on to the library, wondering what clandestine meeting he was getting into with Doctor Carlton. He found the doctor where he said he'd be, standing between two rows of books, holding a book but not reading. He wore the same strange expression as when Blankenship saw him in the street. Carlton nervously glanced from side to side as if expecting someone to be watching.

"I doubt anyone would have reason to follow me," Blankenship said as if reading the young man's thoughts. "What did you want to see me about?"

"It's about Jarvis. I don't know how to say this, but I think he was murdered," Carlton said in a whisper.

Blankenship sank back against the bookshelf as if he had been hit in the gut. Another murder was the last thing Blankenship needed.

"What makes you think that?" he said, trying not to look or sound surprised.

"It's all circumstantial, you understand. I have no real proof, but all the evidence seems to point to his death being murder."

"I didn't take much notice at first. Wasn't any of my business, but when Doctor Mathews said he would take charge of Jarvis' body and do the autopsy himself, he chased me out of the anatomy room to carry out some errand and locked the door. I got to thinking, why be so secretive about an autopsy? We do them all the time. As a resident in training, I usually sit in on all of them. It didn't make sense, but I let it go until I came across the death certificate."

"What did it say?"

"That's just it. He wrote cause of death as heart failure on the death certificate. I couldn't figure why he would have written that on the report when it was obvious to me by the bruises on Jarvis' neck that he had been strangled."

"You saw his neck?"

"Yes."

"When was this?"

"Just as Doctor Mathews brought him in. And that's also curious. Doctor Mathews would never be the one to bring in a body."

"Why not?"

"That's our job. He always gives the grunt work to interns and students. That got me curious. Then I remembered the marks on Jarvis' neck looked exactly like those on that young blacksmith's neck. Doctor Mathews wouldn't allow any of the students to watch that autopsy, either."

"So, what are you saying?"

"That wasn't a rope mark on the blacksmith's neck. A rope doesn't leave three distinct lines like that. Those were finger marks."

Blankenship had suspected the same thing. Nothing about the way the body had been anchored to the tree made sense. The confirmation about the rope marks just added more pieces to the puzzle.

If the murders of Harper and Grimes weren't enough, now he had to add the possibility that Jarvis might have also been murdered. He pondered the possibility that the two deaths were connected. But the only connection seemed to be that Jarvis had discovered Harper was poisoned. If somebody killed him to keep him quiet, why wait so long? Jarvis would have had plenty of time to report his findings. Maybe he figured out who had killed Harper and threatened to tell. Maybe Jarvis needed money. He did have a large family. It takes a lot to keep a family clothed and fed.

"They said Mr. Harper died from cyanide poisoning. I saw his body the day his body was broght to the school. I overheard Doctor Kibby and Doctor Mathews discussing using his corpse for anatomy class, since nobody came to claim it. They said he didn't have any relatives or anybody to give him a proper burial and it seemed fitting that he be used for better purposes."

Blankenship never thought about what happened to Harper's body after Jarvis took care of him. Blankenship figured Harper had been buried in the section of the cemetery designated for the indigent.

"But, that's not all."

Blankenship wasn't ready for any more surprises.

"I believe you should investigate Doctor Haroldson's death."

"Doctor Haroldson? Why?"

"I found arsenic in his body. Arsenic, like many other poisons, leaves traces of itself behind, if you know where to look. Nobody looked. Doctor Mathews signed the death certificate, so nobody questioned the cause of death as heart failure. When he died I had just started my internship and was eager to learn all I could. We were studying the findings of Matthew Orfila. He's a toxicologist. Fascinating work. Anyway, I did a lot of reading on poisons and took tissue samples to study after regular class. Traces of arsenic were in his hair, liver and bowels. Hell, he was full of the stuff."

"So, Charles Mathews did the autopsy and..."

The doctor glanced around again with the same nervous expression. "No. No. Not Charles. John."

"Damn! What were those two doctors up to?"

~ Chapter 26 ~

The Willoughby Medical School occupied a stately three-story red brick building that was once home to the Female Seminary before it moved to a larger facility in Cleveland. The college, the first of its kind built in the Western Reserve, was the central pride of the town and brought prestige and prosperity to the struggling mill town. A rolling expanse of lawn filled an entire city block. Northern white cedars, evenly spaced between gas lamps, lined the stone-paved circular drive leading to the front portico.

He walked along the path that during summer was lined with rose bushes and white and pink peonies. Concrete benches placed along the way gave the town folk a pleasant place to sit and relax. Today, however, the grounds look withered, ready for the coming winter.

Blankenship pulled at the massive oak doors and entered a grand foyer. It was covered in dark, highly polished paneling. His boots echoed off the white marble floor as he walked to the directory board hanging on the wall near the stairway. A large portrait of Doctor Richard Haroldson, dressed in a black robe and wearing a mortarboard with tassel, hung on the opposite wall from the entrance. A conference room stood to the left and the administration office to the right. Straight ahead was a double door marked Assembly Hall. A brass nameplate marked each door.

He paused to read the names. Doctor Haroldson was still listed as director of the school. Blankenship guessed that Charles Mathews used that office now. The laboratory and classrooms were situated on the second floor, as were offices of several doctors and instructors. The dormitory, housing medical students, was shown to be on the third level.

Blankenship took the stairs to the second level. Muffled voices and the sound of an instructor came from one of the classrooms, and the smell of formaldehyde seeped into the hall, apparently from a double-door marked Laboratory. A student dressed in a white lab coat came out of the room, nodded to the chief, and then hurried down the steps.

The first door he came to was inscribed with the name Bruce Kibby. Blankenship wasn't familiar with the name, other than when Ned said he had been in his barbershop. He tapped a knuckle on the door.

"Come in," answered his knock.

The man seated behind the desk rose when he saw Blankenship. The chief recognized him immediately as the man he had seen arguing with John Mathews in the park on Sunday.

"What brings the police chief here?"

Never having been introduced, Blankenship was surprised that the doctor knew who he was. But then he realized this uniform coat and badge were a calling card.

"Don't tell me one of my students has been down at the pool hall raising dust again?" He spoke with a slight British accent.

"No, nothing like that. I just came by for a brief visit. Thought it was time to acquaint myself with the school."

"I'm Doctor Bruce Kibby, an instructor here." He stood to shake Blankenship's hand. "I would be pleased to show you around as soon as I finish grading this last test. It will only take a minute. Please, have a seat," Kibby said, motioned to a chair, and then returned to the paper he had been working on.

Blankenship started to sit, but changed his mind when he saw a hollow-eyed human skull staring at him from a large cabinet. He stepped closer to take a better look. Various sized jars containing black leeches, slithering over each other and sucking the side of the glass, were on the bottom shelf. On the back of the shelf, he spied a box similar to the one he saw in Red Gundersen's barn. The skull and cross bones told him it contained poison. He wanted to open the box and check its contents, but with Kibby sitting so close, he thought better of it. Other containers labeled *Potassium Hydroxide* and *Sodium Hydroxide* sat behind a brown glass bottle of *Carbolic Spray*. Several large jars containing human organs floating in a purple liquid sat on a table next to the window.

His curiosity got the better of him. He picked up the jar tagged *Human Heart*. The heart was sliced in half and floating in a brownish liquid. He had never seen the inside of a human heart. As a hunter, he had cut open many deer, but had never cut open their hearts. Seeing the human organs suddenly brought back the horrific memory of dead soldiers lying on the battlefield with their guts ripped and limps torn off. It wasn't a memory he cared to revisit and was grateful when Kibby interrupted his thoughts.

"Interesting, isn't it?"

"Huh?" he said, jerking his hand away like a child caught with his paw in the cookie tin. "Yes. I've never seen a human heart before."

"According to some of my student's test papers, they haven't either."

Kibby placed the paper he had been grading along with the rest and laid his pencil on top. "Now, what may I do for you?"

"As I said, I just stopped by for a visit."

"Would you like a tour of the school? If so, you're in luck. I happen to be between classes at the moment."

"No, that won't be necessary. I'd rather just talk. How is the school operating now without Doctor Haroldson?"

"As a matter of fact everything continues to run smoothly. I'd even go so far as to say that the school is running as well as before, if not better," Kibby asserted.

"I guess the new director has made quite a difference then?"

"What do you mean?" Kibby asked.

"Who actually pays the bills here?"

"Why, the financial director, of course. Doctor Mathews, along with his staff, oversees the everyday operations of the school. Why do you ask?"

"How many doctors teach here?"

"We have six very fine physicians on our staff. Highly qualified. Came from the best schools back East."

"How is John Mathews to work for?"

"I don't work for him. Charles is the director now," Kibby said, clearing his throat.

"Of course, my mistake. You and John are friends though?"

"Yes, we are very good friends." Kibby sounded jovial.

Very good friends who argue in a public park?

"I am curious about something that you might possibly be able to clear up for me."

"Certainly, if I can."

"How well did you know Pete Harper?"

"Pete Harper? The old man who was found dead in his house last week? The grave digger, I believe."

Blankenship nodded. "That's right."

"Never knew the man personally."

"Can you tell me why he might have been seen around the school? Would he have any reason to be here?"

"I really can't say," he said and picked up a pencil and began twirling it between his fingers.

"I have to follow up on everything I hear. Seems Harper was seen around here sometimes."

"Quite a lot of people come around. They find the school a phenomenon, a curiosity. We train only the most qualified young men in the art of medicine. I imagine that would be a great attraction for a lot of people."

"I know you're a very busy man, so I won't take up any more of your time, but one more question."

Kibby looked at him as if wanting to rid himself of a rodent. "Yes?" he said.

"Where do you get the bodies the students use for their classes?"

"Why from the prison, of course." He stood. "Chief, I would like to chat with you, but I have all these papers." The doctor began shuffling through the papers he had just finished grading only minutes earlier. Blankenship wasn't sure, but he thought he saw Kibby's hands shake slightly.

"Yes, of course, I understand." Blankenship might not know a lot about murder or murderers, but he did know when somebody was lying. Kibby was definitely lying, but he wasn't going to press. Blankenship would wait. He'd get to the truth in time.

"Oh, how's that new young doctor..." Blankenship snapped his fingers as if trying to remember his name, "...Carlton doing?"

Blankenship watched Kibby's expression change.

Kibby grinned with pride. "He is my very best student. He'll make a fine doctor. Correction. He already is a doctor. Graduated last spring. He's doing a short internship and then I guess he'll move on to a larger facility. I believe he has plans for Columbus."

Blankenship thanked Doctor Kibby for his time, left his office, and walked down the stairs. Standing at the bottom, was a pimply-faced delivery boy holding a small box and nervously glancing around.

"Do you know where I can find...ah..." the boy checked the paper on top of the box, "...a Doctor John Mathews?"

"I believe his office is on the second floor," Blankenship said.

The boy looked at the chief, then up the staircase and back to the chief again. He tugged on his shirt collar. "Would you give him this box?"

Before Blankenship could answer, the boy shoved the box into his hands, dropping the box top in the process, and then shot out the door.

Blankenship picked up the lid and put it in place but not before noticing the box contained stationary. The letterhead read: *John Mathews, M.D., 24 Dodson Boulevard, Willoughby, Ohio,* across the top. The unusual watermark suggested the paper was expensive. Blankenship was sure the cost of this paper was beyond his own pocketbook, but then why would he need such fancy stationery?

Blankenship returned to the second floor, found the door marked Dr. John Mathews and tapped on the thick oak.

"Yes? Come in," Mathews called.

Blankenship opened the door and stepped inside. Dr. Mathews, with his sleeves rolled up, was doing knee bends and counting.

"Chief Blankenship? What a pleasant surprise," he said between squats. "Have you found another watch fob?"

"I believe this is yours. A young lad handed it to me downstairs. He seemed uncomfortable about coming up here."

"Just put it on my desk. Twenty-two," he puffed.

Blankenship set the box down next to a stethoscope on the desk.

"Happens from time to time. They hear stories that we give shots to wayward boys," Mathews said before counting twenty-three.

"Doctor Mathews?" a voice called from the doorway.

"Yes, what is it?" Mathews answered with a sharp edge in his voice.

"Can you come to room three? There seems to be some confusion," a young man wearing a white lab coat explained.

"Can't you see I'm busy at the moment?" He squatted again and counted twenty-four.

"Yes, sir, but it's important."

Mathews stood and wiped his brow. "Please excuse me, Chief. I'll be right back." The doctor left Blankenship standing in the middle of the room.

Mathews' office was small, but neat. The furnishings bore no resemblance to those in his home. A plain, glass-front secretary cabinet, filled with medical books and the same journals as in Kibby's office, stood along the far wall next to the only window. Another cabinet with glass doors stood against the other wall, its shelves filled to capacity with medical books. The table standing next to it overflowed with copies of *Lancet Medical Journal*.

Ledgers and letters filled several vertical slots above the writing compartment. A plain maple desk in the middle of the room held a bone-handled ink blotter, a variety of pencils, and a half empty bottle of ink. On the desk sat a neat stack of papers that appeared to be students' tests.

Blankenship thumbed through small pieces of paper pierced on a spindle. Most were notations for appointments — probably with students, from the looks of the messages: *Addison — Fairhaven; Tuttle — laboratory equipment; Haupbell — conference.* The word conference was underlined. At the bottom of the stack was a note with the name Kromer underlined three times.

John Mathews returned, a scowl on his face. "You would think they would know how to operate the machine by now," he said, without explanation. "I apologize for the interruption. Where were we?"

Blankenship took advantage of the timing and asked, "Doctor Mathews, I was just wondering. How can you tell if someone dies from drinking poison?"

"There are many poisons. If it's arsenic we can test body tissues for signs of it. It shows up in the hair if taken over a long period of time, and of course, it can be found in the stomach contents if ingested recently. Most other poisons are more difficult to pin down. Why do you ask?"

"What about cyanide?"

"You want to know about Mr. Harper don't you?"

"That's correct," Blankenship said.

"My personal opinion is that Mr. Harper died from poison, but it wasn't cyanide. He most probably died from food poisoning after eating whatever was in that bowl of molded gruel on his table. I would be astounded if you had smelled its distinct odor when you found him. His house was in such a horrid condition."

"How well did you know Mr. Harper?"

"In what respect do you mean?" Mathews asked.

"Did he ever do any work for you?" Blankenship said, hoping he didn't sound obvious.

"I only knew the man by reputation. I never met him."

The chief thanked the doctor for his time and closed the door behind him. Jarvis was certain that Harper died from cyanide. Why did the doctor contradict him?

Instead of going out the front entrance, Blankenship left by the back door and followed the alleyway around to Clark Avenue.

The grumbling in his stomach reminded him he hadn't eaten breakfast. The Kingsway Inn wouldn't be serving lunch for another hour so he used the time to wander the cemetery. He thought perhaps a stroll through the serenity of the tombstones might soothe his bewildered spirit and clear his head, but deep down, if he really stopped to analyze his motive, he realized that he wanted to take another look around where Harper had worked. He might get a clearer picture of what happened. But as he passed through the gate, a chilled wind like a ghost passed through him. He pulled the collar of his jacket closer to his ears and stuffed his hands deep into his pockets. Gravel crunched under his feet as he treaded the well-trimmed, narrow path. Harper had done a fair job of keeping the grounds clear of debris, unlike his own house. The man was a mystery.

He scuffed his toe on a rock in the middle of the path, picked it up, and tossed it to one side. He wrestled with what he knew about the school. Pieces of the puzzle were beginning to fit together. Somewhere among the rat's nest was the answer he was looking for.

Blankenship wasn't a man to give into a philosophic ponderings, but sometimes he did question what would drive a man to murder. Hatred, greed, lust for a woman? Any one of a hundred reasons was cause enough, he guessed. Which reason lead to Harper's murder? Then there were Jarvis, Grimes, and possibly Haroldson. How did they fit into the mystery?

The chief looked at the different headstones and thought about the people lying beneath them. He removed his hat in respect. What had their lives been like? Walking on, he read each headstone. One name stood out among all the others. *Terrance Kromer.* The date of the stone read: *May 11, The Year Of Our Lord 1869.* Hadn't he just seen that name somewhere? He thought a minute. Oh yes, it was written on a piece of paper on John Mathews' desk. Was there a connection between the two? Most likely there was. Willoughby was a small town.

He stepped aside to avoid treading on the grave. In the next row, he noticed the headstone of an infant next to Kromer's. The headstone, like Kromer's, was fairly new. The inscription read: *Rest My Beautiful One In The Arms Of Jesus Our Savior In Heaven.* The date on the tombstone indicated the child, buried only four months ago, was only three-days old. Babies shouldn't die so young. He shook his head.

Blankenship looked from the infant's grave to Kromer's. His tranquil mood suddenly changed. He didn't like what he was thinking. Didn't like it one damn bit.

He left the cemetery with a strong sense that there was a connection between the rumors about grave robbing and murder. Although he didn't understand or fully believe what the Mathews boy had said, he had to place a new meaning to his story. Could any of this be connected to the disappearance of the little Mathews child? He didn't like what he was thinking.

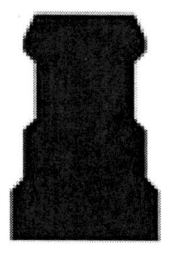

~ CHAPTER 27 ~

Blankenship was deep in thought when he heard the front door of the jail open. He glanced up to see Mr. Grimes with hat in hand, head bowed, standing at the railing.

"Good morning, Mr. Grimes, what can I do for you?"

"I need to talk to you real bad."

"Come on in and sit down." Blankenship held the swinging counter gate open for him.

With a heavy sigh Mr. Grimes took the chair at Blankenship's desk. He reached into his coat pocket and pulled out a thin black book. "The Misses found this while going through Ethan's things. We have no need for his clothes now. The Misses wanted to give 'em to the poor. I boxed them up and took them over to the church this morning, but I saved this." He handed the book to Blankenship.

"God forgive him. He was a good boy, my Ethan. He never meant no harm." Tears welled up in the old man's eyes and rolled down his wrinkled face. He sniffed and wiped his eyes. "Sorry," he said, his voice barely audible.

After a long pause he continued. "I brought the book to you because I figured you would want to know what my boy did. Read it through. When you're finished, me and the Misses would like to have it back. It's all we have left of him 'cept our memories." He paused again. "I know you'll do the right thing."

Blankenship assured Mr. Grimes he would take good care of the book. A pang of sorrow shot through him as he watched Mr. Grimes slowly rise, and then walk out the door, overburdened with despair.

A feeling of dread washed over Blankenship as he held the book. He turned it over slowly. The cover, worn and discolored from age, its edges dog-eared, had no printing on it to indicate its contents.

He opened it. The name Ethan Grimes was written at the top of the first page just above the date 1862. Blankenship realized he was reading the dead boy's journal.

Ethan's handwriting was small but legible. Flipping through the journal, the chief saw that each page was dated. The first page began January 25, 1862, and read: *My pa got a letter from Evan today. He says that he and Emery are fine and that the war is going well. They hope to whop some Rebel ass and come home soon. I hope they are home before harvest.*

Most entries told of the young man's comings and goings and gave an accounting of the day's events. Some were just rambling thoughts. Many days and weeks were skipped all together.

April 20, 1862: *My pa received word today that Emery and Evan were killed at Shiloh about two weeks ago. I can't believe they are dead. I pray they didn't suffer. If I was older I would join up. Ma hasn't said much all day. She just sits in her black dress and stares out the window, holding her Bible and praying. Pa went to the telegraph office to send word to Uncle Lawrence and to make arrangements for the Army to ship Emery's and Evan's bodies back home.*

May 6, 1862: *We buried my brothers today. It rained.*

Blankenship skipped forward several pages.

August 2, 1863: *A storm passed through today and washed out all the roads. Pa says now without Emery and Evan's help there will be more work for him and less money. We don't have a lot to eat and Ma has had to do without broadcloth for her sewing.*

Blankenship was uncomfortable reading Ethan's journal. He felt as though he was intruding into the innermost thoughts of the dead boy.

The next several pages told of the hardship he and his family endured during that time.

He flipped ahead again to entries annotated with the dates of last summer.

July 3, 1869: *Pa hurt his back and is laid up. He can't work like he used to. I'm doing all the labor on the farm now. Got a job at the blacksmith shop. Mr. Johnson taught me how to work with black heat, but I still have trouble cold fitting. Uncle Lawrence came to stay until picking time is finished.*

July 5: *The rain came last week and hasn't stopped. The fields have turn to mush. If it doesn't end soon we will lose all our crops and have nothing to sell at harvest.*

Blankenship remembered the days when the rains saturated the ground for weeks with unrelenting torrents, causing the river to overflow its banks. The same river that dragged the body of the little boy to its bottom then belched him up days later. The rains soaked the streets and created mud so thick and deep no horse could pull a wagon through it without getting bogged down. Even the many layers of straw didn't help.

Blankenship also remembered how the storms, carrying hail, beat the crops, destroying them. Most farmers rely on their fields, not only to feed their own families, but also to take to market. Without crops to sell there wasn't enough money to purchase food, kerosene oil, or material for clothes. Times were hard that summer. Everyone suffered and many families never recovered.

He turned the pages to the beginning of the present year and read on.

June 6: *With both my brothers gone and father ailing so bad, I've looked for extra work, but there just isn't any to be had. Everybody's having a hard time.*

June 10: *I got work helping Mr. Harper in the cemetery. He pays me by the job. It's not much, but it helps a little.*

June 15: *Mr. Harper had me dig a grave today. It was easy to dig the hole because the ground was soft, but the earth was heavy.*

June 20: *Mr. Harper wants me to do a few extra chores around the graveyard. I don't like what he wants me to do. He said I was helping medical science. I figured Mr. Harper knew what he was talking about. They were dead already, and I need the money.*

June 28: *God forgive me — forgive my soul. I didn't mean to hurt her. We were digging up a grave when she just suddenly appeared out of nowhere. She was so small and so helpless. She saw us and began to run, but she tripped over a headstone and fell. Mr. Harper ordered me to grab her. He said we had to stop her screaming before someone heard; we couldn't leave her there for somebody to find. I didn't want to do it. I tried to stop him, but he pushed me aside. I can't sleep nights. I can still hear her screaming every time I go by the graveyard. She's screaming in my head like she did when Mr. Harper slammed the coffin shut. God, please forgive me.*

Was Ethan talking about the Mathews child? Then the thought struck him. "Oh, my God," Blankenship said aloud, "they buried her alive."

His stomach churned. Suddenly he felt dizzy. Bile rose in his throat. He swallowed hard, but it didn't help. He made it out the back door just in time before he threw up. He gagged several times until there was nothing left in his stomach. With the bitter taste still in his mouth, he took a deep breath and leaned against the building for support, letting the cold air hit his face. Even after several minutes, his body still trembled. He wiped his mouth, straightened himself, and spit again. Once his head cleared, he went back inside.

The memory of those long hours that turned into days searching for the child came flooding back. Had anyone searched the graveyard? Of course, they had. Every inch of ground was searched and searched again. But nobody thought to look in the ground. Could Theodore Mathews be correct? Was the little girl buried in the graveyard? But how could the boy have known that? Blankenship didn't believe in spirits talking to the living. The boy had an overactive imagination, that's all.

He found the place where he left off, not really wanting to read anymore, but he had to know if Grimes' journal shed light on where they had buried the child.

There were no more entries for the rest of July, or August.

September 10: *I told Mr. Harper I wasn't going to work for him anymore. I can't stand the sight of the graveyard. Can't go near where she is. He laughed at me and told me to get lost. I could smell liquor on his breath.*

September 17: *I went to see Mr. Harper tonight to ask for the money he owes me. He didn't come to the door. I think he is trying to get out of paying me. I'll have to go back tomorrow to that awful place. I need the* money. The uncle of that little girl was riding out when I got to the house. He looked at me like he knows what I did.

September 21: *They found Mr. Harper dead yesterday. They said he was poisoned. I was going to tell the police chief everything, but lost my nerve.*

September 22: *I wrote a letter to the police chief, telling him that I know who killed Mr. Harper. I can't stand the pain of knowing what I did to that little girl. I know I will burn in hell for what I did.*

That was the last entry.

Oh, Ethan. Why didn't you put it in your journal? Who killed Harper? Where did Harper bury the child?

Blankenship reverently closed the journal, placed it in his desk drawer, and then shut it as if enclosing a holy relic in a tomb. He leaned back in his chair and sat for a long time with his eyes closed listening to the tick-tock of the wall clock. The image of a tiny child being buried alive, branded into his mind. Did she struggle? What were her last thoughts? He got up and paced back and forth trying to shake off the sickening feeling that still crawled around in his stomach.

In need of fresh air, he got to the door just as Mrs. Sawyer, the church organist, rushed in wrapped in a black woolen shawl over her mourning dress and black bonnet.

Mrs. Sawyer spoke softly but adamantly and got right to the point of her visit. "Chief Blankenship, I think something bad has happened in the cemetery."

Now, there's an understatement.

"Perhaps you should sit down here and tell me what this is all about, Mrs. Sawyer," he said, still not in full control of his voice.

"It's my uncle. Clarence Tarrson. You remember him?"

Blankenship didn't know the man personally, but nodded anyway.

"Someone's vandalized my uncle's grave — or worse." She paused as if thinking how to say what came next. "My mother, my aunt, and I buried him two weeks ago. We set out two beautiful vases to mark his grave until a headstone could be made. We set them deep into the ground so the wind wouldn't knock them over." She paused to take a deep breath and then continued. "When we went to visit the grave this morning the vases had been moved. Both were tipped over and laying off to one side."

"And you want me to find out who moved them?"

"Yes. I want you to find out who moved the vases and why someone was poking around in my uncle's grave. I want to know if something has happened to my uncle. You have to look into it."

"Why would you think something has happened to your uncle, Mrs. Sawyer?" He thought he knew the answer, but asked anyway.

She lowered her eyes and twisted a handkerchief in her hands. "The dirt was raked smooth after the funeral. But now it's…well, you can see where it's been dug around in." Lowering her voice to a whisper and said, "I've heard things have been happening in the cemetery. Awful things."

He didn't like what Mrs. Sawyer just told him. Of course, it could be the tale of an overly excitable woman who had gotten herself caught up in the drama and gossip of the past few days, but with the revelation of Ethan's journal still fresh on his mind, and knowing how Harper had stolen possessions from the dead and possibly dug up bodies and sold them to the school, her story was plausible. Either way, he'd have to check it out. It was his responsibility to prevent an ugly situation from becoming worse.

Blankenship followed the woman to the cemetery and inspected the grave. The two vases she claimed to have placed in the center of the plot were, as she said, tipped over and laying off to the side. The earth over the grave had also been disturbed. Blankenship stood looking at what might possibly be the last testament to Pete Harper's heinous act before he was murdered.

Blankenship wasted no time getting back to the office. He sent Stanger to the courthouse in Painesville with a letter to the circuit court judge asking permission to open the grave of Mr. Clarence Tarrson to see if he was still resting in peace.

~ Chapter 28 ~

News spread through town that something extraordinary was about to happen in the cemetery. Suspecting that trouble could easily break out, Blankenship secured his revolver in his waist holster. Something told him he might need a weapon.

By the time Stanger returned from the courthouse with the court order to exhume Tarrson's body, late evening shadows had begun to stretch across town. The weather, which had been mild with only light flurries most of the morning, had turned mean, as if the gods were protesting what was about to happen. Dark, grey clouds hovered like a shroud as a northwest wind blew through the bare tree branches, bringing with it a chilling wet snow.

A crowd had already gathered when Blankenship and Stanger rode into the cemetery. They took up a position near the rear and sat watching the proceedings. Ned Potter and Bernie Holtzman huddled together, their faces filled with curiosity. Mrs. Sawyer wiped her eyes as she rested her head on her aunt, who stood rod-straight clutching her Bible. Mayor Bascom, in his top hat and fur-collared coat, sat in his carriage, shooting daggers at Blankenship. Norville, with paper pad and pencil in hand, nudged his way closer to the grave, writing the next day's headlines.

A group of women from the Baptist Church, some wrapped in blankets, others wearing their finest winter cloaks and furs, stood singing, "Nearer

My God To Thee." Reverend Watkins hovered near the unopened grave reading a passage from the Bible Blankenship recognized as the 46th Psalm. The priest from St. Mary's Parish watched, the hem of his black cassock whipping in the wind.

Some folks braced themselves against the chill by circling a nearby bonfire, trying to keep warm, while others sat in buggies or wagons wrapped in blankets. All wore the same expression of awe and disbelief.

Blankenship sat on Mingo and watched the crowd, unable to understand the depths of people's curiosity for the macabre. Apparently, no one had ever opened a grave before in Willoughby — at least not legally — and no one wanted to miss this, the most exciting event of the year.

The crowd murmured and moved closer when two men with long-handled pickaxes and shovels began cutting into the earth. One man swung the axe and broke the ground while the other heaved the first shovel of dirt from the grave. Two men stood off to the side holding lanterns to give them light.

Stanger shifted his weight in his saddle, observing the drama like a kid seeing his first paddleboat sail across Lake Erie.

The grave diggers continued working laboriously as they removed shovelful after shovelful of dirt from the grave where Mr. Tarrson had been buried, pausing only occasionally to warm their hands over the fire before continuing their arduous task. More and more people arrived, nudging others aside to get a better look. Why in God's name were they here? They should be home sitting by a warm fire or tending to their business. Even children, who should be home doing their schoolwork, ran around getting in the way. Conspicuously absent from the onlookers, however, were the doctors from the medical school.

Seeing the children reminded him that Katie wasn't among the faces in the crowd. He figured she would abhor this scene and stay away. Then he recalled her saying that she wanted to talk with Charles Mathews about Theodore's poor performance in school. She was probably at the school talking with him right now.

Large snowflakes blew in the digger's faces and stuck to their hair. The smaller of the two men swiped at the flakes as if they were flies buzzing him at a Sunday picnic. The snow mingled with the tension in the air and settled over the crowd. After digging for a half hour, the men were only knee deep into the grave.

Lanterns and torches began appearing at the far end the cemetery. In the distance, with his torch held high, Jack Barnes stood among a cluster of men, shouting angry profanity. Their presence made Blankenship nervous. Barnes meant trouble, and the police chief couldn't predict what he was capable of doing if Tarrson wasn't resting in his grave. Blankenship knew that if the body wasn't in its proper place, there would be hell to pay, and Jack Barnes, along with the rest of the town, would be collecting.

Blankenship guided Mingo through the crowd and over to the group of men. "Gentlemen, you wouldn't be here to cause trouble, now would you?"

"This ain't right, Chief, and you know it. We've been told that folks at that school have been up to no good and this proves it," Barnes said, as puffs of air escaped his mouth.

"This proves nothing. I told you before, if there's been any wrongdoing here, I'll see that it's handled in the proper manner."

"There ain't nothin' proper about a man's resting place being disturbed. If he ain't in there, we aim to find out who took him," Barnes said.

"As if we don't know already," a man bellowed from the rear of the group.

"Yeah, we know who's responsible for taking that body," another man yelled.

"Nobody knows anything for sure. Especially you. Understand?" Blankenship hollered over their yammering.

The chief warned the men that if they caused trouble, he wouldn't hesitate to haul them off to jail. They backed off, but resentment smoldered in their eyes.

"Hit something," one of the diggers called from the opened grave, and then threw down his shovel. Men moved closer, pushing and shoving to get a look. The digger began scraping the remaining dirt from top of the coffin, and then with a crowbar pried off the coffin's lid. A paralyzing silence fell over the crowd.

The lid popped open with ease.

"It's empty!" somebody standing near the open grave called out.

Mrs. Sawyer's aunt shrieked and fell faint onto the ground. Women swarmed around her. An outcry of obscenities came from the angry crowd of torch-toting men.

"The school!" a man hollered.

"Yeah, all those body snatching doctors are at that school now," another voice bellowed.

"We'll get that body back or we'll burn that school to the ground."

"Oh, my God! Katie!" Blankenship yelled to Stanger. "Miss Wilson went to see Mathews at the school. She's there now. Let's go!"

The enraged mob had already begun pushing toward the entrance of the cemetery, cursing and shouting. Blankenship attempted to guide Mingo past the crowd, but carriages and wagons blocked his way. He was trapped and unable to spur his horse safely around them.

"They're going to burn down the whole town if we don't stop them."

"What do we do?" Stanger called over the noise.

"How good are you at getting that horse of yours to jump?"

"I think we're about to find out."

"Follow me." Blankenship prayed he hadn't lost the skills learned while serving in the cavalry. He'd have to trust Mingo. Digging his heels into the sides of his horse, he bent forward, and leaped the row of hedges. Blankenship glanced back and saw Stanger's horse, unsure of the task, unwilling to make the jump. Stanger made another attempt only to have his horse balk again, refusing to leap the hedge. Blankenship couldn't wait. He spurred Mingo into a gallop and headed for the school.

The raging mob stampeded down Spaulding Street toward the school, their torches leading the way. Blankenship, unable to move around the crowd, was slowed and failed to reach the school before them. By the time he arrived the hysterical mob had gathered on the lawn, hurling angry shouts, as well as rocks and bottles, at the building.

Blankenship pushed Mingo through the rioters and maneuvered between them and the front entrance. Light from the flames fell on their faces making them look like grotesques masks.

Mingo, instinctively fearing the flaming torches, threw her head back and snorted. Nervously pounding her hooves, and her eyes wide with fear, she reared and came down with a fierce thud, moving the mob back, but as soon as the horse settled down, the mob pushed forward again.

"I want you all to go home before someone gets hurt," Blankenship shouted over the crowd's whooping and hollering. "I'll see to it that Mr. Tarrson's body is returned to his rightful place and the people responsible are arrested."

"Not good enough, Chief," Barnes hollered.

"We aren't leaving here until we know that body is back where it belongs," someone else yelled.

"And if we don't get it back, there won't be one brick left of this building come tomorrow morning," another voice called out.

"Go on now! Go home! You don't want to get yourself into trouble over this."

Mingo's hooves beat the ground.

"Get out of the way, Chief. We have no quarrel with you," Barnes screeched, dodging the horse's pounding hooves.

"You're breaking the law." Blankenship guided Mingo between the men. "Go home," he repeated. "Let the police take care of this."

From over his shoulder he heard the sound of shattering glass. He turned to see a torch had been thrown through the first floor window. The crowd fell silent, but only for a moment. Screams of "fire" erupted as flames shot from the window.

"You fool! You'll burn the building down, and the whole town with it!" Blankenship screamed over the roar of the protesters.

A knot tightened in Blankenship's stomach and then twisted. He had to stop the fire before it spread and destroyed the entire town. But he had to find Katie first.

"You there, go fetch the fire team," Blankenship called to a man standing off to one side. The man took off in the direction of the firehouse shouting, "Fire! Fire!"

Stanger finally arrived, urging his horse through the mass of people.

"What in the hell are they doing?" Stanger shouted to his boss over the clamor.

"Hold this crowd back," Blankenship called to Stanger. "I've got to get into the building. I have to find Katie."

Stanger came up behind one of the rioters, snatched the torch from his hands, and waved it from side to side, jockeying his way to Blankenship. Stanger's forcefulness in moving the crowd surprised Blankenship. He had never seen his deputy move so quickly and with such authority.

The crowd backed up long enough for Blankenship to dismount, toss the reins over Mingo's head, ground tying the horse, and then race into the burning building.

Black smoke had begun snaking out from under the door of the conference room where the torch had landed. He flung open the door, ran to the window, and yanked the flaming drapes from their rods. He stamped at the fire but only managed to fan the flames. Once the fire reached the wallpaper, it blistered its way up the wall, stretching for the ceiling. He knew it wouldn't take long before the entire conference room would be engulfed. He closed the door and backed into the entrance hall.

Blankenship dashed for the stairs. Katie was up there with Charles Mathews. He had to find them and get them safely out of the building. He had made it half way up the steps when Barnes, leading a group of five men, burst in. Blankenship wasn't about to allow them to muscle their way into the school. If Mr. Tarrson's body was there, he would get it back, not the rioting mob. He drew his pistol from his holster and waved it high enough for all the men to see.

"I won't hesitate to stop you from making a bigger mistake than you already have. I will use this. Leave the building, now!" he yelled, motioning with the barrel of the gun.

"We want that body back," Barnes snarled at the chief as he attempted to slide past him.

Blankenship fired a round into the ceiling. The gunshot reverberated off the walls.

The men froze.

"I warned you. Go home! If the body is here, I'll get it back. You can count on that, if the building doesn't burn down and everyone in it first. Now, get back outside, wait for the water wagon and help them put out this fire you started," he yelled.

Tentacles of flames had spread from the conference room and were licking their way up the stairs by the time Blankenship finished arguing with Barnes. With precious seconds lost, he didn't wait to see if Barnes and his henchmen had left the building, but bounded up the stairs two at a time.

On the second floor, students came running from a classroom. "What going on?" one student asked, his eyes wide with alarm.

"Get out of the building now! It's on fire," Blankenship ordered. Without further questions, the students pushed past Blankenship and ran down the stairs, coughing by the time they reached the bottom.

Racing blindly down the hall, Blankenship opened the first door he came to, the one directly above the conference room. A blast of intense heat repelled him. "Katie," he called. No one answered.

In the distance, he heard the clanging of the fire alarm, the pounding of horse's hooves, and frantic calls from the firemen.

Blankenship pushed open the door to Doctor Kibby's office. The doctor was frantically opening cabinet drawers and pulling out papers.

"What are you still doing here? Get out. The building's on fire," Blankenship yelled.

Kibby didn't look up but continued gathering his papers.

"Didn't you hear me? The building is on fire. Get out!" Blankenship grabbed the doctor's arm and pushed him toward the door. Kibby broke loose from Blankenship's grip and ran to his desk.

"My work. My research," Kibby cried, clutching his papers.

"Forget about those damn papers. Get out now!" He shoved Kibby through the door. Seeing the flames, the doctor gave no further resistance and ran from the room and down the stairs.

"What was that noise? Sounded like a gun shot?" Stanger said, running up the stairs, out of breath.

"It was," Blankenship said.

"It sure dispersed the crowd. Especially when Barnes came racing out. Kunkle got here just in time. Together we got the crowd to move back. They're pretty much under control now."

"Good. Come on. We have to find Katie."

"Katie!" Blankenship called again, running down the smoke-filled hall as the smoke stung his eyes.

Halfway down the hall, Doctor Carlton came stumbling from a classroom.

"Have you seen Katie Wilson?" Blankenship asked.

"What's going on out there? I heard people yelling. Is that smoke?" he asked.

"No time to explain. Have you seen Miss Wilson?" he yelled.

Carlton shook his head.

"Is anyone else in the building?"

"I don't know."

"You have to get out of here, now!" Blankenship said and watched the doctor until he disappeared down the stairs.

Smoke had begun to engulf them. Stanger, only a few feet away, was only a dark specter. Blankenship covered his nose and mouth with the bend of his arm and started down the hall opening each door he came to calling Katie's name. Stanger followed, yelling into the rooms on the opposite side. No sound came from any of the rooms. Finally, Blankenship found the door with the name Charles Mathews on it. He burst in.

The room was empty.

~ Chapter 29 ~

"Katie!" Blankenship called frantically. He strained to listen for a response, but all he heard was the popping and crackling of the fire as it seared the wood. He had to find her before it was too late.

There was only one room left. Blankenship's heart sank. He staggered to the last door and flung it open, slamming it against the wall. Inside, Charles and Katie stood at the window like trapped animals as suffocating smoke filled the room and flames lashed at them through the floorboards. The room had become a fiery deathtrap. The floor was certain to collapse any second.

"Hank!" Katie cried and ran to him.

Blankenship took her in his arms and held her tight.

"My God. What's happening out there?" Charles asked. "We heard a gunshot."

"No time to explain. We've got to get out of the building."

With Stanger leading the way, they made their way out of the room and raced toward the stairs, but a massive wall of flames blocked their escape. The intense heat pushed them back. Flames crawled along the floor and lapped at their feet. With no other choice, they retreated down the hall.

"Is there any other way out of the building?" the chief asked.

"No," Charles answered.

Blankenship held Katie close. The smoke stole the air. Coughing and choking, they hurried back to the room. The ceiling was now engulfed had begun falling in around them.

The window was their only means of escape.

Blankenship picked up a chair and started to hurl it through the window when a voice beyond the smoke called from the doorway, "Quick this way! There's another way out of the building. Come on. Hurry."

Holding onto Katie, Blankenship followed the voice that guided the four of them through the searing heat of the smoke-filled hallway. But instead of leading them away from the flames, the voice directed them toward the engulfed stairs. Blankenship balked. He wasn't about to risk his life and the lives of the others. "Are you crazy? We can't get down those stairs."

"Trust me. Go! Go!" the voice insisted.

With no other choice, he did as the voice ordered.

"Hank, I'm scared," Katie whimpered.

He was too, but wouldn't allow his fear to take over and cause them to perish. He had to stay strong.

"Hurry in here," the voice said.

He heard the creaking of what sounded like a door opening, and then a hand pushed at him, and then the door closed. They stood crushed together barely able to breathe. Were they at the mercy of a madman? Was he going to lock them in? Blankenship wanted to lash out, but in the darkness he feared hitting the doctor, or worse, Katie.

"Hold onto each and stay close," the voice instructed.

Still holding Katie's hand and stumbling in the darkness, he followed the voice down a short flight of stairs. The steps were uneven and the walls barely wide enough for an average size man. At the bottom Blankenship heard the striking of a match followed by the flicker of light rising in a lantern.

When his eyes adjusted, he saw that they were standing in what looked like a small supply room. As the light grew it fell across a man's shadowy face.

"Razzy!" Stanger exclaimed.

"What are you doing here?"

"No time to explain. Move!"

Razzy tugged at a wooden handle on the back wall. The wall slid open to reveal a narrow passageway. The walls were so close, they touched his shoulders on both sides.

"Stay close, and hurry," Razzy said.

They trailed behind the lantern's light following Razzy's voice until they came to the end. Razzy handed the lantern to Stanger and pulled at a rusted metal ring attached to a trap door in the floor. The door creaked open exposing a gaping black hole.

"Careful going down the ladder. It's old and a bit rickety," Razzy cautioned as he descended into the blackness below.

Still reluctant but desperate, Blankenship helped Katie down the wobbly ladder to Razzy's waiting grasp. Stanger followed, then Charles with Blankenship climbing down last. Hunched over, they followed the trail of light through the long, dark tunnel that smelled of raw earth; damp and musty, but smoke free.

"What is this?" Charles asked.

"It's part of the old underground railroad," Razzy said.

"I never knew this was here. How did you find this?" Mathews asked.

"Long story, doctor. I'll tell you about it sometime when we aren't so busy."

The tunnel ended at another ladder that led upward. Razzy instructed Blankenship to go first. After climbing a few steps he found a small trap door at the top and pushed it open. He stuck his head through the opening. Fresh air filled his lungs.

Once satisfied that it was safe, Blankenship helped Katie into a large room. The others followed, staying close.

"Where are we?" Stanger asked, looking around.

"It's an old washhouse once used by the residents of the Female Seminary years ago. Some of the doctors use it for storage now," Razzy answered.

"Hank," Katie said, just before she fell limp into Blankenship's arms. He picked her up and carried her over to a barrel and gently set her down. She coughed, gasping for air. Her face was soot-streaked, her eyes red from the stinging smoke, but to him she was beautiful. Blankenship made a feeble attempt to wipe the smudges from her face with his handkerchief, realizing how close he had come to losing her.

"Thank you, Hank," she whispered and leaned her head on his chest.

"Katie, my dear sweet Katie," Blankenship murmured as an avalanche of emotions took hold of him. He could have lost her. He gently kissed her forehead.

Katie rested in his embrace with her head on his chest. Blankenship felt her soft, round breasts rise and fall with each breath she took, her heart beating in rhythm with his. Suddenly she stiffened, pointed to a far wall, and screamed.

Blankenship looked to see what she was pointing at. In the corner, a hand dangled from underneath a tarpaulin.

Stanger was first to reach it. Razzy stayed on his heels carrying the lantern. Stanger pulled back the tarpaulin. There underneath was a body.

Katie screamed again.

"Stanger, take Miss Wilson outside for some fresh air. Quickly, now," Blankenship ordered.

Stanger lifted Katie in his arms and carried her from the washhouse.

"What the bloody hell? Somebody want to tell me what is going on?" Doctor Mathews asked, staring at the body in disbelief.

Blankenship took a closer look at the corpse. The clothes were still intact but badly torn and tattered. The face was putrefied from decomposition and the jaw hung slack.

"Grave robbing, Doctor Mathews. Unless I'm mistaken, I believe this to be the body of Mr. Clarence Tarrson, and the reason behind all the ruckus."

Charles opened his mouth to reply, when a whimpering cry came from the far corner of the washhouse. Blankenship followed the sound to a pile of straw.

"Over here," Blankenship called to Razzy. "Bring the lantern, over here."

Razzy's light fell upon the figure of a boy.

"Theodore? What on earth?" Mathew ran to his son and swept the hair from his eyes. A tiny trickle of blood ran down the side of his head. "Hold the light closer," he instructed Razzy.

"Father…"

"Theodore, what happened to you?" Charles asked as he checked his son's pulse.

"Father, Uncle John tried to hurt me."

"What?"

"I went to talk to him, but he…"

"It's all right, Theodore. It's going to be all right," he said, taking his son in his arms.

Charles looked from the boy to Blankenship. "You must stop my brother, Chief Blankenship. He's become a monster. I should have known something like this would happen sooner or later."

Blankenship didn't bother asking what Doctor Mathews meant. He already had a good idea.

"Do you know where John is?" Blankenship asked.

"If he isn't in his office, he could be anywhere."

Razzy spoke up. "I saw him leave the building just before the fire started. He left through the back door where he keeps his horse tied."

"Razzy, would you please see that Miss Wilson gets home safely?" Then to Charles he said, "Doctor Mathews, I want you to stay here and guard that body. Don't let anyone try to take it. Understand? I'll take care of him later. Right now I have to find your brother."

Outside, the fire brigade worked frantically pumping water onto the burning building. With Kunkle's help and a few of the more sane folks of the town, they had successfully herded the angry crowd back to the road, away from the danger. Much quieter now, people stood as if mesmerized by the flames, its orange glow reflecting on their faces.

Blankenship instructed Kunkle to stay and keep the peace while he and Stanger went after John Mathews. He whistled for his horse. Seconds later Mingo came trotting to him with Stanger's horse close behind.

"How'd you get your horse to come like that?" Stanger asked.

"I'll tell you when we have more time. Right now, we have to stop a killer."

~ Chapter 30 ~

Spits of mud from the horse's hooves pelted the air behind Blankenship and Stanger as they rode hard down the street. Mingo had barely halted on the front lawn of Mathews' house before Blankenship vaulted off.

"Stay here," he ordered Stanger, as he ran up the steps. Ignoring the doorknocker, he pounded on the door. No one answered. Blankenship could hear rustling coming from inside but still no one came to the door. Furious, he hammered on the door and shouted until someone finally responded.

"Where is Doctor Mathews?" Blankenship demanded of the servant who stood there, not saying a word.

"What's all the commotion? Sounds like the fire wagon. Good heavens! Is something on fire?" Edna Mathews said, as she motioned for the servant to step aside.

"Yes, the whole damn town will be on fire any minute. Where's your husband?" Blankenship said.

"Why, I have no idea," she said with a haughty expression.

"Where is he?" Blankenship demanded.

"He isn't at home." She gave Blankenship a look of disdain.

Seeing that he wasn't going to get anywhere with her, and knowing it was illegal to burst into someone's home without a warrant, he turned to leave. He had gotten to the end of the walkway when Blankenship heard the crack of a whip and the pounding of horses' hooves. John Mathews charged past them, whipping his horse into a run.

Blankenship dashed to Mingo and with one leap, swung his leg up and over the horse, and slid into the saddle. "Let's go," he shouted to Stanger.

Mathews rode with his head bent into the wind like a mad man in a blind fury as he urged his horse onward. At the end of Dobson Street he turned north toward the center of town. Ahead, the crowd stood in the middle of the road watching the medical school as it burned. With all the chaos, no one noticed the lone horse and its rider bearing down from a hundred yards away.

What in the hell did Mathews think he was doing? Didn't he see the people standing in the middle of the road blocking his way? Did he even care?

The chief watched in disbelief as the doctor galloped straight for them, making no attempt to change course. Blankenship and Stanger followed, racing to catch him. He hollered for him to stop before he injured or killed someone, but got no response. He considered shooting at him. Even though he had once been a marksman, he couldn't rely on his aim being accurate now after all these years, and he feared hitting an innocent bystander. Instead he yelled for them get out of the way, but it was useless. His voice failed to carry that distance, and with all the bedlam, their attention was on what was happening to the school.

Mathews was about to plow into the crowd when a man looked up just in time to see the horse charging toward them. The man yelled. Women screamed, picked up their skirts, and scrambled out of the way. Men swept children into their arms and ran for safety, leaving a narrow path.

Mathews plunged through the crowd and never looked back.

As quickly as the path opened, it closed again. With all eyes focused on the passing horse, no one saw Blankenship and Stanger barreling down on them.

Blankenship reined in Mingo and motioned to Stanger to follow. He spun his horse around and detoured to Glenn Avenue with the intention of cutting through the alleyway to intercept Mathews before he reached the bridge.

The plan would have worked except when they got to the bridge at the north end of town, Mathews was nowhere in sight. Blankenship brought Mingo to a halt and scanned the road in both directions. If Mathews hadn't come this way, then he must have gone west toward Cleveland. Blankenship turned around and kicked at Mingo's sides, and then took off with Stanger beside him.

They followed Vine Street across the railroad tracks and then to where the road curved north toward the lake. After a quarter mile the road began to narrow; there was no sign of Mathews. The man had simply disappeared. Blankenship turned Mingo in a circle looking for any sign of him.

Stanger rode ahead for a short distance, returned and shrugged. Nothing.

"Where did he go?"

"The train," Stanger cried.

Guessing that Mathews might have gotten on the train, they rode hard toward town and the train depot. If he was wrong, and Mathews hadn't taken the train, the possibilities of where he had gone were endless. When they reached the depot, Mathews' horse rested, tethered near the platform. The ticket seller told them that the 6:45 to Erie had just pulled out of the station. "You just missed it."

"Damn." Blankenship swore. "Stanger, go back to the telegraph office. Send a telegram to the Painesville station. Tell them to hold the train and not allow anyone off. Send it urgent from the police department. And don't let the clerk give you any guff."

"You got it." Stanger said, lashed his horse, and sped off.

For the first time, Blankenship thought he saw a flicker of hope in Stanger. Maybe the boy might work out after all.

Knowing that Mingo would never walk across railroad ties on the trestle bridge, he backtracked and followed the train, riding along the wagon road that went through Mentor. Blankenship spurred Mingo and felt her muscles tighten beneath him as the horse broke into a gallop. Not since he rode with the 8th Illinois Cavalry when he carried messages from the front lines to outlying camps had he ridden so hard or so fast.

It didn't take long before the train came into sight. Blankenship watched the glowing red cinders belch from its smoke stack as it rolled along. Outrunning the locomotive would have been easy, but there was no need. He slowed Mingo into a lope until he reached the Painesville station.

The locomotive was standing at the depot with stream hissing from its boiler when Blankenship rode up. The engineer bounded from the train waving a lantern, getting Blankenship's attention.

"Got a telegram saying I was to hold the train. What's going on?" he asked.

Blankenship gave him an abbreviated version of the events and asked him to help search the train for Mathews.

Along with the stationmaster and a local police officer, they boarded and hurried through the passenger car, checking each seat. Mathews was not among the riders. He searched the smoking, sleeping, and baggage car with the same result. He doubted that a dignified man like Mathews would try to hide in the freight car, but looked anyway. It was fortunate that he did. He found Mathews huddled behind a row of pickle barrels, looking as though he had wrestled a bear. His coat was soiled and his trousers had a long gash in one leg. Apparently Mathews had boarded the train on the fly, catching it just as it rolled out of the Willoughby station.

Blankenship knew from his railroad days that hopping a train to get a free ride happened frequently. He had dealt with freeloaders many times, but not a prominent doctor such as Mathews. Seeing the man sitting there like a nickel bum caught him off guard, and saddened him.

"Doctor Mathews, please stand and step off the train," Blankenship said.

Mathews gave him a look of resignation, but didn't move. Blankenship had hoped not to make a scene, but the doctor gave him no choice. The chief pulled Mathews to his feet, cuffed his hands behind his back, and then hustled him from the freight car. All the while, the doctor never said a word.

Faces stared out the windows of the passenger car as Blankenship escorted Mathews along the platform. That's when the chief realized he had a problem. How was he going to get his prisoner back to Willoughby? He had only one horse and it was a long walk home.

"Thought you might need this."

Blankenship turned to see Stanger sitting in the police wagon, feet propped up, sucking on a licorice stick. He couldn't help himself. He burst out laughing.

~ CHAPTER 31 ~

The ugly scene from the night before resulted in the arrest of six men, with nine people injured — one seriously, and the reputation of the medical school in shambles. Blankenship stood staring in disbelief at the gutted corpse of the prestigious Willoughby Medical School. People wandered along the street looking at what had once been a great institution — an institution with a dark secret.

The fire had stripped away its facade leaving behind a building without a soul. Flames may have destroyed the structure, but something far more sinister had caused its ruin. Muscles and sweat could replace the bricks, but the chief feared nothing could repair its reputation.

The only saving grace was that the fire had been contained and hadn't spread to any nearby buildings. At least the town had been saved from that disaster.

With a heavy heart, Blankenship started to walk to his office. Out the corner of his eye, he saw Mayor Bascom coming in his direction. From the look on his face and the amount of smoke billowing from his cigar, the mayor had worked up a good head of steam.

"I want to talk to you in my office. Now!" the mayor hissed between clenched teeth.

Blankenship drew in a conciliatory breath and followed the mayor down the street to the administration building, knowing this wasn't going to be a tea party.

Gold lettering on the door, large enough to be seen by even the most near sighted person, read: *The Office of the Mayor*. The office was furnished with quality furniture, expensive carpets, and fine drapery. It was obvious where most of the town's budget had been spent.

Without offering the police chief a seat, the mayor immediately began ranting once the door was closed. "How could you allow something so loathsome to happen right under your nose? I always knew you weren't fit to be the chief of police and wear that badge. I'll see to it that you never hold a job in this town again." The mayor tore around his office hurling accusations and threats. He looked as though he would explode with the smoke from his cigar acting as the pressure valve.

Blankenship listened, arms folded across his chest, waiting until the mayor paused for air, and then said, "And what part did you play in all this?"

"What are you talking about?" Bascom turned and glared at him.

"You know exactly what I'm talking about. You knew about bodies being taken from the cemetery and used at the school and yet you said nothing. That's as good as condoning it. You might as well have dug up those bodies yourself."

"That's a lie." Bascom stood with his hands behind his back rocking back and forth on his heels.

"I have proof," Blankenship said in a calm, calculated voice.

"You're stark raving mad." The mayor raised his fist and waved it in the chief's face.

"Nope. Don't think so. Your nephew told me about the conversation he had with you when Charles Mathews' watch fob came up missing. He and Razzy saw Harper carry a body in the back door of the school — a body obtained in a most reprehensible manner. You knew about it, didn't you?" Blankenship took his time watching the mayor's reaction. "You knew all along but did nothing. I want to know what your involvement was in all this. Or should I just let Norville turn his pencil loose? I can back up everything I say."

The mayor spun around, his mouth open as if to say something, then stopped and suddenly began coughing. Blankenship couldn't tell if his face was red from hacking or from being cornered.

"Want to tell me about your involvement now, mayor?"

"Posh," he said.

Bascom wasn't giving in.

"Have it your way. Norville loves a good story." Blankenship started for the door.

"Wait."

Bascom flopped into his high-back leather chair, took a handkerchief from his pocket, and mopped his brow. "The school was the central pride of this town. It brought money and people. Important, influential people." His words came out in short, raspy breaths, as if speaking was difficult.

"You wouldn't be talking about folks who control the vote, now would you?" Blankenship jabbed.

"The school was the only thing holding this town together. I've watched businesses come and go; nothing has ever happened to this town like that school. Willoughby is known for having the best medical school west of the Alleghenies. And, yes the people who came discovered they liked it here so they stayed and became voters. But it's more than that and you know it. Without that school this town would cease to exist."

"So why ruin it by robbing graves?"

The mayor squirmed in his chair. "The school was in deep financial trouble. Doctor Haroldson might have been a good doctor and good teacher, but he didn't have a head for making wise financial decisions. The school was losing money every year."

"But enrollment was up. Tuition should have covered the expenses."

"That's true, but Haroldson was ill for some time and could hardly teach his classes, let alone preside over the running of the school. The board of trustees didn't want it known that he was unable to manage and that there might have been problems. That would have hurt enrollment. So we just had someone else take over the daily operations."

"Who?" The chief planted his hands on the mayor's desk and leaned in, and looked him in the eyes.

"John Mathews. Only a few of us on the board knew that John was in charge. We kept it quiet. He would have been appointed as the new director, but John had another problem — his wife. Seems she has very expensive tastes."

Bascom wiped his brow again and grumbled under his breath. Blankenship liked seeing the mayor squirm.

"The trustees didn't realize anything was wrong after John took over — not at first anyway. We didn't look that closely."

"You had a responsibility as a trustee to the people of this town and you didn't feel it was important enough to look closely? Excuse me if I find that a bit contradictory."

"As I said, everything appeared to be in order. It was only after Bert LaRue threatened to foreclose on the mortgage that we discovered the truth. When LaRue called for an audit, the board went over the books and found John had embezzled from the coffers. Probably to pay for Edna's fancy clothes, furs, and that house." He sounded sour, or was it jealousy?

"And what part did you play in all of this?" Blankenship stepped away from the desk.

The mayor hesitated for a long time before answering. "As you said, I did nothing. What was there to do? I figured things would work themselves out in time. I had a few sleepless nights over it, you can be certain of that."

Blankenship didn't like the way the mayor made the statement sound like an absolution. He wasn't going to let him off that easily.

"Knowing about it and doing nothing makes you as guilty as John Mathews for the embezzlement." He spit the words. "I'm not too sure the citizens of this town will let you off so easy just because you had a few sleepless nights."

The mayor buried his head in his hands. He didn't appear so pompous now.

"What was your role in influencing the prosecutor not to press charges against Charles Mathews?"

"I couldn't allow you to arrest him for murder. Everything would come out if there were a trial. The school would be ruined. Just suspecting him and taking him in for questioning was enough to cause letters and telegrams to flood my office." Bascom shifted again, then added in a lowered voice, "Besides I knew he was incapable of murder."

"What about the bodies? Who procured them? Who paid for them?"

"I don't know. I guess John did. He handled all financial matters before Charles took over. John had devised a way to save money. That's all. What could it hurt?"

Blankenship couldn't believe what he was hearing. Bascom was trying to weasel out of his responsibility. "You guess? You don't know, or you haven't checked into that too closely either?" Blankenship shouted.

"I don't have to be talked to like a common criminal," Bascom said. "And I don't have to sit here and take your insubordination."

"You're right. You don't have to take it. I guess the citizens will be your judge and jury come next election."

Blankenship paused at the door long enough to allow his words to sink in. He wasn't a vindictive man, but he enjoyed getting in one last dig. "And by the way, I bought Doc Haroldson's property. Got a good deal, too." He no longer feared the mayor could have him fired, and watching Bascom's expression change was worth a million dollars.

He hadn't told anyone about the contents of the letter he received from the Michigan attorney; figured it wasn't anyone's business. It seems that the father of a young soldier whose life Blankenship had saved at Seven Pines showed his appreciation by leaving him a large sum of money in his will. It wasn't enough to make him wealthy, but it was enough to buy Haroldson's property with enough left over to start his horse ranch.

~ Chapter 32 ~

"Why John? Why? I don't understand. Why did you do it?" Charles stood peering through the bars, waiting for an answer.

Blankenship leaned against the wall of his office listening, wondering how something so evil had gotten this far and what had pushed John over the edge?

Norville sat at Blankenship's desk with pencil and paper in hand writing his next headline–a headline that would sell every paper he printed.

John Mathews sat erect on the edge of the cot in the holding cell, curling and uncurling his fists, sending a chilling, deadeye stare through the bars at Blankenship. His hair stood out on the sides of his head like dried, tossed straw.

"It should have been mine." John finally spoke. His words hissed like water spitting on a hot griddle. "I should have been named director of the school. I was the one who ran the school. I saw that the books balanced. It was me who padded the budget so the board of directors never guessed the school was in financial trouble." He paused, and then turned to look at his brother. "I held on, Charles. Held tight. Wasn't that worth any small infraction for what I would gain? Haroldson always promised that I would be his successor, not you."

Stanger nervously stood by with baton in hand as if expecting John to bolt from the cell.

"It was my destiny to be the head of the greatest medical school in the Western Reserve. But Haroldson wouldn't resign, wouldn't quit even though he was too sick and too old to handle the enormous challenges of running such a large institution." John paused again and leaned back. "He just wouldn't give in. So I helped him along. With him out of the way, the board of directors, seeing how well I ran the school, would appoint me as the new director."

He took in a long, deep breath before continuing.

"The Honorable Doctor John Mathews, trusted member of the town council, deacon in the church, fine upstanding citizen. That's me, Charles, not you. It should have been my name on the door." He paused again as if lost in his thoughts.

"But no, they named you the director." John stood and stepped toward his brother and pointed at him. "*You* pull a lot of weight in the community now. When *you* say jump, people jump; no questions asked. I'm the older brother. I'm the one people should be jumping for. I'm the one who worked to save the school. It should all be mine." His voice trailed off and the look in his eyes became distant.

Everyone in the room waited for John to continue. The popping of the fire in the stove and the tick tock of the clock on the wall were the only sounds in the jail.

Suddenly, John began to speak again, his eyes wild like a trapped animal. "I know how to hold on, Charles. It wasn't just your game, you know. Remember how we used to play Hawk when we were children? I was good at it. Better than you. Remember the mouse we found? I held on. You got squeamish. You let go, but I never did. I knew how to grab it and hold on until it succumbed. I squeezed it ever so carefully between my fingers until its ribs broke and it suffocated. I could hold on for hours. I liked watching its legs twitch while the blood and mucus ran out its mouth." His fingers pinched together holding the imaginary victim.

"Taking the bodies was my idea. All mine," he said as if proud of the fact. He threw his head back and gave a demented howl, the kind of sound that could only come from someone who had lost touch with reality.

Stanger stepped away from the cell.

Charles hung his head as if drained of all emotion — all energy.

"But that no account Harper wanted more money to keep his mouth shut. He wasn't satisfied with what I gave him. The last time he brought us a body he said he wanted more money or he would have a little talk with you." He glared at Blankenship.

That must have been the body of Tarrson they found in the washhouse, the chief thought.

Blankenship finally broke in and asked, "How did the watch fob get into Harper's house?"

"Oh yes, the watch fob. That was fortuitous. *Through Difficulties to Honors.* Grandfather was correct in selecting that particular phrase for the inscription. You have all the honors. I have all the difficulties."

Then turning to his brother with an evil grin, he said, "That's when fate stepped in, my dear brother. I found your fob lying on the floor under the chair where you had placed your coat. It must have fallen out. You thought that little weasel took it." He pointed to Stanger. The young deputy shifted uncomfortably from one foot to the other, his chin jutted out in defiance.

"I would have left it there, but then I had the most brilliant idea. I saw a way to eliminate both of my problems in one squeeze. Yes. I took your fob and put it in Harper's house when I took care of that little problem."

John rubbed his hands together, stood, and then began pacing his cell.

"Harper liked to drink. I laced his whiskey with a dash of cyanide. Wasn't that clever? That piece of slime grabbed at the bottle of whiskey like it was a bag of gold. It was delightful watching him chug it down. I waited for him to die, but the bastard just sat there looking at me. He vomited, but still wouldn't die. That's when I took his neck into my hands and squeezed until he died."

Mathews paused for a moment as if recalling his actions. "I watched him struggle for his last breath. Watched him twitch. He died very slowly."

He ran a finger along his mustache. A wicked sneer spread across his face and then his expression became somber again. "With you out of the way, locked behind bars or better yet hanging from the gallows, the trustees would have to select me, the rightful person, as the new director. They should have chosen me from the start."

Charles seemed to shrink in size. As if unable to bear the weight of his brother's hatred, he lowered himself into a chair and hung his head.

Blankenship wondered just how much Charles knew about his brother. The remark he made while in the washhouse indicated he knew something like this would happen one day. How long had Charles known about his brother's mental state?

John spoke again. "I knew when Blankenship discovered the fob, he would think it was yours. You see I have mine. What else would he think with his limited intelligence? He's not like us, Charles," he snarled.

Blankenship wasn't going to allow the comment to bruise him. He began directing the questioning in order to get the unpleasant ordeal over with.

"Why plant the blackmail letter?"

"That was a stroke of genius, don't you think? I had fun with that. I knew it would stir the pot. Make it appear as though Harper was into extortion – blackmail. Wanted to give the chief something to do while he chased you down. I just gave him a little squeeze." He pinched his fingers together again. "I stuffed the letter into his pocket. Didn't want it to look too obvious."

"What part did Doctor Kibby play in your plot?" Blankenship asked.

John didn't answer right away, but sat back down and stared at his brother. His cold eyes chilled the room. Blankenship couldn't understand what could cause a man's heart to be filled with such hatred. He was looking at pure evil.

John shifted slightly in his chair, then said, "That no-account. He wouldn't cooperate. But he kept his mouth shut. He knew he'd lose his job otherwise."

"Why did you kill Andy Jarvis?" Blankenship asked.

Blankenship heard Norville gasp. He stopped writing and looked up at his friend, flabbergasted.

"He figured out what I had done. He claimed he knew how Haroldson had died, and began to make threats. The little worm said he was going to expose me if I didn't confess. I waited for him in the alley behind the bakery. I knew he went there every morning. It was easy to take him down. I will say, however, he put up quite a fight. Made it more exciting. I liked seeing him struggle. "

"How many bodies did you take from the cemetery?" Blankenship asked.

"I didn't count them."

"Good God, John. How long did you think you could get away with this?" Charles interrupted.

John ignored his brother's question.

Blankenship had heard enough. He had a full confession in front of witnesses. He wanted to find out who the other players were in his scheme.

"Why did you kill Ethan Grimes?" Blankenship threw the question at him and hoped for the right answer; after all John Mathews had no reason to hold anything back now.

This time it was Stanger's turn to gasp. Blankenship actually felt sorry for him. No one should have to witness such insanity.

"Too bad about the lad. Seemed like a nice boy, but you have to understand; he knew too much. Harper had become lazy and hired the kid to do his dirty work. He saw me at his house that night. I couldn't take the chance that he would say something, so I made sure that he didn't."

"Why did you hurt my son?" Charles leaped toward his brother.

Stanger jumped up, putting himself between Charles and the cell. With a stern expression, he guided him back to his seat and cautioned him to calm down.

"I never planned on him getting in the way," he continued. John paused, relaxed his hands and looked at his brother. "He knew about Anna. As God as my witness, I had nothing to do with her death, and I wouldn't have hurt Theodore. I just needed him out of the way for awhile."

"Anna! Death!" Charles screamed. This time he made it to the bars before Stanger could restrain him. Charles reached through as if to grab him, but John was too far away. "What do you know about Anna?"

John lay back down and closed his eyes. It was as if he had crawled into a fantasy world he had created in his mind. Everyone in the room waited for John to speak again but he said no more.

Charles let out a long sigh and looked up at Blankenship. "What will happen to my brother now? It's obvious my brother is mentally ill, Chief."

"We'll have to wait and see what the county prosecutor has to say. In the meantime, he'll be bound over to the county prosecutor for the murder of Harper, Jarvis, and Grimes. They might also include Doctor Haroldson. They'll let us know when the trial will be."

Charles slowly stood, nodded, and then left the jail, his head down like a broken man with a million regrets.

"What was John talking about? What did he know about the Mathews child?" Norville whispered to Blankenship.

"That's a strange story, but the boy came to me with an odd tale about knowing where his sister was. Told me I should look in the cemetery. Of course, we had looked there. I personally checked the grounds several times. I couldn't make heads nor tails out of what the boy was saying and sent him home to talk to his parents. I guess he went to talk to his uncle instead."

"How did you know he killed Harper, Hank?" Norville asked.

"After you pointed out to me that Harper couldn't have written the blackmail letter, I figured the paper might have come from his killer. The letter had been written on a very fine grade of stationery. There was a watermark just visible at the tear. I hadn't put any meaning to it at first, but when I saw that the box of stationery delivered to John's office at the school was the same quality and had the same watermark as the paper Jarvis found on Harper, and the one left by Ethan Grimes' body, I began to suspect. Then Doctor Carlton told me about the autopsy, and how he found cyanide in Haroldson. I put two and two together."

Blankenship rubbed his chin.

"With all of Mathews' cunning, he made one big mistake. He described Harper's house. He told me he never had any dealings with Harper; said he had never been to his house. Yet, he described the house as being in a horrid condition and that there was an overturned bowl of stew on the table. How would he have known that if he hadn't been there?"

"What's this about Anna?" Norville asked, his voice still low.

Giving Stanger something to do to get him out of the office, he told him to go get water for the coffee pot. Stanger didn't object, but reluctantly put on his coat and left by the back door.

"That's something you don't want to know, and must never, I repeat, never put in your newspaper."

"But I…"

"Listen to me, as a friend. Never print what I'm about to tell you."

Norville put down his pencil and folded his hands together over his notepad and sat listening. Blankenship knew his fingers were itching to pick up his pencil.

"John must have known or suspected that Harper had something to do with her disappearance. But admitting it would have ruined his bigger plan."

Blankenship pulled a chair around and sat facing Norville. Saying the words out loud pained him. "Like I said earlier, Theodore came to me the other day with an outlandish tale of knowing that his sister was in the graveyard. He said I was to look next to heaven. It made no sense to me, but when I was walking through the cemetery the other day I saw that the grave next to Kromer's had an epitaph that read, *Rest My Beautiful One In The Arms Of Jesus Our Savior In Heaven*." The date of death on the tombstone was three days before Kromer was buried. I know it was stretching the possibility, but when I read Ethan's journal telling about what he and Harper did to the child and that she was next to heaven, everything else seemed to fall in place. Grimes' journal said he saw John leaving Harper's house the night of the murder. It didn't take much to put everything together."

Blankenship locked the front door to the jail. He slumped into his chair, leaned back, and closed his eyes, hoping to never repeat the past two weeks. Murder, deceit, and destruction were not something that happened in a small town like Willoughby.

~ Chapter 33 ~

Blankenship stood with his hat in his hand, remembering the times before when he knocked at Mathews' door. None were ever good. Theodore answered his knock. The police chief spoke softly and asked to speak to his father. The boy showed him into the parlor never taking his eyes off the policeman as he backed out of the room.

Charles Mathews entered the parlor, shook Blankenship's hand and offered him a seat.

"I'll stand, thanks." He hesitated. "But you need to sit down," Blankenship added and rested his hand on Charles' shoulder.

He pulled Ethan's journal from his pocket and handed it to him. "I think you should read this, but I warn you, it isn't going to be easy."

"What's this?"

"Go ahead. Read it."

Charles reluctantly opened the journal and began reading. The turning of each page was the only sound in the room. With the last page read, Charles closed the book, and then placed his elbows on his knees and wept.

"What's the matter, Charles?" Martha said, coming into the room.

Charles rose, walked over to his wife, took both of her hands in his, and then looked into her eyes. He hesitated for a long time as if trying to find the right words. "Sit down, dear, I have something to tell you. It's not good, I'm afraid." He paused to wipe at his eyes before speaking. "Martha, Chief Blankenship has brought us a young man's journal that reveals where our baby Anna is."

"Anna?" her eyes widened. "They've found our baby?" she grasped his arm. "Where is she? Is she alright?" A hopeful glee showed in her eyes.

"No, Martha."

Charles opened the journal then closed it again. His voice broke several times before answering her.

It pained Blankenship to see such a strong man in this kind of distress.

"This is Ethan Grimes' journal," he said. "It seems he was working in the cem..." His voice broke again. "It seems he was working in the cemetery the night that Ann...the night Anna went there."

"Went there? What do you mean, she went there?" Her eyes searched her husband's face for an answer.

"They... that is Mr. Harper and this Ethan Grimes found her there and... killed her."

Martha's face turned white as fireplace ash and her hands began trembling.

"They buried her in a grave they were robbing."

"No. No. That didn't happen. They didn't kill my baby."

Martha looked from her husband to Blankenship, her eyes begging for him to say it wasn't so. When the chief didn't say anything, she let out a woeful moan that turned into a howling scream that pierced his heart. She clutched at her skirts and then flung herself back against the sofa. Her screams cut through the room like a train whistle in the dead of night.

Charles grabbed both her arms and told the chief to hold her while he ran to his office. He returned shortly with his medical bag, took out a hypodermic needle, and then filled it with morphine from a small bottle. He pushed the sleeve of his wife's dress above her elbow and stuck the needle into her arm.

She tried to resist but within seconds she grew calm. Her head rolled from side to side, as she closed her eyes and whispered Anna's name.

"Why, Charles?" she said, her voice only a whisper. "She was just a baby. Why?"

Charles held her hand and swept hair from her face.

"Can we bring our Anna home now, Charles? I want my baby home." Her words faded into slurred sobs, then she fell silent.

"Yes, bring Anna home," Charles said to Blankenship

Blankenship told Doctor Mathews that he would make the necessary arrangements to have the grave opened where he felt their child was buried.

Charles nodded.

~ Epilogue ~

A plume of dust rose against the horizon as a surrey traveled along the road leading to the ranch. Blankenship recognized the driver immediately by the way he sat hunched over holding the reins as if letting go would send the horse and driver plummeting off the road.

Blankenship waited by the fence until the buggy stopped and Norville climbed down.

"Good to see you. You're early," Blankenship said and slapped his friend on the back.

"I wouldn't miss this for the world. Bet she's excited. How is she?" Norville reached into the back of the surrey and retrieved a colorfully wrapped box.

"I've never seen her so wound up," Blankenship said.

"Well, it is her special day."

"What's in the box? More toys to spoil her?" Blankenship asked.

"Sure, why not? It's not everyday that my godchild turns five. Where is she?" Norville asked, looking over Blankenship's shoulder toward the house.

"She's inside helping Katie prepare for the party. Come on around to the barn," Blankenship motioned for Norville to follow him. "Got something to show you."

Norville followed Blankenship to the stable and into a far stall.

"She's beautiful," Norville said, reaching to touch a colt, careful not to agitate the mare.

"Born just two days ago."

As Blankenship took the reins of the mare, Cleo came trotting toward Norville. She gave a loud meow and stretched her paws up to greet him.

"Ah, Cleo. I've missed you. How's my favorite cat? I bet you've become the queen of the barn." He bent to pick her up but she scampered away.

"I think she wants you to follow her," Blankenship said.

Norville followed the cat to an adjoining stall and looked in. There in the corner was a box with six fuzzy kittens. Cleo jumped into the box and nudged one of the kittens toward him.

Blankenship chuckled. "I think she just selected one for you."

Norville picked up the gray and white cat that looked just like its mother. "I'm honored." Norville stroked Cleo's head before putting the kitten back with the others. Cleo nestled in with her brood and began purring.

If Blankenship didn't know better, he thought he heard the self-assured, at times overbearing newspaperman, sniffle.

"You can get the kitten next month after it's weaned, but you can come see it anytime."

Norville threw his shoulders back, stuck out his check, and smiled like a proud papa.

Blankenship led the mare out of the stable and into the corral. The colt followed, staying close to its mother.

"What does Mary Beth think of the colt?" Norville asked.

"She was there for its birth. Thought she might as well see how it all happens."

"What did she do?"

"She was a real trooper. Stood and watched without saying a word, then immediately named it Charlie. She reluctantly renamed it Charlene when I told her it was a girl."

"Come along, Katie is expecting you." Blankenship closed the corral gate behind them. "I think she's waiting for you to test the icing for the cake."

"Ah, a woman after my own heart."

"Just remember her heart is taken."

The two men walked along the fence back to the house.

"I see you got the other corral finished. Sorry, I couldn't come to help."

"I understand. We had plenty of men here to help with the fencing and to raise the barn. You did miss some of Katie's best fried chicken and rhubarb pie, however."

"Actually, that's what I'm truly sorry about. I love Katie's pies," Norville confessed. "You've come a long way from that guy who said he was only going to stay in Willoughby for a couple seasons then move on. Whatever happened to him?"

"He fell in love, my friend."

"I hear that's the downfall of every great man."

"Great or not, I'm happy."

"So, I see. You got the horse ranch and the woman you love. Can't beat that."

"I still don't know what would have happened if McFarland hadn't left me that money. I still can't believe it sometimes."

As they reached the porch, Mary Beth came running out of the house, her golden ringlets tied with yellow ribbons that matched her dress.

"Uncle Adam, you're here," she said, and threw her arms around Norville.

"Mary Beth, give Uncle Adam room to breathe," Katie called from the doorway.

"What did you bring me? Let me see. Let me see."

"Mary Beth! Watch your manners. It isn't nice to presume," she scolded.

"What's presume, mommy?"

"It's what well-mannered little girls don't do. Now, scat. We still have a lot of work to do before your guests arrive." She gave Mary Beth a gentle tap on her behind to move her along.

"Adam, it's so good to see you," Katie said, turning to Norville and giving him a peck on the check.

"Katie, you look beautiful as ever," Norville said.

Blankenship thought so too. In fact, everything in his life was more than he ever hoped for. The horse ranch, thanks to the generous gift from Buford McFarland for saving his son's life, was the first of many wonderful events. The next was Katie's answer to his somewhat awkward proposal, followed by a beautiful wedding, then the arrival of Mary Beth a year later. Yes, his life was full.

"Katie's been planning this birthday party for months. A herd of elephants couldn't stop her from the fun she's having," Blankenship said to Norville as they entered the house.

Norville stuck his head into the kitchen. "Hmm. Smells great. Some spread you're making. I see you have outdone yourself with this party," he said, spying the table laden with platters filled to the brim and the special chocolate birthday cake sitting in the middle.

"You'll have a full page for your newspaper," Katie said. "And I expect the front page, too."

The men made themselves comfortable in the front room. Blankenship took two cigars from a humidor and offered one to his friend. Norville lit it, and then said, "Too bad Charles Mathews isn't here to enjoy this party. I'm sure he would like to see how Mary Beth is doing."

"We had quite a time with her there for awhile when she was born, that's for sure. Good thing he was there for us," Blankenship said, shaking the frightful events of Mary Beth's difficult birth from his thoughts. "Saved her life. Can't ever thank him enough. Too bad he chose not to stay in Willoughby, but Columbus gained a great teacher."

"Probably too many bad memories here with his brother going to prison. Edna went back to England, you know. Guess she couldn't afford the gossip and lack of income."

"Yes, I heard."

"So, who is coming to this shindig?" Norville asked.

"All the children in the county from the looks of the invitation list. Mary Beth knows just about everybody, it seems. She's invited Stanger, of course. She expects a tin of licorice from him." Blankenship puffed on the cigar, savoring its robust flavor.

"He sure turned out to be a surprise. Never dreamed he'd end up taking your job after you resigned as police chief. He's doing a fine job, too."

"Bet that made Bascom proud."

"Too bad the folks voted him out of office," Norville laughed.

"Yes, I know. I was one of the voters."

The End